"You're worried f...

Brandon colored. "M...
I'm more concerned a...

Elizabeth put her hands on her hips... ...
you agree that I'm some kind of fortune hunter?"

"No." He puffed out a breath. "Elizabeth, please. Consider my offer. I will make no demands of you. You and the boys would have a secure home, a place in the community. I can protect you. But if marrying me is unthinkable, even under those terms, I'll understand."

"Frankly," she told him, "I don't know what to think. I'm willing to believe we've both grown since our days together in Cambridge. But a marriage of convenience? I had once hoped for more."

He nodded. "So had I. But we are different people now. I promise you all my support, all my respect. I hope more will grow with time."

Time. Might as well say *chance*. He was asking her to risk her future on him. How could she?

"All I can say," she told him, "is that I'll give the matter due consideration. Good day, Pastor."

* * *

Lone Star Cowboy League: Multiple Blessings

Regina Scott has always wanted to be a writer. Since her first book was published in 1998, her stories have traveled the globe, with translations in many languages. Fascinated by history, she learned to fence and sail a tall ship. She and her husband reside in Washington state with their overactive Irish terrier. You can find her online blogging at nineteenteen.com. Learn more about her at reginascott.com or connect with her on Facebook at Facebook.com/authorreginascott.

Books by Regina Scott

Love Inspired Historical

Lone Star Cowboy League: Multiple Blessings

The Bride's Matchmaking Triplets

Frontier Bachelors

The Bride Ship
Would-Be Wilderness Wife
Frontier Engagement
Instant Frontier Family
A Convenient Christmas Wedding

Lone Star Cowboy League: The Founding Years

A Rancher of Convenience

The Master Matchmakers

The Courting Campaign
The Wife Campaign
The Husband Campaign

The Everard Legacy

The Rogue's Reform
The Captain's Courtship
The Rake's Redemption
The Heiress's Homecoming

Visit the Author Profile page at Harlequin.com.

REGINA SCOTT

The Bride's Matchmaking Triplets

HARLEQUIN® LOVE INSPIRED® HISTORICAL

Special thanks and acknowledgment
are given to Regina Scott for her contribution
to the Lone Star Cowboy League: Multiple Blessings miniseries.

Recycling programs
for this product may
not exist in your area.

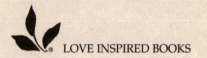

LOVE INSPIRED BOOKS

ISBN-13: 978-0-373-42526-6

The Bride's Matchmaking Triplets

www.Harlequin.com

Printed in U.S.A.

Yet to all who received Him,
to those who believed in His name,
He gave the right to become children of God.
—*John* 1:12

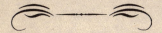

To Meryl, Lola Jo and all those who open their hearts to children who need them; and to the Lord, who adopts us all into His family.

Chapter One

"And which of our fine gentlemen have you chosen to be your husband?"

Elizabeth Dumont tried not to cringe at Mrs. Arundel's question. Instead, she picked up one of her three precious charges and handed a triplet to the lady. One look at little Theo, and Mrs. Arundel's stern face melted like snow in the sun.

"I've actually advertised for a position," Elizabeth said, bending to pick up the second baby as another woman—Mrs. Tyson, if she remembered correctly—pressed closer, the scent of her lavender cologne like a cloud surrounding them.

The snug boardinghouse room felt even more cramped with her three visitors this morning. How much nicer it would have been to receive the ladies in her own home, as her aunt had done as Cambridge's most famous hostess. Elizabeth could picture the babies playing on a rug at her feet, tea and cakes waiting on a side table. But right now, this room, with its flowered wallpaper, chintz-covered iron bedstead, porcelain washstand and sturdy walnut dresser, was the best she could do. She was just thankful David and Caroline McKay had given her the three high chairs and large crib they had used when caring for the boys.

"You don't need a position," insisted blond-haired Stella Fuller, wife of the local sheriff, as she came forward to take the last baby. "There are plenty of men in this town worth marrying. You just have to pick one. I did."

Elizabeth had heard Stella had been a mail-order bride, just as Elizabeth had planned to be.

As Stella laughed, little Jasper grinned in her arms. Eli was looking up at Mrs. Tyson, brown eyes wide, as if trying to memorize her kind face. Theo wasn't nearly so sure about Mrs. Arundel, for his lower lip trembled. He glanced at Elizabeth as if afraid the woman was about to make off with him.

Elizabeth knew the feeling. Ever since she'd been given charge of the boys three days ago, she'd wanted to gather them close, smooth their dark hair, whisper comfort in their ears. Maybe it was because they were so little and helpless, maybe it was because they were orphans like her, but Jasper, Theo and Eli touched her heart more than any of her other charges in her four years of being a governess.

"I hear Clyde Parker is looking for a wife," Mrs. Arundel offered. "He has a fine ranch not too far from town. He might not object to red hair." She bounced Theo on her hip, and he frowned at her.

Elizabeth tried not to frown as well. She'd never had anyone complain about her long red hair, now carefully bound up in a bun at the top of her head. Until the time her uncle had been sent to prison for swindling others, she'd received nothing but compliments on her looks. After that, people tended not to want to look at her at all, as if she'd somehow been tainted by the scandal.

"James Forrester needs a wife too," Mrs. Tyson put in. "His two boys have settled down nicely since they joined the Young Ranchers program."

"His boys are nearly grown," Stella pointed out. "I'd think you'd want someone younger to be father to the triplets." She bent and rubbed her nose against Jasper's, and he squealed in delight, winning a smile from all the ladies.

Mrs. Tyson looked to Eli and sighed. "I simply cannot understand a mother giving away a child. Has no relative come forward since Bo Stillwater found the boys abandoned at the fair?"

"Not one," Elizabeth told her, feeling a little guilty for the relief that statement brought. "The Lone Star Cowboy League advertised in newspapers all over the state, even offered a reward for information about the mother, but the one couple who had asked about the situation later sent word they weren't related after all."

Theo started fussing then, and Mrs. Arundel hurriedly handed him back to Elizabeth. He leaned his head against her shoulder, thumb going to his mouth. Elizabeth drank in the soft weight in her arms, the scent of fresh soap.

Please, Lord, couldn't I be their mother?

She stifled a sigh. She'd just asked for the impossible. While she believed God could do anything, He had never moved mountains in her life. He didn't heal her aunt of the stroke that had left her bedridden or send Elizabeth a new position or husband to support her when her last position ended. Instead, she found herself in Little Horn, a governess-turned-mail-order-bride, whose groom had changed his mind and married another. Any day she'd receive an answer to the advertisements she'd posted seeking a position, and then she would have to give Jasper, Theo and Eli to someone else to raise.

She hugged Theo closer.

"What about Pastor Stillwater?" Stella asked, perking up and causing Jasper to raise his head in expectation. "He's young enough to be a father."

Elizabeth's stomach dipped, and she started shaking her head.

Mrs. Tyson must not have noticed, for she nodded eagerly. "He's such a nice man. Everyone respects him." She tickled Eli under his chin, and he squirmed with a bright giggle that made Elizabeth want to hug him close as well.

"We are very fortunate to have a gentleman of Mr. Stillwater's character as our minister," Mrs. Arundel agreed, her face becoming all prim and proper. "He comes from near Boston, you know. He is very well connected."

Oh, but Elizabeth could tell them stories about Brandon Stillwater's supposedly excellent character. She clamped her mouth shut. Watching her, Theo did the same.

"Compassionate to the less fortunate," Mrs. Arundel continued.

Focused on himself.

"Kind."

Selfish.

"Humble."

Arrogant!

The other ladies were smiling their agreement. Elizabeth dropped her gaze to Theo, whose brows were once more furrowed, as if he was concerned about what he saw in her blue-green eyes. She was concerned about her feelings as well. She'd thought she'd put aside the disappointment and hurt she'd felt when Brandon had abandoned her four years ago.

Then three days ago she'd arrived in Little Horn and encountered the minister as he was marrying her groom to someone else. She still wasn't sure which had shocked her more: finding David McKay about to wed or seeing Brandon again for the first time in years.

Now Eli started fussing as well, and Mrs. Tyson rocked him, making cooing noises that seemed to calm him. By the way his little mouth pursed, he was trying to mimic her.

"It's getting close to their next feeding," Elizabeth explained, going to set Theo in one of the high chairs. It was crammed next to the wheeled handcart the babies' mother had left them in. Just looking at the care that had gone into the construction of the conveyance told her Jasper, Theo and Eli's parents had loved them. So did the note that had been found with the babies. When she'd agreed to be their nanny, David McKay had given it to her to read.

To the Lone Star Cowboy League: Please take care of my triplets. I'm widowed and penniless. The ranch is dried out. I can't stay there and provide for my babies. I'm also very sick and am going to where I was born to meet my Maker. One day, if you could make sure the boys knew

*I loved them, I'd be obliged. They were born
September 30. Was the happiest day of my life.*

The league had been seeing to their care ever since.
First Louisa Clark, daughter of the town doctor, had
taken a turn, but an illness had required the babies to
be moved elsewhere. Caroline Murray, the woman who
had married David McKay, had been hired to serve
as nanny for the babies and David's daughter, Maggie, but Caroline and the widowed father had fallen in
love. When she'd injured her arm saving Maggie from
a flash flood, it had been clear a new nanny was needed
to care for the orphaned triplets. And Elizabeth, abandoned by yet another man she'd thought she'd marry,
had been available and ready to help while she looked
for something permanent.

A shame she'd fallen in love as well, with three little boys she had no hope of keeping. Even if she could
have persuaded the ranchers of the Lone Star Cowboy League to allow her to adopt the triplets, she had
no way to support them. With her skills, she might
have applied to be a cook, seamstress or some kind of
teacher. But Little Horn had a teacher and seamstress;
no one seemed to need a nanny or governess; and the
only cooking jobs available would require her to go
on cattle drives, spending weeks on the trail, where
women were rare and babies could not go.

No, she would have to give up her charges unless
God intervened.

A knock sounded on the door, and, with a look to
Elizabeth, Mrs. Arundel went to answer. Brandon
Stillwater stepped into the room with a compassionate, kind, humble smile Elizabeth was certain must

be false. His sandy-brown hair was as thick as she remembered, combed carefully back from the high forehead her friend Florence had called noble. He stood
tall, confident and reserved in his brown frock coat:
the perfect minister. The look in his quicksilver eyes
said he had come to help.

But how could she accept help from a man she could
not depend on?

Brandon smiled at the ladies in his congregation
who had come to visit the triplets that morning. Mrs.
Arundel puffed up as she usually did in his presence;
the feather in the hat resting on her graying curls stood
at attention as if even it was determined to have him
know its wearer was a proper Christian lady. The
brown-haired Mrs. Tyson was beaming at him in such
a motherly manner that he was reminded of the sixteen jars of peaches she had provided him recently.
Mrs. Fuller, however, had a speculative gleam in her
golden-brown eyes that made him wonder what the
women had been discussing before he entered.

And then there was Elizabeth. *Miss Dumont*, some
part of him chided. She had made it clear four years
ago that she was no longer interested in having him
court her, so he would have forfeited the right to use
her first name as well. At least, in public. His heart,
he feared, still defaulted to Elizabeth.

She was regarding him now, her eyes the exact
shade of the Charles River on a sunny day. The fine
silk gowns she used to wear had been replaced by
a practical dun-colored twill skirt and brown-and-
green-striped blouse with the puffy sleeves that were
all in fashion, if the ladies of his congregation were

any indication. She'd covered her clothes with a cotton apron already decorated by working with the triplets. And she held herself as if she were royalty and everyone else was merely here on her sufferance.

"Come to see the babies too, Pastor?" Mrs. Fuller asked with a grin. "Or someone else?"

He ignored the implication, bending to put his head closer to the baby who was squirming in her arms. This had to be Jasper. He was the most rambunctious, always laughing or playing. Theo, on the other hand, was shy, hugging his nanny close more often than not. And Eli was the watchful one, taking his cue from his brothers. Now Jasper flashed a grin that showed two white teeth before reaching for Brandon.

"And how are our little men today?" he asked, opening his arms to offer to take the baby.

Elizabeth stepped between him and Mrs. Fuller. "Quite energetic, as you can see." She intercepted Jasper before the baby reached Brandon. Jasper pouted as he peered over her shoulder at him.

Brandon knew the feeling of frustration. It came over him every time he was in Elizabeth's company.

She set Jasper in the chair next to Theo's. Mrs. Tyson brought her Eli, who reached out a hand to grasp Theo's as he sat in the third chair.

"As I was saying, it's just about feeding time," Elizabeth told her company, "so it might be best if you leave me to it." She smiled at the women. "We all know the damage a baby can do to a nice dress."

The women all chorused agreement, patting down their cotton skirts as they took their leave and headed for the door. Mrs. Arundel paused to eye Brandon.

"A baby can damage a fine suit as well, Pastor," she

informed him, as if he hadn't already been christened by each of the triplets since his brother had found them at the county fair six weeks ago.

"Then I'll just have to rely on the Lord's mercy and the skill of the kind ladies who do my washing," he replied with a smile.

The older woman glanced at Elizabeth, brows narrowing. "But you can't stay. It isn't proper."

Not proper for him to care about three babies left alone in the world? Even if the little fellows hadn't tugged at his heart, as the minister of the only church in Little Horn, it was surely his duty to see to their well-being. He was called in to comfort and mediate in most areas, from praying over sick children to finding homes for orphans like Jo and Gil Satler to stopping the feud between Dorothy Hill and Tug Coleman and their families.

"Not proper at all," Elizabeth agreed, arms crossed over her chest. "And I know Reverend Stillwater is very careful about his reputation."

There was an edge to her words, as if trying to live up to his calling was somehow shocking. She'd known him since he'd attended divinity school at Harvard. What else would she have expected him to become but a minister?

"It's all right," Mrs. Tyson said, stepping back into the room. "I can stay a little longer. You go ahead, Margaret. I'll join you for tea in a bit."

With a nod, Mrs. Arundel sailed from the room, her feather high.

And he had a chaperone. He could have told Mrs. Tyson that she had no need for concern. Elizabeth Dumont would have no use for him even if he proposed marriage right then and there.

The older lady went over and clucked at the babies as Elizabeth moved to the dresser against the far wall and picked up one of the jars of applesauce crowding the surface. He was pleased to see the ladies of his congregation had been equally generous to the babies as they were to him. The gingham-topped jars of pears would be from Mrs. Dooley; he had a dozen like them at the parsonage. Betsy McKay had likely donated the stewed plums, the purple glinting in the light. For the triplets' sake, he hoped the applesauce had come from Lula May McKay, for she was one of the best cooks and canners in the area, not to mention being the leader of the Lone Star Cowboy League.

Elizabeth came back to the high chairs carrying the jar and a silver spoon. Once, she'd presided over an entire table laden with silver and fine china and crystal. Her long red hair had been smoothed into a tight bun, and the emeralds at her ears and throat had called attention to her almond-shaped eyes. The smile she'd offered him across the table had been bright, eager, almost as if she couldn't wait to learn more about him.

Now her smile seemed brittle as she reached for a wooden chair against one wall. Brandon hurried forward to lift it for her, positioning it in front of the high chairs. Mrs. Tyson nodded approval, but Elizabeth narrowed her eyes at him as if suspecting he had ulterior motives.

What did she think he was going to do, pull it out from under her?

Putting her back to him, she perched on the chair. The sunlight from the window across from her blazed fire along her hair and made him wish he still had the right to touch the gleaming tresses.

Help me, Lord. I don't know what I did to earn her wrath. Show me how to behave toward her.

Elizabeth remained focused on her charges. "All right, little bird," she said to Jasper. "Open wide your beak." She dipped the spoon in the jar and brought it closer to him. Jasper opened his mouth for the applesauce.

Theo reached for the spoon and ended up knocking it aside, splashing fruit across the chairs. Eli set up a howl.

"Oh, dear," Mrs. Tyson said. "Let me see if I can find something to clean that up." She hurried to the dresser and began rummaging through the items left for the babies.

Elizabeth wiped applesauce off her cheek with one finger. "Well, that didn't work."

Brandon stepped forward and picked up the crying baby. "I'll take Eli. Can you handle the other two?"

Her gaze snapped to his, and there was fire in those eyes. "Certainly, Mr. Stillwater. That's what the Lone Star Cowboy League is paying me to do, remember?"

Of course he remembered. He'd been at the wedding when David McKay had made the suggestion. It was only right that David find some way to support Elizabeth, after she'd come all this way to marry him only to find him marrying another. The rancher had sent her a telegram telling her of the change in plan, but it had never reached her. Still, Brandon couldn't help wondering why Elizabeth had agreed to marry David in the first place.

Now he merely nodded. "I meant would you prefer

me to take Theo as well so you can focus on Jasper," he said, moving back from the high chairs as much to separate Eli from the food as to distance himself from her anger.

"We're fine," she said, turning her attention to the two remaining babies.

"Babies can be such work, the little dears," Mrs. Tyson put in with a commiserating look to Brandon. She bent to clean up the floor.

Elizabeth moved Jasper and Theo farther apart, then took turns feeding them a spoonful of the applesauce, her movements brisk and efficient. Mrs. Tyson hovered behind, ready to step in if needed. Brandon rocked Eli, the baby warm in his arms. As Eli's cries quieted, he looked up at Brandon, trusting.

When had Elizabeth lost trust in him?

He'd thought them destined for marriage, partners for life. She'd been everything he could have dreamed of in a wife back then—caring, loving, generous. Even now, she cajoled the babies into eating, praised them for waiting to take their turns and set them to beaming happily. Their brother in his arms reached for her as if he simply had to get closer.

Brandon had felt the same way once. She'd been the one to break things off, to marry a wealthier, more socially prominent man, she'd said. Yet here she was, a mail-order bride of all things. Much as he loved Little Horn with its wide-open spaces and kindhearted people, the community was a far cry from the society she'd been raised in near Boston.

So what had happened to bring Elizabeth Dumont back into his life again?

Chapter Two

Elizabeth forced her shaking hand to steady on the spoon. How dare Brandon question her ability to care for the triplets? She was a good nanny, for all she had not imagined herself in the role. Anyone might have found three babies a little challenging.

Though, she had to admit, he looked remarkably comfortable dealing with the boys. He was rocking Eli back and forth, the baby gazing up at him as if he was the most important person in the world.

She'd looked at him that way once.

She would never forget the day they'd met. Her aunt Evangeline had been hosting one of her famous dinner parties. It was well-known around Cambridge that Mrs. Dumont, wife of the influential financier, welcomed only the most interesting people to her table, so an invitation was cause to preen. As her niece, Elizabeth had dined with senators, adventurers, novelists, artists and scientists. That evening, attendees around the white damask-draped table had included the mayor and his wife, a man who had invented some sort of circuit for conducting electricity, an award-winning poet and the dean of the divinity school with his most promising student.

Brandon Stillwater.

As the least most notable person in the room, besides her, he would have had every right to sit quietly, speak only when directly addressed. Indeed, he had been quiet the first part of the meal. Then the inventor, a Mr. Lombard, had begun a paean to man's ingenuity.

"Why, even now, in New York, a pneumatic system brings warm air in winter and cool air in summer," he boasted, the sleeve of his black dress coat coming perilously close to dipping into his creamed asparagus as he waved a hand.

"Amazing," the mayor proclaimed. "We may have to rethink our futures, gentlemen. Science seems to have the upper hand."

Brandon had merely offered them all a charming smile as he reached for his crystal glass. "I think I'll stick with the Author of invention instead of the implementer." And he'd calmly taken a sip as if giving them all a moment to think about what he'd said.

How could she not be drawn to such a man? He was only a year older than her, yet he seemed so confident, so sure of who he was and what he was meant to do. She'd envied him that.

"Ready for this little fellow?" he asked her now, smiling on the infant in his arms. She remembered how it felt to be cradled close, those strong arms around her, making her feel safe, loved.

Elizabeth scooped up a baby and shoved him at Brandon, anything to stop these memories. "Here," she said. "I'll take Eli. You take Jasper."

If he was surprised by the urgency in her voice, he

didn't show it. But as they exchanged babies, his fingers brushed her sleeve and a tingle ran up her arm.

Why was she still so aware of him after all these years? Even as she began to feed Eli, Theo watching them, she felt Brandon beside her. He held each baby so gently, every movement effortless. No other man had ever made her feel that she could rely on him no matter what.

A shame that feeling had turned out to be false.

She offered Eli another spoonful of applesauce, which he gobbled down. The men she had counted on had proven singularly unreliable. Her uncle, legendary for making fortunes, had been exposed as a swindler, stealing from clients to increase his coffers. The men who had flocked to her aunt's table had quickly distanced themselves from scandal. The gentlemen who had seemed interested in courting her had followed suit. And Brandon…

Really needed to leave her room before she forgot herself and gave him a piece of her mind!

"You needn't wait around, Pastor," she said without looking at him. "The triplets and I are fine. We have Mrs. Tyson to help. You've done your duty by looking in on us."

Mrs. Tyson smiled at her as she went to hang up the dirty cleaning rag. Brandon didn't say anything, but his arm brushed her shoulder as he set Jasper back into the high chair. She turned without thinking, and her gaze met his. His silver eyes should have looked cold, forbidding, but now they drew her in like cool water on a hot day.

"Seeing to the well-being of those we care about is never a duty, Miss Dumont," he murmured. "It is a privilege." He held her gaze a moment longer, as if making sure she heard him. Such a heartfelt look, with his lips turned down in sympathy. She should agree, smile back. But she knew his tricks now. She was neither an awestruck girl nor a member of his flock who needed schooling. Elizabeth turned her face resolutely toward the babies. A moment later, she heard the door close behind her.

Mrs. Tyson came to lay a hand on her shoulder. "Pastor Stillwater is a good man. I'm sure he was only trying to help."

Had she looked as if she was about to breathe fire at the minister? She certainly felt as if she could. Instead, Elizabeth gave the lady a bright smile. "But why should I trouble your pastor when I have all you lovely ladies to help?"

Mrs. Tyson's round face turned a pleased pink. "We are delighted to help you, dear." She bent and picked up Theo, whose eyes were already drifting closed. "Such darling boys. They make me miss my own sons."

Elizabeth was almost afraid to ask, but it seemed the right thing to do. "What happened to your boys?"

Mrs. Tyson straightened slowly, then carried the baby toward the nearby crib. "They are grown men now. They had to leave to find work during the drought, but I have hopes they might return soon. In the meantime, if you need anything, please send word." She laid Theo in the crib and smiled down at him a moment before helping Elizabeth transfer the other two into the crib as well. Then Elizabeth saw her out.

As she shut the door behind Mrs. Tyson, Elizabeth drew in a breath. At least that was over. Glancing back, she saw that all three boys had dozed off. In the silence, she could hear the clock ticking on the dresser.

Peace. Quiet.

Normally, that would be a blessing. Caring for the triplets was exhilarating and exhausting. She appreciated the moments when she could relax. But now all she could think about was Brandon Stillwater and the life she had once known.

Not for the first time, she wished Aunt Evangeline was still alive. Her aunt, who had raised Elizabeth after her parents' death when she was a toddler, had always encouraged her to dream big.

"You could be an explorer, discovering new plants and animals," she'd said, excitement dancing in her green eyes. "Or a novelist, unleashing the potential of the human heart. Only the best for you, my dear Elizabeth."

Sometimes, sitting around the dinner table with people so famous and talented, she had thought she had found her calling, to be a society hostess like her aunt, bringing people together, sharing knowledge, encouragement. Other times, she wondered. Why must she be the one to listen to other people's adventures? Why couldn't she have adventures of her own as her aunt suggested?

Brandon had seemed to understand when she'd emboldened herself to confess her yearnings. After that first dinner, he had called whenever he could slip away from his studies. Studying, it seemed, wasn't too difficult for him. They'd talk in her aunt's opulent sitting room, take walks in the nearby park. They had been strolling beside an ornamental pond in the center of the park one Sunday afternoon when she'd told him she wished she might do something more.

"My brother, Bo, says the same thing," he'd answered, bending to pick up a stone from the path and toss it into the pond.

She hadn't met his brother yet. She hadn't met anyone in his family, although she knew his mother had passed away and his father was an invalid. Aunt Evangeline said Mr. Stillwater senior was a fine gentleman who had run a prosperous business in Cambridge. Elizabeth had wondered why Brandon hadn't introduced her, but she was certain it was only a matter of time.

"And what sort of adventures does your brother want to have?" she asked, lifting her green silk skirts away from a puddle in the path.

Brandon smiled. "He wants to move to Texas and build a cattle ranch. He's been studying under a rancher here, and he thinks he's ready to take on the frontier."

"Like a cowboy in the dime novels?" Elizabeth grinned. "How marvelous! What could be more thrilling than fighting desperadoes to carve a home in the wilderness?"

Brandon tossed another rock in the pond with a plunk. "Well, the Texas Rangers make short work of any desperadoes, from what I understand. But Bo will certainly be carving at the wilderness." He glanced her way. "He wants me to go with him."

To Texas? The image that came to mind, of a woman in gingham skirts shooting her own dinner as she rode across the plains, was brave and bold and a little scary. She wanted adventure, but perhaps she ought to start with something more tame.

She'd linked arms with Brandon. "Too bad you're

already being considered for a position at St. Matthew's. We can cheer your brother on from here. Just think how much fun it will be to sit around the hearth and read his postcards."

She'd never dreamed necessity would drive her to this Texas town, or that she'd discover Brandon here as well.

She went to the window now and gazed out at Little Horn. The boardinghouse was near the end of Second Street, with the church and school among the buildings opposite. She could see the doctor's house between them. Louisa, the doctor's daughter who had first cared for the triplets, had married Brandon's brother, Bo. The two men were twins, it seemed. Why hadn't she known that? Why hadn't she been good enough to meet his family?

Why hadn't she been good enough to be his wife?

She could still see Florence's face as her friend had relayed the hurtful message a few days after the scandal about her uncle had become common knowledge.

"He releases you from any agreement you might have thought the two of you had," she'd said, pretty face scrunched as if she'd felt Elizabeth's pain. "As a minister, he must protect his reputation. He hopes you'll understand."

But she hadn't. He'd claimed to love her. Though he hadn't proposed yet, he'd given her every indication that he would do so soon. They'd shared a tender kiss that had left her breathless.

She was still the same person, for all her uncle had been sent to prison, his properties foreclosed to pay off those he'd swindled. Why must she be punished for his actions?

She'd wanted to go to Brandon, beg him to reconsider. If there were those who would condemn him for associating with the family of a convict, surely there were others who would praise him for his charity. But Florence had convinced her that Brandon would not see her, so she had soldiered on alone.

And Brandon had headed west to become pastor of the church in Little Horn. His reputation must have remained spotless, for everyone in the area seemed to adore him.

Eli whimpered in his sleep, recalling her to her duty. The little sweetheart was growing another tooth on the bottom, the pearly nub just breaking through, and she knew his tender gums kept him from sleeping soundly.

Her heart, it seemed, was just as tender when it came to Brandon Stillwater. Only this time, she would listen to her head instead, and it cautioned her to keep her distance.

How was he supposed to keep his distance? Brandon's legs ate up the dusty ground as he headed for his next appointment at the railway station. By word and deed, Elizabeth made it clear she had no use for him. But he was the minister. Having no parents, Jasper, Theo and Eli were under his care, for all he could not see to their needs on a moment-by-moment basis. He had every right and responsibility to check on them, to make sure they were safe and well cared for.

He couldn't deny she was doing a good job. The boys seemed content in her company, happy even, especially after being shuttled between houses since their mother had abandoned them. Elizabeth was good to them, efficient, yet gentle, taking the time to talk to and touch her little charges as if she were their mother.

She'd make a marvelous mother and a wonderful wife.

A wife for someone other than him. He had to remember that.

The best thing he could do was keep busy, which shouldn't be hard. He had a long list of tasks today. Amos Crenshaw had asked him to stop by to discuss the house the railway was building for the stationmaster and his family. Brandon ought to check on Tug Coleman and see how the widowed rancher was faring after the wildfire that had destroyed part of his spread. Then he'd swing over to Dorothy Hill's to make sure the feisty widow and her brood were helping repair the damage as she'd promised. He had a sermon to develop before Sunday and the Harvest Festival to plan.

But even after Amos gave him some excellent news he knew would make David McKay rejoice, Brandon's feet drew him back to the boardinghouse that afternoon. This time, he didn't even have to go inside, for Elizabeth and the babies were out front. She'd managed to wrestle the handcart down the stairs and was just rearranging the babies inside it, back bent and glorious hair hidden under a straw hat. But it was the person standing next to her that had Brandon hurrying forward to help.

Constance Hickey, church pianist and all-around busybody, was lecturing Elizabeth as he reached their sides.

"And cod-liver oil," she said, shaking a bony finger at the babies as if scolding them. "One dose in the morning and one at night. It will help them develop strong constitutions."

The babies all nodded, but Brandon thought it was more likely they were following the movement of Mrs. Hickey's finger than agreeing with her recommendation.

"I'll be sure to bear that in mind," Elizabeth said. Brandon thought he might be the only person in Little Horn who would have detected the annoyance under the polite response.

"Good afternoon, Mrs. Hickey," he greeted the older lady. "How kind of you to take an interest in our triplets."

The thin woman raised her head, aiming her pointed nose in his direction. "And did not our Lord demand that we help the poor and lowly like Miss Dumont?"

Elizabeth's lovely lips tightened. It had to have been one of the first times she'd heard herself referred to as either poor or lowly.

"Oh, I doubt our Lord would have considered Miss Dumont in need of our charity," he told the older woman. "Her skills in caring for the triplets are notable."

Mrs. Hickey frowned. "And exactly where did she learn, a young lady like herself? Has no one checked her references?"

Brandon knew David McKay must have some knowledge, or he would never have sent for her when he'd thought he needed a mail-order bride to help raise his daughter, Maggie. But Brandon hadn't been able to figure out a way to ask without raising questions.

Elizabeth cast Mrs. Hickey a glance. "I was a governess in Boston, and the household had two younger children along with my older charges. The nanny and I often assisted each other."

Mrs. Hickey blinked her blue eyes. "A shame you were discharged."

Where had that rumor started? Brandon frowned, and the babies gurgled as if in protest, but Elizabeth raised her head.

"I wasn't discharged," she told Mrs. Hickey, voice as tight as her look. "My charges were about to go off to school, and the youngest ones were not yet ready for a governess. And then my only living relative, my aunt Evangeline, died, and I simply wanted to be somewhere else."

So she truly was alone in the world, like the triplets.

"I'm sorry to hear about your aunt," Brandon murmured. "She was a grand lady."

Mrs. Hickey turned to him, gaze avid. "Oh, did you know her, Pastor?"

"No!" Jasper declared.

While Mrs. Hickey frowned at the baby, Elizabeth's look shot to Brandon, panicked. So she didn't want the town to know about their past. He hadn't been overly eager to share either. How did you admit that the only woman you'd ever wanted to marry had refused you? The fact called his character into question, or hers.

"Everyone from the Boston area knew Mrs. Evangeline Dumont," Brandon said, and he felt Elizabeth relax. "The lady set a fine table, with only the best on it and around it."

Elizabeth returned her gaze to the babies, who beamed at her. "She never lost her interest in people, even though the stroke left her unable to do the things she loved most."

The stroke hadn't just affected her aunt. It seemed to him Elizabeth had chosen a path much narrower than she'd once dreamed. All of society had been open to her, yet here she was, focused on three little boys. Why?

No way to ask that question with Mrs. Hickey watching them both so eagerly.

"Ah, I fear I have detained you, my dear Mrs. Hickey," Brandon told her. "I'm sure you had business elsewhere this afternoon, industrious lady that you are."

Her smile wavered. She couldn't very well admit she had nothing better to do than vex Elizabeth. "Yes, well," she said, taking a step back. "I am very busy. You will heed my warning about the cod-liver oil, won't you, Miss Dumont?"

"I will give it due consideration," Elizabeth promised her.

With another glance between Elizabeth and Brandon, the pianist turned and headed toward the doctor's office, very likely intending to instruct the physician on some point now. The boys waved their fists in farewell.

"Do not tell me she means well," Elizabeth threatened Brandon, "for I won't believe it."

"She delights in knowing more than anyone else, about everything," he said. "So long as you remember that, you won't have any trouble with her."

Elizabeth shook her head. "You must not have noticed the way she looked at you. You better watch your reputation, Pastor. You wouldn't want to be seen with a discharged governess who was left at the altar. People might talk."

"I've never been particularly concerned about what anonymous people have to say," Brandon told her. He bent and seized the handles on the cart, and the triplets started bouncing up and down in anticipation of the ride. "Now, where can I take you and the boys?"

That look in her eyes told him she would have preferred to tell him where to go, and it was as far away from her as possible. But she nodded across the street. "The triplets and I have been cooped up in the boardinghouse for three days now. I was hoping to cross to the grass and let them out on the quilt. If you would be so kind, Reverend?"

Of course she wouldn't call him Brandon. They were supposed to be strangers. Besides, times had changed since they'd last known each other. They had changed. He wasn't a man bent on courting her. He was her minister, just as he was the minister for everyone in Little Horn. His only concern should be for her spiritual growth and comfort. If she had been anyone else, he would have done his best to charm her, putting her at ease. But his winning ways no longer seemed to work on Elizabeth.

So he trundled the cart across the rutted street for the grassy field between the parsonage and the church, the creak of the wheels playing them along.

The good citizens of Little Horn had designed the church grounds, like the church and parsonage, with the community's needs in mind. Between the two buildings lay a sweep of grass, wildflowers nodding here and there, just waiting for a church picnic or baseball game. Amos Crenshaw kept it in order, even going so far as to carry water to it during the drought so the grass wouldn't dry out. Brandon positioned the cart in the shade of an old live oak and helped her spread the large brightly colored quilt beside it. Then they arranged the triplets in the middle.

At nearly eleven months old, they were crawling well. Jasper, as usual, was the most adventurous. Elizabeth must have realized it, for she positioned herself between the tree and the edge of the quilt as if to prevent his escape. Rolling over on his side, Eli tugged at a block of red gingham on the quilt as if eager to get to the grass beneath. Theo sat and regarded the nearby daisies as if suspecting they had designs on his brothers. Jasper set off across the quilt and paused a moment beside Elizabeth before attempting to scale her lap.

She smiled at him, making the day brighter. "Clever boy. You wait and see, Pastor. Jasper will turn out to be an explorer."

Brandon smiled. "I think Eli's going to end up mayor of Little Horn by the way he manages his brothers."

She laughed, and the sound bathed his heart in light. "Can't you just see them," she asked, "tall and strong, crowding in the doorway with daisies from the fields, come to wish their mother happy birthday?"

So she could still dream. He remembered the hopes she used to share—visiting Europe, opening a school for girls, driving a carriage across the whole country.

"What happened, Elizabeth?" he asked. "Why did you become a governess in Cambridge? I thought you wanted to marry."

Her sunny smile turned stormy. "I did want to marry. The man I'd hoped would be my groom abandoned me. Or don't you remember telling me your reputation was more important than I was, Mr. Stillwater?"

Chapter Three

She must have looked as angry as she felt, for Brandon recoiled from her. So did the triplets. Jasper's face puckered. Eli curled next to him. Theo stuck his thumb in his mouth, a tear rolling down one chubby cheek.

Brandon reached out and scooped him onto his lap. "Easy there, Theo. Elizabeth isn't angry with you. She couldn't be. She thinks you're going to grow into a fine man. I'm the one she doesn't like. She said she couldn't marry a country parson."

Elizabeth stared at him. His eyes looked as sad as Theo's.

"I never said I didn't want to marry you," she protested. "And I certainly never called you a country parson. You were going to serve at St. Matthew's, a fine respectable position."

Theo leaned against him as if ready to defend him. Brandon patted his shoulder. "You knew I wanted to go to Texas with Bo. And Texas wasn't good enough for you."

She spread her hands. "Look at me, Brandon. Here I am, in Texas!"

Her voice was rising again. Jasper let out a squawk as if determined to be louder. Eli's gaze darted between her and Brandon. Theo plastered himself against Brandon's chest. Even the bushes at the edge of the lawn rustled as if in agitation.

She forced herself to calm, to speak quietly and evenly. "I don't understand why you have that impression of me. I never said money and position were important."

He raised a brow. "That's not how John Hood's sister explained it."

Poor Florence, to be caught in the middle of such a difficult situation. She'd been as caring as her brother, who had been in Brandon's class at the divinity school.

"I'm sure it wasn't easy for her," Elizabeth said. "When my uncle was arrested, everything changed. I was so caught up in caring for Aunt Evangeline that I couldn't do more than survive each day. Some of Aunt Evangeline's more colorful acquaintances stuck by our side, but Florence was the only person who came by regularly."

He nodded. "She was the one who brought me the news about your uncle's arrest and your aunt's stroke. I was surprised you didn't come yourself."

There was more pain than censure in his voice. Just thinking about that dark time made an ache rise inside her. She reached for Eli and pulled him onto her lap. The baby rested his head against her, a comforting bundle.

"I couldn't leave Aunt's side, so I asked Florence to help me reach you. I thought you would want to know what was happening, that you'd want to help. But Florence said you couldn't risk being seen with me."

He frowned. "Why would there have been any risk to me by being seen in your company? You weren't the criminal. Your uncle was."

She could not have misunderstood Florence. Her friend had been quite clear on the message. Her face had been anguished, dark curls trembling, and she'd barely been able to force the words from her lips.

"You were hoping for an appointment at a prestigious church, Brandon," Elizabeth reminded him. "Having a wife associated with scandal might have hindered that."

"I never considered that," he insisted. "I wanted to go to you, help you any way I could, but Florence said you refused to see me. Because of the funds needed to pay for your aunt's care, you had no choice but to marry a better connected, wealthier man. It sounded as if you had him all picked out. With your aunt's parties, you had plenty of candidates to choose from, each more eligible than me."

What was he talking about? Hadn't he realized she had looked at no one else once she'd seen him? "I didn't have another groom in mind. Florence knew that."

He cocked his head. "I thought you needed money to pay for your aunt's care."

"I did. That's why I became a governess. All my income went to fund nurses."

Now all three babies were watching her, and Eli's and Theo's lips were trembling as if in sympathy. Jasper looked more as if he wanted to fight her battles instead, little hands fisted.

Brandon straightened, rubbing his free hand along his pant leg. "I don't understand. You needed me. I wanted to help. What went wrong?"

What indeed? It was easy for him to claim all innocence now. Yet she could not convince herself he would lie to her face. No member of his congregation was present. The triplets weren't likely to remember this conversation by the time they could speak enough to tell anyone about it. And no one in Little Horn would believe her over their beloved pastor. Why posture?

Elizabeth made herself shrug, then snuggled Eli closer. "It seems to have been very easy for us to believe the worst of each other. I'd say our attachment was never meant to be."

He frowned as if unwilling to believe that. How could he deny it? Back then, she'd been unsure of herself, awed by everyone she had met at her aunt's table. Why would the marvelous Brandon Stillwater find her worthy to be his wife?

But she was no longer that wide-eyed girl with dreams bigger than her capabilities. Now she knew just what she was made of, had been tested and survived. Now she knew what she needed.

A steady position or a steady husband. Brandon Stillwater would be willing to offer neither.

Once again she was calm, composed, the baby cradled in her arms, but this time Brandon thought Eli was more of a shield to keep him at a distance. Jasper, leaning on her legs, made another attempt to crawl over them for the freedom beyond, and Brandon grabbed the baby's foot and pulled him into the scope of his arms. All the while he tried to orient himself to a world that had shifted.

Our attachment was never meant to be.

Though he'd thought he'd put it all behind him four

years ago, though he was certain he'd moved forward with his life, something inside him rebelled. He'd believed her need for position and privilege had driven them apart. She seemed to think his need for a spotless reputation was to blame.

She was right—it had been easy to believe those statements and to think the worst of each other. Only, he knew that her assumptions about him were false.

Florence had been anguished when she'd brought him Elizabeth's answer to his plea to reconsider her decision to throw him over. A slender, dark-haired girl with the appropriately pious attitude of the daughter and sister of clergy, she'd gazed up at him, blue eyes shining with tears, fingers pressed against his arm.

"I'm so sorry, Brandon, but Elizabeth is adamant that you will not suit. She needs a man of wealth and position to counter this scandal if she is to regain her place in society. Knowing how she was raised, I'm sure you understand."

He'd understood. His family did not take part in society, for all his father had once been considered a gentleman. Marcus Stillwater had managed his affairs well. Everyone who met him at civic functions and during business considered him a determined, successful man.

But his father had doubted himself—his abilities, his place in other people's affections. Brandon had never been sure why. His grandfather had died when he and Bo were little, but family stories told of a harsh man. Or perhaps the responsibility of building his business had weighed on their father. Either way, to bolster his flagging confidence, his father had cut down every other member of the family. Nothing Brandon's mother could do was good enough. Nothing Brandon and Bo did was acceptable. It seemed only by making others feel small had his father been able to feel big. If Brandon had had a nickel for every time his father had called him worthless, he might actually have been the wealthy man Elizabeth had needed.

Given that upbringing, Brandon could well imagine he wasn't good enough for her. Even while they were courting he'd wondered why she would settle for a divinity student when the very best of Boston society came to call. Still, he'd thought himself genuinely in love, had convinced himself she felt the same way. Florence had tried to console him, but he had pushed her and everyone else away, determined only to finish his studies and escape the stifling confines of Cambridge.

"I don't believe our love was never meant to be, Elizabeth," he told her, alternating his gaze between the babies he jostled in his arms. Both were regarding him as if fascinated to hear how his story would end. "Circumstances prevented it from continuing. That's all."

He could hear her sigh. "Perhaps you're right. But those circumstances haven't changed. I still need a way to support myself, and you still have a responsibility to your congregation."

A responsibility he took seriously. His kitchen was stocked by well-meaning young ladies who had hopes of one day changing their name to Stillwater. But he had an inkling that being married to the local minister would not be the glorious position they all envisioned. His wife would have to be willing to have her life interrupted for the illness, injury and death of others, the destruction of other people's hopes, their property.

She'd have to celebrate every wedding, birth and civic commemoration, be part of planning each church activity and contribute to every charitable cause. Women for miles around would call on her, expecting to find her house perfect, her life perfect.

He'd seen his mother wilt under impossible expectations, although of a different kind. He did not feel comfortable foisting that burden on another.

"For the moment, you have a way to support yourself," he said, nodding to the babies. "But I'll ask around, see if there's another family in the area who needs a governess."

Some of the fire seemed to have left her. "Thank you. I'd appreciate that."

"It would be my pleasure. And I hope, Elizabeth, that, whatever our differences in the past, we can be cordial now."

He chanced a glance her way to find himself slipping into the blue-green depths of her eyes.

"Cordial," she said, and the word held a world of doubt.

"Friends, even," he insisted, giving the babies an extra jiggle that made Jasper smile. "I am the minister of Little Horn, after all. I'm expected to be friendly with everyone."

The fire flashed once more, as if she was building up a head of steam.

"Well, certainly we should be friends, Pastor Stillwater," she drawled. "After all, I wouldn't want to damage your reputation."

Brandon blew out a breath. She simply could not accept his word that his reputation was not the issue.

"This isn't about my standing in the community," he tried again. "It's about what's best for the triplets."

Her look eased, and she returned her gaze to Eli, whose eyes were closed as she rocked him in the warm shade. "I suppose you're right. They get upset even when I raise my voice."

So did he. He would much rather put a smile on her face, make her laugh, than be cause for consternation.

"Then let's start over," Brandon suggested. "Pretend we just met." He gave her a nod. "How do you do, Miss Dumont? I'm Brandon Stillwater, the pastor of the Little Horn church. I'd shake your hand, but mine seem to be full at the moment."

She shifted on the quilt, the movement making Eli crack open his eyes a moment.

"A pleasure to meet you, Reverend," she said softly, as if afraid to believe they could return to anything approaching normality. "I'm Elizabeth Dumont, and I have the honor of looking after these three delightful gentlemen." Her smile faded. "At least for now."

Both of Brandon's babies were nodding off as well. He crouched and laid each on the quilt. Elizabeth did the same, and he pulled up the edge to cover them all.

"What will happen to them after I'm gone?" she asked, straightening as he did.

She was leaving? Well, of course she'd leave if she couldn't find employment in Little Horn. Why should that fact concern him?

"David McKay is planning to set up a children's home," he told her, offering her his hand to help her rise. Her fingers were supple in his, yet they had a strength he didn't remember from before. "I learned today we may have a house."

Behind him, he heard a rustling sound, as if something moved among the bushes at the end of the yard. Before he could turn and look, Elizabeth brightened. "Oh, that would be wonderful."

"It won't be ready for a while," he cautioned, focusing on her. "The railroad is building a new home for our stationmaster, Mr. Crenshaw. As he won't be needing the one he had built before he became stationmaster, he's offered to donate it to the church. It will need to be renovated first. Those funds will have to come from the Lone Star Cowboy League, as the church benevolence fund is empty after seeing to those affected by the drought."

"Will you need someone to run it?" she asked, cinnamon-colored brows up in obvious hope.

Brandon shook his head. "I'm fairly sure the league will want a couple, and I quite agree. It won't just be the boys, you see. Other orphans are scattered about the area, living with distant relatives or friends of the family who are hard-pressed to care for them. The house will be full before we even open the doors."

"I suppose it will be good for the boys to have other children around," she allowed, tucking a strand of red hair back behind her ear. "I've seen how much they enjoy Maggie's company."

David McKay's eight-year-old daughter, Maggie, was something of an adventurer, climbing out of her bedroom window to escape scolds, swimming in the stream on their ranch with the skill of a fish. David had told him how she'd come to regard the triplets as her little brothers and had been inconsolable when they had to leave the Windy Diamond, the McKay ranch.

She'd found solace only because she'd gained a mother in Caroline.

"They'll have brothers and sisters at the children's home," Brandon promised Elizabeth. "And I still haven't given up hope that someone will want to adopt all three."

Something flickered across her face, and he wasn't sure if it was emotion or a shadow from the tree.

"They're such darlings," she murmured, gaze on her slumbering charges. "I can see Jasper as the leader, guiding his brothers. Eli is going to be the planner, determining how to make Jasper's ideas real. And Theo will be the one who comes to his mother and confesses all before anyone gets into trouble."

He smiled. "Bo accused me of that often enough. Our mother had the sweetest look. One moment in her company, and you just had to unburden yourself."

"You have the same kind of smile that invites people to confide in you," she said. "I'm sure everyone in your congregation finds it easy to talk to you."

She had, once. He could remember long walks through the park sharing hopes for the future, sitting on her aunt's front porch talking until the stars brightened the night sky. Brandon shook his head. "You better be careful, Miss Dumont. I think you just gave me a compliment."

She raised her chin. "It wasn't a compliment. It was an opinion. After all, Mr. Stillwater, we just met, remember." She batted her lashes at him, and Brandon grinned.

"Ahem."

He glanced up to find Mrs. Hickey standing at the corner of the parsonage with Mrs. Bachmeier and

Amos's wife, Susan, crowded on either side, eyes wide. Behind him, he thought he heard footsteps hurrying away, but when he glanced back, he saw no one.

"It's time for us to clean the parsonage, Pastor," Mrs. Hickey announced, although he was certain the ladies had just been in to sweep and dust earlier in the week.

Brandon offered them all a grateful smile as he turned to face them. "Very considerate of you, but everything seems fine at the moment."

Mrs. Hickey drew herself up. "Nonsense. We cannot have our minister living in squalor. Cleanliness is next to godliness. Everyone knows that."

Brandon inclined his head. "I applaud your determination. Since you feel so strongly, do what you must to rid my house of any sign of squalor, ladies. I'll just help Miss Dumont return the triplets to the boardinghouse."

Mrs. Hickey brightened. "Oh, is Miss Dumont having trouble managing the little foundlings? Perhaps we should speak to Lula May McKay about finding another nanny. I always thought they would do better with one of our own instead of a stranger."

He was ready to protest that Elizabeth was no stranger, but she gave an almost imperceptible shake of her head. Right. She still refused to acknowledge their past in public.

"Miss Dumont has the trust of the Lone Star Cowboy League," Brandon assured the women. "And mine."

Mrs. Bachmeier and Mrs. Crenshaw nodded, but Mrs. Hickey looked disappointed. Beside him, Elizabeth offered him a smile that made him insufferably pleased with his ability to ease troubled waters.

"Well, hurry along, then," Mrs. Hickey ordered.

"I'm sure we'll have all kinds of questions about what to do with various items. Unless, of course, you'd just like us to sort things willy-nilly."

Brandon nearly groaned aloud. The last time Mrs. Hickey had organized his study, he hadn't been able to find his sermon notes for days.

"I'll be right back," he promised the ladies before turning to Elizabeth. "I hope you don't mind."

"Not at all. I can see you have very important things to do, Pastor." Her voice hinted of a laugh.

He did have things to do, and now he had to do them with an audience. He glanced down at the babies. All three had opened their eyes and were regarding him with such seriousness he had a feeling he was supposed to beg their pardon too.

He'd been concerned about his congregation, he'd been concerned about the triplets. Now he found himself more concerned about Elizabeth's future. He knew it wouldn't be easy finding a governess position among the ranching families surrounding Little Horn.

But if gossip about him and Elizabeth began to spread, she might never find an employer. The Lone Star Cowboy League might even have to rescind the offer for her to care for the boys.

It very much looked as if Elizabeth Dumont had become his responsibility. A responsibility that, for once in his life, he wasn't sure he was capable of meeting.

Chapter Four

Elizabeth thought of Brandon many times over the next few days. He wanted a fresh start, a chance for the two of them to begin again as friends. She ought to accommodate. For as long as she was in Little Horn, he would be her minister. He'd promised to help her find a new position. And he clearly cared about the boys. But it was difficult shifting her heart away from the hurt of their parting four years ago.

As Sunday rolled around, she knew she had to try harder. Like it or not, she realized, a minister's reputation was important to his calling. She truly didn't want to give anyone the impression she was disappointed in Brandon. She put on her best dress, a peach-colored taffeta with black lace in the center of the bodice and double rows of black bric-a-brac trimming the long sleeves and graceful hem. She combed her hair up and covered it with a peach-colored hat with a black lace veil. It was foolish, really—one baby finger poked in the wrong place would send the confection tumbling from her head, but for some reason she felt like taking the risk and looking more like a lady than a servant for once.

It must have worked, for one of the older men in the boardinghouse spotted her as she stepped out into the hallway and volunteered to haul the cart down the stairs for her. His roommate offered to carry two of the boys while she took the third.

"Cute little fellers," the man who had carried the cart said with a smile that spread his thick mustache. He bent to chuck Theo under the chin as the boy snuggled in Elizabeth's arms. The baby promptly burst into tears, and the man backed away, panic on his rugged face.

"It's all right," Elizabeth said, to him and to Theo. "He's just a little shy."

The ladies of Little Horn, on the other hand, were anything but shy as Elizabeth crossed the street to the churchyard. They clustered around the cart the moment she bumped it against the steps. She wasn't sure what to do with the thing, but Mr. Tyson, a burly man with dark hair and kind eyes, helpfully angled it under the steps.

His wife took Jasper. Annie Hill, a cheerful young blonde who helped Louisa at the doctor's office, took Eli, and Elizabeth kept Theo. His button-brown eyes looked out of a troubled face as they all found seats near each other in the crowded church. Across the way, the boys' previous nannies, Caroline and Louisa, smiled a welcome, each sitting beside her new husband. Elizabeth had to force herself not to look twice at Bo Stillwater, for he was identical to Brandon, sandy-haired, tall and strong.

She made herself look at the church instead. The last time she had been inside the Little Horn chapel was when she'd discovered David McKay with Caroline. Then her gaze had been all for the couple and the minister in the wedding. Now she took note of the polished walnut pews running on either side of the aisle, the fresh whitewashed walls and the simple wood cross behind the altar. She recognized the trim figure of Constance Hickey as the woman marched up to them.

"Here," she said, thrusting three wrinkled pieces of paper at her. "I found these on the piano. They're clearly for you." She peered closer. "Who do you think left them?"

Elizabeth had no idea. Balancing Theo on her hip, she shuffled through the simple pencil drawings. The first showed a sad-faced woman bending over a cart, the babies watchful, with pies in a circle all around them. Elizabeth had heard the story about how Brandon's brother had found the babies in the pie tent of the county fair. Was the woman the boys' mother? The picture was too crude to tell anything of her features or coloring.

The second drawing showed two women with the babies between them. Caroline and Louisa, perhaps? The last showed a woman and a man in a frock coat, holding hands, and the babies circling them. Did someone know about her and Brandon's past? She willed herself not to blush.

Annie looked around her arm, and Elizabeth hurriedly folded the sheets closed.

"I know," the girl said. "Those must have come from the Good Samaritan."

Mrs. Hickey perked up.

"Very likely," Mrs. Tyson said with a nod. "Someone has been doing good deeds for the triplets since they arrived, but no one has caught sight of the person."

"Miss Louisa—Mrs. Stillwater—thought it might

be the babies' mother," Annie said. "But no one's seen a strange woman in town."

"Except Miss Dumont," Mrs. Hickey said, watching Elizabeth.

Was the woman intent on starting *that* rumor now? Elizabeth opened her mouth to protest, then hesitated. What would they do if she claimed to be the boys' mother? The Lone Star Cowboy League would be bound to give her the boys. They might even help her support them.

But no, she couldn't lie. The boys deserved to know their parents, both the ones who had birthed them and the ones who would raise them.

"Miss Dumont arrived in town weeks after the babies were found," Mrs. Tyson pointed out with a look to Mrs. Hickey. "And she only came at David McKay's request. She can't be the triplets' mother."

Mrs. Hickey sniffed. "I suppose not. But you tell this Good Samaritan, whoever he is, that I am not the postmaster." She picked up her skirts and swept to the piano in the corner, where she positioned herself on the bench, fingers poised.

So the boys had someone else looking out for them. Elizabeth glanced around the church again, wondering who it could be. No one seemed to be watching to see how she'd taken the drawings, but perhaps the Good Samaritan was being cautious. Still, helping the babies was a kindness. Why keep it a secret? As if the matter concerned him too, Theo cuddled closer when Elizabeth stood with the others and sang the opening hymn. In Mrs. Tyson's arms, Jasper clapped his hands as if trying to keep time, and Eli rocked himself against Annie, wrinkling her red-and-yellow flower-printed cotton dress.

Mr. Crenshaw, the stationmaster, came to the pulpit. He must be the deacon. Elizabeth followed along with the prayers and readings, all the while making sure her boys weren't any more of a distraction than necessary. Her thoughts were distracted enough. Why would the Good Samaritan draw her and Brandon holding hands? Had she done something that made it appear they were a couple?

Then Brandon stepped up to the pulpit, and she couldn't look away. At more than six feet tall, he had had a presence even when he was just a student at the divinity school. Now, though his brown frock coat, waistcoat and trousers were plain and functional, he looked every inch the compassionate, dedicated minister. He leaned forward and smiled, and the whole church seemed to brighten.

"We've been talking about the Israelites leaving Egypt," he said, glancing around at the people who had come to worship. Elizabeth found herself trying to catch his gaze and chided herself. She no longer had to posture for Brandon's attentions. She had more important matters to attend to. She turned her smile on Theo, who smiled back.

"God provided the Israelites a way through obstacles, both natural and made by human hands," he continued, voice warm and thoughtful as he straightened. "Through a series of plagues, He convinced the King of Egypt to let them go free from slavery. With a miracle, He made a way for thousands of people to pass through the Red Sea unharmed. He guided them by day and by night."

How nice to have a God so attentive, to work such wonders. Of course, He'd likely had to perform such feats to save a nation from bondage. That didn't mean she should expect Him to do the same for her and the boys. Didn't the Bible say not to put the Lord God to the test?

"Without God's help," Brandon was explaining, silver gaze ever-moving, "they would have continued in slavery. Even the right to raise sons was denied them. They were, in effect, orphans, until God made them His family."

She glanced at the boys. All three had turned their heads toward Brandon. They knew the sound of his voice, trusted it enough to listen. When had she lost such childlike faith?

Could she find it again?

On the altar, Brandon leaned toward the congregation again with a smile, as if he was about to impart a secret. "We have among us today a number of orphans, children left by parents who passed on or could no longer pay their way. They too are part of God's family. And I believe God is calling on us to help them."

Around her, men straightened on the wooden pews, ladies raised their heads.

"Even though the drought appears to be behind us, for which we thank God, the effects remain for many in our community," he told them. "Times for them are hard. We cannot allow our hearts to grow hard as well. Jesus welcomed the little children, warned against hindering them from learning about Him. And He said that when we offer a cup of cool water or a set of warm clothes to those in need, we offer them to Him. There are many needs in Little Horn. Pray this week about what God would have you do to help meet them."

Elizabeth glanced at Mrs. Tyson to see her wipe a tear from her cheek. Annie held Eli as if she'd never let him go. Theo turned in Elizabeth's arms and gazed at her so somberly she could not forget that she was the one he and his brothers relied upon.

Am I doing what You want me to do, Father?

Just then the piano began tinkling under Mrs. Hickey's fingers, and the congregation rose for the concluding hymn. Elizabeth would have liked a moment or two to think about what Brandon had said, but as soon as the song ended, she was surrounded.

"I kept some of our sons' baby things," Mrs. Tyson said, rubbing a hand over Theo's dark hair and earning her a frown from the touchy baby. "They certainly aren't going to need them again. I'll bring them to you this week."

"The blackberry preserves are just about set," another woman put in. "I'll give you some."

Other ladies offered blankets and bonnets. Gents asked if Elizabeth needed help with handling the cart or chopping firewood for the hearth in her room. Jasper and Eli ate up the attention, and even Theo broke into a giggle as Stella tickled him. All Elizabeth could think was that Brandon wielded a great deal of power in Little Horn, for the townsfolk certainly listened to their minister.

One of the last to come forward was Mrs. Hickey, and she was towing an older man with a wide girth.

"Miss Dumont," she said, pointed nose in the air, "this is Clyde Parker. I understand from Mrs. Arundel that you are desirous of making his acquaintance."

And the way her wiry brows came down told Elizabeth that the pianist suspected nefarious purpose in the request.

The fellow frowned at Elizabeth. A bulldog of a man, with a neck nearly as wide as his chest, he splayed his bandy legs and put his hands on his hips, eyeing her up and down. His clothes were clean, but wrinkled and well-worn. His battered felt hat seemed as ancient as the lines in his weathered face. Oh, dear. Wasn't he one of the men who had been suggested as a husband for her?

"Ma'am," he spit out with a nod of his graying head. He eyed Theo in her arms as if she held a snake. "Pleased to meet you. I hear you'd like to stay in Little Horn."

"No!" Jasper told him. Mrs. Hickey recoiled, and Mr. Parker frowned. Mrs. Tyson stepped back to quiet the boy.

"It's a pleasant town," Elizabeth assured the rancher, wondering how to gracefully make her escape. "Everyone has been so kind."

"Pastor Stillwater knows her family," Mrs. Hickey informed Mr. Parker. "He says they were fine people."

He hadn't actually said that, and Elizabeth knew many did not consider her uncle so fine anymore.

Mr. Parker nodded. "References are always good. And it seems you like children."

She liked Jasper, Theo and Eli. "Do you have children, Mr. Parker?" she asked, turning the questions on him.

"My wife, God rest her soul, and I were never blessed." He cleared his throat as if it hurt to remember, and Elizabeth could not help but like him for that. Then he narrowed his eyes at her. "So, can you cook?"

She had been hoping to interview with someone in the area as a nanny or governess. Did he intend to interview her as a wife? She could think of no kind way to answer him.

Instead, she sniffed the air and made a face. "Oh, dear. I fear I may need to take care of a matter. If you'll excuse me."

Mrs. Hickey and Mr. Parker took one look at the baby in her arms and melted back from her as if little Theo carried yellow fever. Elizabeth turned and hurried out of the door. She knew she'd have to fetch Theo's brothers at some point, but for now she just wanted freedom.

She nearly bumped into Brandon on the front steps. He caught her arm. "Easy. Everything all right?"

Elizabeth pasted on a smile as several of the departing ladies glanced their way. "Fine. Your sermon was very effective. Everyone is offering help."

He smiled. "Glad to hear it. Let's hope the members of the Lone Star Cowboy League are similarly accommodating when I tell them we have a house for the children's home. Say a prayer. They're meeting after service."

She wanted to wish him well. It sounded as if a children's home was badly needed. But if Brandon succeeded in giving one to Little Horn, she could well lose the boys, and her opportunity to get to know him again, forever.

Brandon stood on the steps, listening to praise for his sermon, commiserating about family concerns and generally bidding farewell to the last members of his congregation. All the while a part of him was aware of Elizabeth at the foot of the steps, settling the boys into the cart.

It had been the same way during service. While he'd made it a point to meet the gaze of every member in attendance at least once, he'd felt himself drawn to her. He'd seen those cinnamon brows rise in surprise, those peach-colored lips purse in concern. He generally spoke about what the Lord put on his heart. He shouldn't crave her appreciation.

But he did. And he couldn't help feeling that by championing the children's home he'd somehow disappointed her.

He couldn't afford such concerns now. He'd asked Lula May McKay to call a meeting of the Lone Star Cowboy League for right after service, and he knew he had some persuading to do.

Please give me the words, Lord.

It seemed he'd had to choose his words carefully his whole life, to keep from hurting his already-wounded mother, to prevent a blowup with his father. The trait naturally flowed into his work as a minister. Words chosen carefully built sermons, mended hearts and healed lives.

"Powerful sermon, Pastor," Mrs. Hickey said, strutting out of the church and pausing to frown across the yard. Brandon thought she might be looking for her husband, a warmhearted man who called the community dances, but he knew the moment she spotted Elizabeth, because her gaze narrowed and one foot began tapping under her blue skirts.

"I'm glad you appreciated it, Mrs. Hickey," he said,

drawing her gaze back to him. "But then, I don't have to tell you to care for widows and orphans. You were among the first to reach out to the triplets."

She raised her head, the soft pink roses on her hat belying the sharpness of her gaze. "I believe charity starts at home. I expect you'll be joining us for dinner, Reverend. I plan to eat at four."

Was he now her charity? Something within him protested. "That's very kind of you, I'm sure, but I fear I have other plans."

Her brows came up. "Oh?"

"I was going to see if Miss Dumont and the triplets wanted some dinner," he told her.

She sucked in a breath, no doubt ready to launch into a scold.

Brandon met her gaze. "After all, what use is a minister who doesn't practice what he preaches?"

She deflated. "True, true. Well, next Sunday, then." Head still high, she clomped down the steps. Brandon thought about following her, intervening in anything she might say to plague Elizabeth, but Lula May appeared in the doorway of the church just then and beckoned him inside. It was time to present his case. With one last look at Elizabeth, in a peach-colored dress that only made him think of her lips, he followed the lady into the quiet of the church.

The members of the Lone Star Cowboy League had wandered to the front of the chapel. With fewer people gathered in the pews, their voices echoed to the beams overhead. Every rustle of cotton against wood, every shift of a heavy body spoke volumes. He only hoped his proposal would speak as loudly.

His brother, Bo, gave him a grin of encouragement

from the front row. Brandon knew all the other members. Dark-haired CJ Thorn, one of the founders, had once held himself aloof and somber. Now, thanks to his wife, Molly, infant son and twin nieces, he tended to smile more often than not. He curled his long body next to Edmund McKay, who somehow managed to make the pews seem small.

McKay too had stayed away from people until the widowed Lula May had taken him under her wing and shown him what family could mean. Caroline Murray had done the same for Edmund's brother David, who sat forward on his seat now, hat turning in his hands, as he waited for the meeting to start. Leaner than his brother, David met Brandon's gaze and nodded encouragement, green eyes bright in the shadows of the church.

Edmund, CJ and Bo had been amenable to David's earlier proposal to build a children's home, Brandon knew. According to David, it was the older cattlemen who had balked. They always seemed to count pennies rather than needs.

They clustered together now, as if uniting against whatever idea would be proposed: lean and cautious Abe Sawyer, stocky and cranky Clyde Parker, hard-as-nails Gabe Dooley and ruddy and cantankerous Casper Magnuson. The last scowled at Brandon as if he suspected the sermon earlier had been leading up to this.

He would not be wrong.

"Order," Lula May called, and the men fell silent. There was a reason the cow pony breeder had been made league president. The only woman in the group, the petite blonde with red in her hair had a way of making her presence felt.

"We have one item of business today," she announced, intelligent blue eyes pinning each man in his seat. "And that is the matter of the children's home we agreed to fund."

Sawyer, Parker and Dooley leaned back and crossed their arms over their chests. Magnuson did the same, even though his old friend Saul Hauser had recently passed on, leaving children behind. Nothing like having support.

At Lula May's nod, Brandon stood and spread his hands. "Gentlemen, madam president, thank you for your concerns about the most vulnerable among us. The triplets, the Satler siblings and the other children scattered across the county need our support."

"Something has to be done," Magnuson allowed, lowering his arms.

His cronies cast him a look as if to accuse him of giving in too soon.

"Something has to be done," Dooley agreed. "We said we'd help. But let's not get carried away. There's only so much money."

"True," Bo put in. "But there isn't a civic fund, and the church fund already goes to pay for religious activities, community gatherings and the school."

"We could always levy taxes," Lula May suggested sweetly, a determined gleam in her eyes. "Say, on every head of cattle on the range and every acre of farmland."

Edmund shook his head, a grin winning free. Brandon wouldn't have been surprised to see him applaud his wife's audacity.

Dooley, Sawyer and Parker shifted in their seats. Magnuson tugged at his collar. "Enough of that kind of talk now. Someone might get ideas."

Brandon hid a smile. "Then the Lone Star Cowboy League is our best, least expensive option to fund a children's home."

Parker snorted. "Least expensive? You didn't hear McKay's proposal. Gardens, their own bedrooms, training for employment. Why give all that to orphans?"

"Why give those to any child?" David countered, gaze darkening. "Because we want them to grow up to become contributing members of society."

Parker turned his scowl toward the young rancher.

Brandon held up his hand. "What if I told you I could give you everything David originally asked for, at less than half the cost you imagined?"

Sawyer and Dooley perked up. Magnuson leaned forward. Parker's scowl eased just the tiniest.

CJ spoke up. "I'd say I'd like to hear more, Pastor."

Brandon drew in a breath. They were ready to listen. He went on to explain about the Crenshaw house and his hopes for an easy renovation. He added that the Arundels and Mercy Green had agreed to help provide food for the home. By the time he had finished, they were all nodding.

"It just might work," Sawyer said. "Several families in the area are having trouble caring for kin left orphaned. This could really help them."

Bo winked at Brandon.

Lula May beamed at them all. "It seems we have an accord, gentlemen. We already agreed that David and Pastor would oversee the project. All in favor of funding Pastor Stillwater's proposal?"

"Aye," everyone but Parker chorused.

"Opposed?" She speared Parker with her blue gaze. Parker clamped his mouth shut.

"Motion carries," she declared. "Now, if there's nothing else…"

Brandon held up his hand again. "One other concern, if I may."

Parker groaned, but his friends silenced him. Lula May nodded for Brandon to continue.

"The league is currently funding Elizabeth Dumont to care for the triplets," he told them. "When they move into the children's home, she will need another position."

"Don't expect us to pay for that," Sawyer ordered.

"There must be someone who needs a cook or nanny," Dooley put in, glancing around as if he hoped to find one among them.

"Most folks hereabouts prefer family to help raise children," Lula May replied thoughtfully.

"And most cooks have to travel with the herd," Bo added.

Brandon had known it would be hard to find Elizabeth other work, but hearing their reluctance just steeled his resolve. She'd lost her place in society, her position as a governess and her potential husband to another woman. She deserved something of her own.

"You're all worried for nothing," Magnuson grumbled. "She's a fine-looking woman who loves children. Someone's going to marry her. You wait and see."

Though Lula May looked unconvinced, most of the men were nodding again, even David, Bo, Edmund and CJ. Brandon knew he should protest. Elizabeth shouldn't have to sell herself in marriage to support herself. Then again, what if she met a man she could love and who loved her in return? Wouldn't that make life better for her again? His responsibility toward her would diminish to that of a pastor for his flock. Magnuson's suggestion was logical.

He simply could not understand why the thought of Elizabeth marrying made him feel as if he'd failed.

Chapter Five

Caroline and Louisa accompanied Elizabeth back to the boardinghouse and helped her change the boys into fresh diapers. At just over five feet tall, with soft brown hair and warm brown eyes, Louisa gave off an air of competence and kindness no doubt earned from years helping her physician father and invalid mother. A good half foot taller, Caroline was more energetic; her light brown hair, sparkling hazel eyes and bright smile inspired confidences. Coming from a musical family, she had a natural presence. Each had spent time caring for the triplets before Elizabeth arrived, and both had gone out of their way to make her feel welcome in Little Horn, even though it was hard to get into town often from their ranches.

Today, they gathered on the floor, heedless of their pretty church dresses, and played with the boys as they chatted with Elizabeth.

"Look how big you've grown," Caroline told Theo, who was crawling toward her with an eye to the sling that protected her healing arm. She carefully moved her arm aside as Louisa distracted him by clapping her hands.

"I can't imagine a mother leaving them," Louisa said as the boys converged on her. Jasper sat and began clapping along with her, off beat and grinning. "I pray for her every day."

"That reminds me." Elizabeth rose to fetch the drawings that Mrs. Hickey had found on the church piano. "These were left for the boys. Any idea who the artist might be?"

Louisa flipped through the pictures, then handed them to Caroline. As if determined to look as well, the boys headed back her way.

"Someone has an eye for detail," Caroline said with a glance up to Elizabeth.

Had she noticed the picture with Elizabeth and Brandon holding hands? Elizabeth willed herself not to blush. "Is it possible the mother is still here?"

Caroline handed the pictures back to Elizabeth and frowned as if wondering the same thing, but Louisa shook her head. "She can't be. Only a handful of people have moved to Little Horn in the last three months, my family among them. Everyone knows when there's a stranger in town."

"But no one is a stranger for long," Caroline countered, giving Eli's toe a tug as he scooted past her, following the pictures. "That's one of the things I love about this town."

"But if this is the work of the Good Samaritan," Elizabeth protested, "why hide it? Why not come forward?"

Caroline and Louisa exchanged puzzled glances.

"Perhaps the person is shy," Louisa suggested. "And doesn't want the attention."

"The Good Samaritan prefers to keep hidden," Caroline agreed. "Someone even sneaked onto the Windy Diamond and folded the laundry when we had the triplets. Too bad the helper hasn't returned since." She let out a gusty sigh that had Louisa and Elizabeth giggling.

But Elizabeth kept wondering about the matter after her friends left. If the Good Samaritan could do kind acts for Louisa when she had been living in town and Caroline at the Windy Diamond, that meant the person had to have a horse and time to travel to and fro. Any member of the ranching families would likely be too busy, but how could anyone from the town families make it to the Windy Diamond and back without someone noticing?

And how had Jasper managed to get all the way to the bed and pull himself up on his chubby legs without her noticing? Now he balanced precariously, face alternating between a grin and a frown of concern. His brothers were positively bouncing as they waited their turn.

What would she do when the triplets went to the children's home?

She shook the unwelcome thought away. They needed her now. That was what mattered.

She let them play awhile, taking a turn with each at holding their hands and letting them make halting steps around the room. But each step reminded her of others to come—the first time they walked alone, the day they started school, the year they rode a horse—steps she would miss. Oh, but she had to think of something!

She put the boys into the high chairs, fed them some

of the canned fruit and vegetables she had been given and cleaned them up afterward. Normally, one of the ladies brought her dinner, but she hadn't received a visitor since Caroline and Louisa had left.

She was just considering breaking into the canned peaches herself when a knock sounded on the door. She went to answer it eagerly, but instead of Mrs. Tyson or Stella, Brandon stood waiting on the landing. Gone were the brown frock coat and trousers, the starch-collared shirt. Now he wore a rough canvas coat, short-collared cotton shirt and dark Levi's, making him look more like the easygoing cowboys and ranchers of his congregation than the proper minister.

"Miss Dumont," he said with a charming smile, "I believe I have the honor of dining with you this afternoon. That is if the other gentlemen clamoring for your attention will allow it." He peered around her at the babies, who gabbled a greeting.

The invitation reminded her of dinners with her aunt. Those seemed miles away and hundreds of years in the past now.

"It's very kind of you," Elizabeth assured him, "but you've seen what it's like trying to take care of them, much less having a civilized dinner."

He bent and picked up a wicker hamper she hadn't noticed at his booted feet. "Mrs. Tyson anticipated as much. She made us a picnic. Would you like to eat in the field by the church?"

Would she! At times, the walls drew too close. Elizabeth shot him a grin. "If you'll help me with the boys, we'd be delighted to join you."

A short while later, they were spread out on the grass. All three boys were crawling about, exploring, while Brandon handed Elizabeth goodies from the hamper—sliced ham, corn rolls with fresh butter, newly picked apples and cider from the previous crop.

"Easy there, little fellow," Brandon cautioned when Jasper showed every intention of climbing into the hamper after a bright red apple. "You probably need to wait a few months before you try one of those."

"Less time than you might think," Elizabeth said, reaching for the baby and pulling him back. Jasper wiggled in her arms, and she distracted him with a bit of ham. "He's already grown four teeth, and two more are coming in."

Brandon peered closer at Jasper's brother who was also making for the hamper. "Eli's sporting a mouthful as well. The ladies better start watching where they put their fingers." He turned the baby in the opposite direction, and Eli headed toward Theo, who looked a bit alarmed.

With a cry of triumph, Jasper seized a black beetle and brought it toward his mouth. Elizabeth snatched it away. The baby pouted a moment, then set off hunting once more.

"Maybe a picnic wasn't such a good idea," Brandon ventured, tugging Eli off Theo, who promptly snuggled up against Elizabeth.

"It would have been the same at the boardinghouse," Elizabeth reminded him, leaning over to detour Eli from a patch of daisies that didn't deserve his tough love. "They're at the age when they want to move, to try everything. I hope your plans for the children's home take that into account."

"I'll see what I can do." He popped a piece of ham into his mouth with one hand while tugging Jasper back onto the quilt with the other. "The Lone Star Cowboy League agreed to fund the endeavor, so I'll be starting work on the project tomorrow."

Elizabeth smiled at him. "Oh, Brandon, that's wonderful. Congratulations."

He shrugged, gaze on the baby attempting to scale his long legs. "The triplets convinced them more than any words from me."

She liked how he didn't take too much credit for the feat. "What's the first step?" she asked, rubbing a hand on Theo's back. He lay his dark head against her skirts and breathed out a happy sigh.

Brandon picked up Jasper and settled him across one knee, jiggling it up and down as if the boy was riding a horse. Jasper crowed with delight. "David McKay and I are going to plan out each step so we know exactly what should be done, when and by whom."

"I'd be happy to help," Elizabeth offered. "After being a governess and now a nanny, I'm beginning to have a good idea of the situation needed to raise children in groups."

Brandon leaned back, letting Jasper splay out on his belly. "Oh? What would you suggest?"

"Easy line of sight." When he raised a brow, she hurried on. "Think about it. Particularly with the triplets, would you want walls and corridors to separate you while you're doing your chores? The person running the children's home will still need to cook and clean and wash, you know, all while watching over the children."

He nodded, capable hands holding the baby. "That makes sense. We may have to knock out a few walls or add others to make that happen. What else?"

"Fireplace screens," she told him. "Ones strong enough to keep a toddler from tumbling into the flames."

Brandon winced. Jasper, watching him, furrowed his brows.

"And really," Elizabeth couldn't help putting in, "you must give the children at least a few toys to play with. I'm sure they will have chores and schoolwork, but every child needs time to just dawdle."

"Dawdle." His voice was thoughtful. He peered closer at Jasper. "What do you think, little man? Do you like to dawdle?"

In answer, Jasper bounced up and down in his grip, ready to ride again.

Somewhere near at hand, a door slammed, and a woman's voice echoed across the grass, hard and angry.

"I don't care what Pastor Stillwater says. Tug Coleman is a low-down, hard-hearted old codger, and I won't help him one more moment."

Brandon sighed, a significantly less happy sound than the one Theo had made, then set Jasper back from him and rose. "Excuse me a moment." In three strides, he was around the corner of the parsonage.

Elizabeth shook her head. So this was the life of a small-town minister—settling disputes, moving civic projects forward. Somehow she doubted he'd learned such skills at Harvard. Ministers there had been lofty-minded individuals, bent on the contemplation of scriptures and their learned interpretation. When did Brandon even have time to plan his sermon?

Just as they had the last time she'd been on the lawn, the bushes at the end of the grass rustled, and all three babies paused in their crawling to watch. So did Elizabeth. She'd been relieved to find Little Horn remarkably civilized after the stories she'd read about the Texas frontier. But the church was at the end of the street, and all around it grasses waved toward the hills and stony outcroppings in the distance. Had some animal crept closer, lured in by the thought of making the babies its next meal? She reached out and gathered Jasper and Eli closer to Theo.

"Who's there?" she demanded. "If you're here for trouble, go on, scat!"

The bushes rustled again, with more conviction this time, and Elizabeth was certain she caught sight of blue jeans and a pair of wide brown eyes. They had a visitor, and a shy one at that.

She softened. "It's all right. I won't hurt you. Are you here to see the triplets?" She held out one hand. "Come on, then. We'd be happy to meet you."

As if emboldened by her speech, a boy of around four or five squeezed past the greenery, followed by an older girl. Both had brown hair, the girl's close to her face, the boy's curling down over his forehead. The shape of their thin faces said they were siblings. Jasper, Theo and Eli immediately wiggled as if determined to get closer to the newcomers.

Elizabeth offered the pair a smile. "Hello, there. I'm Miss Dumont and these are Jasper, Theo and Eli. Who are you?"

The girl dropped down onto the grass and held out a hand toward the babies. After a moment's hesitation, Elizabeth allowed Jasper to crawl toward her.

"I'm Gil," the boy said, and the maturity in his tone told her he was older than she had first thought. "That's Jo. You're the lady taking care of the babies now."

"That's right," Elizabeth said.

"They've had a lot of mamas," Gil said, sounding envious.

His sister didn't speak as Eli crawled over to her as well. She stroked the hair back from Jasper's face, her own look soft.

"And where is your mother?" Elizabeth asked, wondering whether the children might have come with whoever Brandon was placating.

Gil pointed upward. "In heaven with Pa."

They were orphans like the triplets? Sadness lanced her. "My parents as well. You must miss them."

He nodded, face far too solemn for a child. "A whole lot. But Mrs. Johnson says we should be happy they're in a better place." He hitched up his dusty pants, which had been rolled at the hems to keep from dragging in the dirt. "I reckon she's right. Her place ain't so good, and she don't like us much."

He sounded so sad she hurt for him. "Well, I like you, Gil. And Jo too."

The girl ducked her head, but Gil was eyeing the picnic basket.

"Are you hungry?" Elizabeth guessed. "There's ham and apples still in that hamper. Help yourselves."

They fell on the basket like locusts on Nile grass. Jasper, Theo and Eli looked impressed.

Mouth stuffed with ham, Jo glanced up and met Elizabeth's gaze. She sat straighter and nudged her little brother, who swallowed the bite of the apple he'd taken.

"Please and thank you, ma'am," he said.

The words were so run together she wasn't sure he even knew their meaning. His sister did, for she smiled her approval at him.

"Do you go to school?" Elizabeth asked the girl, keeping an eye on the babies, who were once more converging on the hamper as if emboldened by Jo and Gil's repast.

The girl ducked her head.

"Jo don't talk," Gil said, reaching for another piece of ham. Jasper opened his mouth, but Gil shoved the food into his own mouth. Jasper pouted.

Was his sister mute? She certainly wasn't deaf. She reacted now to Eli's squeal for attention, patting the baby's back with a soft hand. Then her head turned, and Elizabeth heard footsteps coming closer. Jo scrambled to her feet and tugged on her brother's shoulder.

"It's all right," Elizabeth assured them, rising as she sighted Brandon around the side of the parsonage, Annie Hill beside him. "It's just the pastor and a friend."

In answer, Jo and her brother scrambled back into the bushes. Jasper's face clouded, Eli's lower lip trembled and Theo started crying. Elizabeth knew just how they felt. It was as if their friends had deserted them.

Who were Jo and Gil, and what connection did they have with the triplets?

Brandon caught a glimpse of the Satler siblings slipping away from the parsonage and sighed. Only the other day, he'd spoken with Mrs. Johnson, who had taken the children in, about being more involved in the orphans' lives. Unfortunately, the woman was overwhelmed. She and her husband were struggling to make ends meet here in town while raising their own three young children. Jo and Gil were mostly left to themselves, sometimes riding around the range on an old mule. Who knew what kind of trouble they could get into that way?

Just another reason the children's home was needed.

"Oh, there are my darlings!" Annie Hill's exclamation recalled him to his purpose at the moment.

"Miss Hill," he said, "have you met Miss Dumont?"

"I'm just Annie," the girl said with a smile as she dropped down next to the triplets, her flowered skirts pooling about her.

"Louisa introduced me to Annie," Elizabeth told him with a smile to the girl. "She helped me in church this morning. I know she's very familiar with our boys."

Our boys. The words seemed to lodge in his heart. That was why he was creating the children's home, to make sure their boys had a loving place to live until they were ready to go out on their own. That was what every child deserved, just like David had said. Brandon and Bo had struggled to find that place, especially after their mother had passed.

The babies were crowing their delight at Annie now, surging across the grass to reach her side. She gathered them all into her lap, cooing and crooning.

Brandon sat next to Elizabeth. "Annie brought her mother to town this afternoon to see me," he explained, careful to leave an opening for the young lady to share the full reason for her visit.

Annie nodded. "Ma and Mr. Coleman don't get along," she explained to Elizabeth, hands patting baby shoulders and backs. "Pastor's been trying to get them to see reason. I thought he could talk to Ma some more."

He was no longer sure talking would help. The Hills

and the Colemans had been living in the area before he and Bo arrived and chartered Little Horn, and their enmity had been evident even then. The Hills accused the Colemans of stealing their prize possession, a diamond ring that had been in the family for generations. The Colemans insisted the ring was theirs, won by rights in a bet.

The families' heated interactions had escalated recently when Annie and Tug Coleman's oldest son, Jamie, had fallen in love. Brandon had hoped the engagement would bring the families closer, but the wildfire that had swept through both ranches had everyone on edge.

"She says she won't help Mr. Coleman unless he apologizes and gives back the ring his family stole from us," Annie was saying now. "I told her Mr. Coleman says his family didn't steal anything. He's never even seen that old ring. But she won't believe him. She called him a liar to his face. Men like him don't stand for that."

He imagined not. Tug was a bear of a man on his best days. Still, he generally cared about providing for his family to the point where he'd humbled himself to accept help from the Lone Star Cowboy League to repair his fences and outbuildings. The Hills had a similar need. Brandon had convinced the league to provide funding for the materials only if the families worked together. Now that plan was in jeopardy.

"We'll have to find a way to get them talking again," Brandon said, rubbing his chin.

Annie sighed, picking Jasper up and giving him a hug. Eli raised his hands for a turn as well. "I don't know, Pastor. She's terribly angry."

"Does she like babies?" Elizabeth asked.

Brandon cocked his head. Elizabeth's look was narrowed, as if holding in deep thoughts. "Why do you ask?"

She smiled. "You must have noticed the effect the boys have on people. It's hard to yell at someone with a baby in your arms."

He had cause to know the truth of that statement. He suspected Elizabeth had had to talk to him about their past in part because she had been trying to keep the boys calm.

"Tug has a heart for children," he acknowledged. "He used to help with Sunday school."

Annie rubbed her nose against Jasper's, and even Theo cuddled closer to her. "And Ma thinks the triplets are adorable. She'd adopt them if we had room for them."

"I know how she feels," Elizabeth said, reaching out to touch Theo, who was hanging off Annie's leg.

Did she mean she also wanted to adopt Jasper, Theo and Eli? Even with a position, how could she afford to care for them? The boys were already outgrowing her room at the boardinghouse. And if she was working, who'd care for the babies?

What she needs is a husband.

He shut the thought away. She'd come here to be a mail-order bride, but David had told Brandon he was certain he'd seen relief on her face when he had proposed a position instead. Despite Casper Magnuson's claims that the men in town would be happy to offer Elizabeth marriage, Brandon should focus his efforts on helping her find work.

"Here's what I propose," she said, oblivious to his

chaotic thoughts. "Tell your mother Pastor and I will bring the triplets out your way, but she has to accompany you to the Coleman ranch to see them."

Annie nodded. "That might give her a reason to go on Coleman land."

"We'll give Theo to your mother," Elizabeth explained, "and Eli to Mr. Coleman. That should stop anyone from yelling for long."

"It might work," Annie said. Her smile grew. "Oh, thank you, Miss Dumont! I was at my wits' end."

Brandon knew how she felt. But he thought Elizabeth's presence might work to the good as much as the presence of the babies. She'd always made people feel welcome, valued.

What could he do to make her see the value in him once more?

He nearly shook his head to clear it. Where were his thoughts this afternoon? It shouldn't matter what Elizabeth thought of him. The only approval he should seek was that of his Lord.

It wasn't as if Brandon and Elizabeth were courting. He'd told her he wanted to start over as friends. He was the Little Horn minister, respected in the community, a force for good in the area. He could not allow residual feelings for Elizabeth to interfere with his purpose. For that was all these feelings could be—leftovers from their time together in Cambridge.

Then as now, they were two people with different goals. He had to remember that. There was no future with Elizabeth, only today.

A shame some part of him protested otherwise.

Chapter Six

They fixed the momentous visit between the Colemans and the Hills for Tuesday. Then Brandon and Annie helped Elizabeth take the triplets back to the boardinghouse. Brandon seemed inclined to linger.

"No pressing engagements this afternoon, Pastor?" she asked as Annie gave each of the boys a farewell hug and kiss.

"None," he replied. "After my Sunday morning sermon, the good people of Little Horn often leave me alone Sunday afternoons, except for a dinner engagement."

His smile was as polished as ever, so why did she detect a hint of sadness under it? She walked him and Annie to the door, watching as they started down the stairs. No, there was something bothering him. Those broad shoulders were just a bit slumped. It seemed the pastor didn't like being alone. Between having a twin brother and living in the dormitory at the divinity school, perhaps he'd never lived by himself until he'd moved into the parsonage. Was he lonely?

She was.

She straightened her spine and turned to the boys, who perked up in the crib.

"Nonsense. How could any lady be lonely with three such handsome gentlemen beside her? You are such dears, do you know that?"

Theo and Eli nodded, smiling.

"No!" Jasper crowed with a grin.

Elizabeth knew it would be challenging to bring all three babies out to the Coleman ranch with only her and Brandon in the wagon, so she asked Mrs. Tyson to watch Jasper at the boardinghouse. Theo and Eli looked none too pleased about leaving their brother behind. Both faces puckered above their blue shirts, and tears pooled in Theo's eyes. She made sure to give them an extra hug and smile encouragingly as she carried them out. For all she knew, it might have been the first time the boys had been parted.

But once Brandon set out with them in the wagon he had borrowed from the Crenshaws, they brightened and gazed about themselves with wide eyes as they sat on Elizabeth's lap.

Elizabeth was just as interested. Though she'd seen a little of the country around Little Horn when she'd come in on the train, she had spent her first week and a half in town. Now the land opened up around her. Golden grasses waved from either side, while live oaks grew in clusters, their leaves whispering in the breeze as if they spoke to each other. Hills rose in the distance, and she thought she saw the flash of red and white that spoke of cattle moving in the shade.

"As wild as you wanted?" Brandon asked.

She smiled at him. Today, he was once more the

quintessential minister, coat and waistcoat somber, shirt crisp and collar stiff. His only concession to the warm, sunny day was the dun-colored hat on his head. She'd heard such hats were called Stetsons, for their maker, and that they were required wear in Texas. The broad brim shaded his eyes, making them look deeper, darker. She forced herself to return her gaze to the scenery.

"It's more beautiful than I expected," she said, watching the swirling blue-green waters of a stream that wound through the valley. Something flashed, and she realized it was a fish jumping.

"It's good to see new growth," Brandon said with a nod toward the wildflowers that poked up heads of red and orange along the bank. "We've had a drought for the last six months. It's been hard on the cattle and crops alike."

"Will everyone have enough for winter?" she asked, settling Theo a little closer on her lap. On the other side, Eli reached out and grasped his brother's hand.

"Very likely now that we've had some rain. But the winters here are very different from what we lived through in Cambridge. The nights are cooler, but the days are still pleasant. You can grow crops right through, so long as you have water. And no snow."

Elizabeth turned her gaze on him, noting the smile hovering about his lips. "None?"

He shook his head. "Not a flake. I heard one tried to land on Clyde Parker's ranch once, but he shot it down."

She stared at him a moment, then burst out in a laugh that made Theo and Eli smile. "Now I know you're teasing me."

He held up one hand, the other firm on the reins.

"It's the truth—I promise. In the four years I've lived in Little Horn, it's never snowed once."

Elizabeth gazed out at the land again, marveling. All her life, she'd spent the winter bundled up against the cold, inside and out. Jasper, Theo and Eli would never have to put woolens on under their clothes to keep warm or duck past eaves to avoid icicles. But that also meant they'd never sled, skate on an icy pond or build a snowman.

"It's different here," she said.

He sobered. "It is, and it isn't. The animals and plants might look unusual, and the weather is more mild, but people are the same wherever you go."

That could also be a good thing or a bad thing as far as she was concerned. People had been unkind in Cambridge after her uncle's thefts had been uncovered. Even though that was four years ago, would the people of Little Horn turn on her if they knew about the scandal? And what of Brandon? Would he really put aside his reputation to come to her aid?

She drew in a breath. Best not to think about things that might never come to pass. She should focus on what was happening now. She kept her arms around the boys as the wagon bumped over uneven ground. As if they thought it was for their entertainment, they giggled.

"They were born to be ranchers," Brandon said with a smile.

"Do you think so?" She eyed both boys, who were poking at each other good-naturedly.

"Their mother couldn't have come from too far away," he reasoned. "And most people around here are ranchers or farmers. That's what they raise their children to become."

Elizabeth frowned. "You make it sound as if the children have no choice. What if one wants to be a poet or an artist?"

He shrugged. "It wouldn't be easy to make a living as a poet in Little Horn. Not too many opportunities for sponsors. And only so many people can afford paintings or have a place to hang them. The closest thing we have to an artist is Mrs. Longfeather, and she has to travel around the area to the other towns to sell enough of her jewelry to make ends meet."

Elizabeth settled the boys closer. "Well, I say the triplets can be anything they want. Isn't that right, boys?"

Theo and Eli chattered at her, faces animated.

"Far be it from me to argue with such logic," Brandon said with a smile. "If I had my say, every child in Little Horn would grow up with a bright future. No one would be sad or scared or lonely."

The faces of their young visitors at the picnic Sunday came to mind, peaked, unsure, yet willing to offer friendship to three orphaned babies.

"And some apparently are," she told him. "When you were talking to Annie on Sunday, two children came to see the boys. The girl didn't speak, but her brother said she was Jo and he was Gil."

Brandon nodded. "The Satlers. Their father died a couple of years ago. Their mother tried to make a go of the farm, but she took ill and passed on this spring. No one's been able to get a word out of Jo since."

The poor thing! "They're some of the children you

hope to help with the new children's home, aren't they?"

"Them and several others in the county. It's best if family can keep the children in familiar surroundings. But sometimes circumstances make that impossible."

"Like with the triplets," she acknowledged. "No mother, no father, no known family."

He nodded. "Exactly. Mind you, I had some doubts when I heard David had proposed an orphanage. I suspect I was remembering my Dickens—cold, dark workhouses and stern taskmasters."

"'Please, sir, I want some more?'" Elizabeth quoted from *Oliver Twist*. "Surely your children's home will be better than that!"

He flashed her a grin that made something flutter inside her. The boys wiggled as if they wanted to get closer to him too.

"Of course," he said. "You should hear the plans David has for it. Bedrooms instead of a dormitory, a mother and father to manage things. The Crenshaw house is just across the street from the school and church, so the children can easily attend both, and you can be sure I'll be checking in often."

Like he did with the boys. Commendable. Boston had had an infant asylum for motherless babies like the triplets, but she seemed to recall an annual inspection by the clergy, not the watchful care Brandon supplied.

A butterfly bobbed over the wagon just then, and Eli reached for it. She held him back from damaging the fragile wings. Theo patted his shoulder as if in sympathy.

Elizabeth had more sympathy for the changing landscape. Here the grass was withered, missing entirely in places to show blackened ground beneath. The dirt shifted in the breeze like a writhing snake. The scent of charred wood seemed to hang in the air. Eli wrinkled his nose as if he smelled it too.

"What happened here?" she asked.

"Wildfire," Brandon explained. "The same storm that broke the drought brought lightning. The skies were red for miles."

Elizabeth hugged the boys close. "Does that happen often?"

"Not too often, but still too frequently," Brandon said. "You wanted adventure, remember?"

Perhaps not quite that much adventure to see homes damaged and lives threatened. For the moment, she was content to ride alongside him with the boys in her arms.

He pulled off the road onto a dusty track that led up to a long, low house and a weathered barn. A man was out front, setting a bar back into the corral fence. He stopped and watched as Brandon reined in the horses, but his bearded face broke into a grin as his gaze rested on Elizabeth and the babies.

Tug Coleman was a large man who seemed to be in his midforties, his broad shoulders and rough clothing making him look as if he were chiseled from the rocks that ringed his ranch. He ambled over now and held the horses as Brandon climbed down.

"Mornin', Pastor," he said. "What brings you out this way?"

Was that wariness she heard in his gruff voice? Was he feeling a bit guilty for not working harder to mend the rift between his family and the Hills?

Brandon clapped him on the shoulder before continuing around the team to Elizabeth's side. "Miss Dumont and her charges needed some fresh air, and I knew you would welcome our young gentlemen."

Tug's grin widened. "Of course I will. Always loved children. Makes me sad mine are all nearly grown. And I know the girls will be disappointed they missed this. They're off helping at the Carsons' with my two youngest sons." He raised his voice. "Jamie! Company!"

Theo and Eli blinked as if impressed by his volume.

A young man loped out of the barn. Unlike his dark-haired father, he had hair the color of ripened wheat, and there was something warm and likable about his handsome features. So this was Annie's betrothed. He took his father's place at the head of the team with a welcoming smile to Elizabeth and Brandon.

Tug came around and opened his arms. "You just hand me those young'uns, Miss Dumont. We'll see they have some fun."

With that smile on his face, Elizabeth could well believe it. She handed him Eli first. The baby settled against his broad chest, then reached up to finger Tug's bearded chin as if fascinated by the hair. Theo went next, lower lip trembling. But he rested his head against Tug as if sure he'd be safe in the big man's arms.

Tug's craggy face softened. "Well, aren't you little gents?"

Brandon stepped up beside him and raised his arms. "Allow me to assist you, Miss Dumont."

For a moment, she could see herself nestled close, head on Brandon's shoulder, feeling equally safe and comforted. She shook herself and managed a smile as he lifted her from the bench and set her on her feet. As she stood in his embrace, he bent his head, and she had the insane notion that he meant to kiss her. Even more insane was her reaction. She could feel her lips pursing in anticipation!

Instead, Brandon's breath brushed her ear. "It's working already. Well done, Elizabeth."

If he'd known the direction of her thoughts, she was fairly sure he would not be offering such praise.

He straightened before she could comment on her plan or the fact that he had used her first name. Very likely it had been habit from their days of courting, but she found she liked the sound of it even more now. It had been a long time since a gentleman had called her Elizabeth. With her employers and charges, she had always been Miss Dumont. The name felt distant somehow, as if it were meant to be changed to something more important.

Like Mother.

Tug was jiggling the babies up and down so that they giggled. As Brandon went to help Jamie with the horses, Elizabeth mastered her wayward thoughts and smiled at their host.

"Pastor Stillwater said you are good with children," she told him.

A rosy red suffused his broad cheeks. "I've had a lot of experience. My sweet Hazel gave me three sons and two daughters."

She thought those blue eyes looked brighter. Eli must have thought so too, for he patted the rancher's shoulder and chattered his support.

"How long has she been gone?" Elizabeth murmured.

"Five years," he answered, stilling his movement of the babies. "But the ache of her passing has eased some." He glanced up, then his brows came thundering down. "What's *she* doing here?"

Elizabeth followed his gaze to the ranch road, where a wagon and team were kicking up the dust that had barely settled after the passing of Brandon's wagon. Through the cloud, she spotted Annie at the reins, an older woman beside her.

"I let Mrs. Hill know the babies would be out her way," Elizabeth told him. "She loves children too."

"Humph" was all Tug Coleman could say as the wagon drew to a stop near the barn. Elizabeth's plan was about to reach the next phase. She could only hope she hadn't landed herself and Brandon in trouble.

Brandon closed the corral after his borrowed team and hurried to where Dorothy Hill sat glowering on the bench of her wagon. Already Jamie was going to help Annie down, completely ignoring the team of horses fretting in the traces. Worse, Brandon could see that Elizabeth's smile had turned brittle as the ranchers faced off.

"Mrs. Hill," Brandon said, going to the lady's side. "How nice to see you."

She stuck her stub of a nose in the air. Everything about Dorothy Hill was no-nonsense, from her short, stiff blond hair to her solid frame. Now her pale pink lips thinned into an unforgiving line.

"It's nice to see the babies," she allowed, somehow managing to avoid looking at Tug. "But it was a long way to come on a busy wash day. And now this." Her lips tightened.

Brandon wasn't sure whether it was the sight of Tug or something else that had set her off. "This?" he asked.

She glared down at him. "I wouldn't expect a fine gent like you to understand, Pastor, but *someone* needs to see to my horses."

"That's a Hill for you," Tug shot back. "Always blaming someone else for something they should have done."

Jamie, who had been murmuring something in Annie's ear, left her to hurry forward and take charge of the team.

"Don't unhitch them," Dorothy ordered. "I won't be staying long." She twitched aside her iron-gray skirts and offered Brandon her hand to help her step down from the bench.

Elizabeth hurried up to her as she descended. "How do you do, Mrs. Hill? I'm Elizabeth Dumont, and I'm delighted to make your acquaintance. I've heard a lot about you."

Foot on the ground, Dorothy eyed Tug. "Nothing good, I warrant."

Elizabeth colored. "Actually, quite good. I've heard you know how to raise children well, and I was hoping to ask your advice. Caring for three babies is such a delight, but at times I simply feel overwhelmed."

Did she? From what Brandon had seen, she managed the challenge brilliantly. But there was no doubting the earnestness of her gaze. He wanted to step in and help her himself.

Dorothy was no more immune to the plea. Her look softened. "I imagine it can be hard. My three boys were a few years apart, and they were still a handful. I'd be glad to help."

Elizabeth took her arm and drew her closer to Tug. The gruff rancher stiffened, and Theo let out a wail.

Dorothy shook her head. "Now see what you've done? Give him to me."

Mouth set tight, Tug handed her the crying baby. Brandon fought the urge to intervene. As if Elizabeth sensed his confliction, she laid a hand on his arm. Those blue-green eyes were encouraging.

"There, now," Dorothy crooned in a sweet, soft voice Brandon had never heard come from her mouth before. "It's all right, little man. Tug Coleman might be big and brash, but he's been a good father to his little ones."

Tug stared at her. So did Theo. Then he sighed and laid his head on her shoulder, thumb going to his mouth.

"Well, look at that," Tug marveled. "I'm impressed. You know your way around a baby."

Dorothy granted him a tight smile. "I should. I birthed four of them."

"And a fine bunch they are," Brandon put in. "You are both to be commended for raising a family alone."

Dorothy nodded, and Tug looked thoughtful. Brandon could only hope Tug was finally realizing he and Dorothy Hill had something in common.

"I'm sure it wasn't easy," she allowed, "raising girls with no ma."

Tug shrugged. "No harder than raising boys with no pa, I reckon."

Dorothy reddened. "So you think my boys aren't manly enough, do you?"

Beside him, Elizabeth stiffened. Brandon felt the shift in the wind as well.

"That's not what Tug said," he put in, but Tug had already drawn himself up.

"They're fine boys," he insisted, jiggling Eli, "*despite* their upbringing."

"Oh, I see what you're trying to do," Dorothy told him, jiggling Theo. "You just can't acknowledge I could be better than you, at anything."

Theo glanced up at her angry face and whimpered.

"You're upsetting the baby," Tug accused.

Eli began crying as well.

"Perhaps I should take them," Elizabeth said, stepping forward with concern on her face.

Dorothy held Theo out of reach. "I was doing fine until a certain fellow raised his voice!"

"Both of them were fine before you showed up," Tug countered.

Both babies were howling now, tears streaming down their faces. Annie left Jamie's side to hurry toward them.

Brandon stepped between the ranchers. "That's enough. Mrs. Hill, give Theo to Elizabeth. Tug, hand me Eli."

He must have put enough authority in his voice, because both complied. It took a few minutes, but he and Elizabeth managed to calm the boys. To do them credit, Dorothy and Tug looked more concerned about the boys than their feud, for once.

Annie, however, was inconsolable. Face sagging, she glanced between the babies, then at her mother and Jamie's father.

"You'll never be civil, will you?" she demanded. "Nothing I say, nothing Pastor Stillwater says, will ever satisfy you. I thought spending time with the babies would bring you to your senses, but you can't even be nice for them. I don't know why I even hoped."

As their faces fell, she turned away from them to Jamie, who still held her mother's horses.

"We might as well give up," she told him. "I can't live this way. I'm sorry, Jamie, but I can't marry you."

Chapter Seven

"Oh, Annie, no!" The words were out of Elizabeth's mouth before she could think better of them. Who was she to champion love when she'd let hers slip away?

"It's for the best," Dorothy said, gathering her daughter close. "My father always said you can't trust a Coleman."

"I should have known a Hill couldn't be counted on to keep her word," Tug replied, voice hard.

"Pa!" Jamie abandoned the horses to rush forward. "You aren't helping!"

"Neither are you," Dorothy accused, releasing her daughter to see to her team. "Come on, Annie. We're leaving."

Annie sucked back a sob, holding up a hand to keep Jamie from touching her. "No. I don't want to go with you, Ma."

Jamie brightened until she continued, "And I don't want to go with you either, Jamie. I'm staying with Miss Dumont and the babies."

With me? Elizabeth started as Annie pasted herself against her side. Jamie's body tightened as if he'd been struck, but Annie's mother drew herself up as if prepared to fight.

One look at the girl's tear-stained face and Elizabeth felt a similar protectiveness rising up inside her. "You're welcome to stay with me as long as you like, Annie."

Dorothy grabbed the reins and dragged her horses around, all the while glaring at Brandon. "See what comes from meddling, Preacher? I thought that good book of yours counseled against it."

"The Bible encourages us to do unto others as we would have done to ourselves, to love our neighbors," Brandon told her, voice kind. "If I was feuding with my neighbor so badly I drove my daughter to sorrow, I'd want someone to intervene."

Dorothy hauled herself up into the seat. "Who asked you? I'm fine on my own. I expect you home for chores, Annie." She slapped down on the reins and set the team rushing out of the yard.

Tug waved the dust away from his face. "Good riddance is what I say."

Jamie was watching Elizabeth and Annie. "I'm sorry our parents can't get along, Annie. But that doesn't change how I feel about you. I love you."

Pain reverberated in the words. Though he couldn't be much more than nineteen, Jamie was deeply in love. By the look on her face, so was Annie. Elizabeth hurt for them both.

"I love you too," the girl said. "But what kind of life could we have with them always at each other's throat? Can you imagine Christmas like that? Church services? Either I'd come to resent you or you'd come to resent me, and I can't bear the thought."

As his son's face shattered, Tug stepped forward. "I'm sorry, Annie. You're a fine girl, for all you're a Hill, but I don't think your ma will ever settle down."

Jamie whirled, eyes blazing. "Maybe she would if you'd ever leave her be. Annie's right. There's no hope for either of you."

Brandon laid a hand on Jamie's shoulder as Tug took a step back, mouth hanging open.

"There's always hope," Brandon told Jamie. "But Mrs. Hill and your father have to be the ones to embrace it."

Jamie hung his head. "Then they're never going to make peace."

Theo reached for Annie just then, and Elizabeth let him go into the girl's arms. As Brandon continued speaking to Jamie and Tug, Elizabeth led the girl to the wagon.

"Take some time," she encouraged her. "You don't have to make a decision now."

Annie shook her head, blond hair coming loose. "It's done. Jamie and I can never be together." She buried her face behind Theo's dark head.

Elizabeth wasn't ready to give up. Funny how four years had changed her perspective. When she and Brandon had parted, she'd been certain she was justified in her actions. She would never speak to him again. He'd left her, after all, in her hour of need. Looking back now, she could see mistakes on both sides. They should have met, talked about their concerns. They might still have decided to part, for she wasn't sure she would have been brave enough to move to Texas then. Or they might have found their way back to each other. Both had been too quick to give up.

She stayed with Annie as Brandon went to hitch up the team for their trip back to town. Tug and Jamie stood at one side, steps apart but miles distant. Tug rubbed his arm as if feeling a pain somewhere deeper. Jamie's tortured gaze remained on Annie. The girl did not glance his way again as Brandon drove away from the house.

"I'll speak to your mother," Brandon promised Annie as the wagon started down the road. "Tug is already regretting his words. We can smooth this over."

It was good of him to offer. It seemed he was called on to play peacemaker often in this town.

"Thank you, Pastor," Annie said from her place in the wagon's bed, her head still turned down to Theo in her lap. "But it won't do any good. Much as I wish it were otherwise, I can't make them behave." She sighed. "I suspect in time I'll have to look for someone else to marry, though my heart won't be in it."

Elizabeth had felt the same way when she'd advertised to be a mail-order bride. With her aunt's death, her last tie to Cambridge had snapped. She'd wanted to go somewhere, anywhere, even if it meant marrying a stranger. Now she could only be grateful that David McKay had found a bride he could love, leaving her free.

But free to do what? She'd been a competent governess, but pursuing that course meant leaving the triplets behind.

She must not have been the only one thinking hard, because they were a quiet group on the ride back to town. The movement of the wagon lulled the babies to sleep, their little bodies cuddling against Annie and Elizabeth. Brandon gazed out over the team, face troubled. Elizabeth was certain he didn't like the results of their efforts.

"I'm sorry," she murmured to him. "I really thought this would work."

"It almost did," he replied with a sad smile. "It was a good idea, Elizabeth. Tug and Dorothy are just a lot angrier than I thought. A shame we can't get them to see that they only hurt themselves by holding grudges."

A shame indeed. She knew the hurt that came with hanging on to past disagreements. She'd been angry with Brandon for years. Laying down the pain had somehow felt like betraying her feelings, her dreams. But she certainly didn't want to end up like Dorothy Hill, pushing everyone, even her own daughter, away.

She glanced at the man holding the reins. He'd been strong today, firm in his convictions and determined to show Tug and Dorothy what it meant to live at peace. Though they'd failed to convince the pair, Elizabeth couldn't help being proud of him. If only she could believe his reputation wasn't the driving force behind his actions. After all, who trusted a pastor who could not help the members of his congregation when they needed him?

They reached the boardinghouse a short while later. Mrs. Tyson took one look at their faces and her own face saddened. While Brandon and Annie settled the boys, Elizabeth checked with the boardinghouse owner to make sure it was all right for Annie to stay with her. The bed was plenty big enough for two, but she wasn't sure about the arrangements David McKay had made for the cost.

"That's fine for a day or two," Mrs. Causewell, the boardinghouse owner, agreed with a wave of her hand.

"But it must be getting crowded up there." She fished in her apron and handed Elizabeth a letter. "By the way, this came for you."

Elizabeth thanked her and took the letter upstairs. All three babies were asleep on the bed, and Brandon was talking quietly with Annie as they watched over the trio. By the way the girl kept nodding, Elizabeth thought he was offering advice. Elizabeth bent her head and opened the letter. The light in the room seemed to dim as she read.

Her face must have mirrored her feelings, for Brandon looked up and hurried to her side.

"What is it?" he asked. "Bad news?"

Elizabeth folded the letter shut, fingers trembling. "Good news, I suppose. Someone responded to my ad. I've been offered a position as a governess, in San Francisco."

San Francisco? The biggest city on the West Coast, it had to be nearly two thousand miles away from Little Horn. And the stories that were reported occasionally in the Austin paper were not complimentary.

"It's a wild place, I hear," he said. "Drinking, violence, mayhem."

Elizabeth raised her brows. "That bad, Pastor?"

Maybe worse. But then, he'd feel the same way about any place that took her away from him.

He nearly jerked back from her at the thought. He had no claim on her affections. Besides, who was he to order her life?

And was San Francisco truly any worse than any other town out West? Very likely there were more than a few wealthy folks in the city built by gold. Someone must need a governess.

Or a wife.

He forced his lips to smile. "You could do just as well in Little Horn without having to move again to another unknown place. Give me time to find you a position here."

She eyed him a moment, and he could almost see the thoughts fluttering like caged birds behind her eyes. Had their time together in Little Horn proved to her he was a man who could be trusted? Was she willing to forego the lure of a fancier city to stay here near the triplets she claimed to love?

"One week," she said. "And then I'll have to send a response."

One week. Relief surged through him. He and Bo had once calculated that there were more than a hundred families within a day's drive of Little Horn. Surely one could use a governess.

His brother was less optimistic when they met at the café the next day. Having recently married, Bo was in town less and less these days and had only come in today to pick up some nails from the general store. But anytime he called, Brandon was ready to meet him.

Most people would see Brandon and his brother as mirror images, but he saw the subtle differences between them. Bo's chest was broader, his arms more muscular from working on the ranch. His coloring was darker too, from spending days in the sun, despite the Stetson he perpetually wore. Now they took off their hats in unison and seated themselves at one of the checkered-cloth-covered tables in Mercy Green's café.

"Everything going well at the ranch?" Brandon

asked, not even bothering to pick up the printed menu. He knew what he wanted, could smell it on the air in the neat little restaurant.

"Perfect," Bo promised him. "And Louisa keeps me as well fed as Ma did."

They shared a smile at the memory.

The dark-haired Mrs. Green came up to their table. "What can I get you fine gentlemen?"

"Apple pie," Brandon told her.

"Peach," Bo put in.

She shook her head. "I don't know why I bother to ask. Coming right up."

As she moved away, Brandon braced his hands on the clean cotton cloth. "I need your help, Bo. I have one week to find Elizabeth Dumont a new position."

"One week?" Bo leaned back from the table. "What's the hurry?"

As Brandon explained the letter Elizabeth had received, Mrs. Green returned with generous pieces of pie. Brandon and Bo chorused their thanks, then bowed their heads to ask the blessing.

"These are proud people," Bo reminded him when they'd finished, "willing to offer help but seldom asking for it themselves. If their children need tending, they rely on family and friends."

Brandon nodded, digging into the apple pie. Mercy Green might not be the best cook in the area, but the lady, like her café, was warm and welcoming.

"David McKay had a governess," Brandon pointed out. "Two in fact."

"One his daughter ran off and one he married," Bo countered. "But he's the oddity, Brandon. A governess is for a tenderfoot from back East." The tines of his fork pierced the flaky crust, and Brandon knew he couldn't wait to dive into the peach pie. Their mother had baked the best in Cambridge, which was why he rarely ordered it anywhere else. No other pie had ever come close to his memories.

"And we all know how badly these East Coast boys fare in Texas," Brandon couldn't help teasing him.

His brother grinned. "We're oddities too."

"And that means there must be two or three others in the area. I just have to find them."

"You're the minister," Bo said, forking up a mouthful of pie. "You hear about everyone's needs."

"Which reminds me." Brandon hitched forward on the seat. "Tug Coleman and Dorothy Hill went after each other yesterday, despite attempts by Elizabeth and me to make peace. Will you mention the matter to Lula May? We may have to use the Lone Star Cowboy League's influence to get them to work together again."

Bo shook his head. "I'm beginning to think those two are a lost cause."

"Annie feels the same way. She broke off her engagement with Jamie."

Bo whistled. "That must have been some ruckus. Sorry I missed it."

"I'm sorry Elizabeth had to witness it. It wasn't exactly a testament to Christian kindness."

Bo cocked his head. "That's twice now you've used her first name. Should I be calling on folks about arranging a wedding instead of finding a governess position?"

Brandon felt his face heating. "Slip of the tongue. Don't refine on it."

Bo shrugged. "I just thought since she was the one who broke your heart in Boston…"

Brandon choked on his pie. "Not so loud!"

"What? Is it a secret?" Bo lowered his voice even as he raised his brows. "You better be careful, brother. Someone might put two and two together."

"And get sixteen." Brandon sighed. "Miss Dumont is a member of my congregation and the person caring for three infants you and I both feel responsible for. I promised to help her seek permanent employment. That's all."

Bo held up his hands. "All right. You told me you were over the girl you left Boston to forget. I remember the scandal with her uncle, how he swindled all those folks. I didn't ask questions. I was just thankful you decided to come West with me."

So was Brandon. He'd needed a way to start over again.

"But I think you should ask yourself why you're so concerned about Miss Dumont now," Bo continued. "She survived the scandal. She got herself all the way out here, and it sounds like she's doing a good job with the triplets. Now she has an opportunity in San Francisco. It seems as if she can take care of herself."

He couldn't doubt it, not after watching her with the babies and some of the more difficult members of his congregation.

"She's already uprooted herself twice," Brandon told his brother, pie unheeded before him. "Once when she had to leave the life she'd known to be a governess and once to come out here. If she wants to stay in Little Horn, she should have that opportunity."

"*Does* she want to stay in Little Horn?" Bo challenged.

Brandon frowned. "Of course she wants to stay. She loves the triplets."

Bo's face softened. "Everyone loves the triplets. Louisa and I would have adopted them and so would Caroline and David if we hadn't thought family would be found. No word there, I suppose."

"None." Brandon shifted in his seat. "And now we'll be setting up the children's home for the boys and others like them."

Bo scraped the last of his pie off the plate. "It's a good idea, but I can't help wishing..."

"The triplets had a family," Brandon finished. "I know. I feel the same way. They've been moved around so much in the last few months. They just need a stable environment, even if it's a children's home."

His brother nodded, and their talk moved on to other matters before Bo had to head back to the ranch. But the conversation remained on Brandon's mind. Perhaps that was why he called at the boardinghouse later that afternoon.

"Miss Dumont has many callers," Mrs. Causewell informed him when she answered his knock. "It's not natural."

"Little Horn is fond of its triplets," Brandon said with what he hoped was a charming smile.

Mrs. Causewell scowled. "All those visiting ladies are bad enough. It's the gents that concern me."

One foot on the stairs, Brandon paused. Between his brother's conversation and this woman's grumbling, it would be all too easy for a rumor to start.

"I hope you know, ma'am," he told her, "that as a minister I visit all those in need."

She waved a hand. "Certainly, Pastor. But you tell me one good reason for Clyde Parker to visit. He went up a quarter hour ago."

Parker? Brandon knew he was frowning as he started up the stairs. Parker had been one of the few ranchers in the area when Brandon and Bo had arrived. The tough veteran had weathered storms and loss alike. Tradition was all-important to him, next to tight control of finances. What business could he have with Elizabeth or the triplets? Had he decided to take Brandon's sermon to heart? Was he here to offer some kind of help?

The door was ajar as Brandon reached the landing, and he could hear a high voice, likely Annie's, crooning nonsense words. Over it, Elizabeth's voice was firm.

"Thank you for the offer, Mr. Parker. I will consider it along with the other."

Offer? Why would Parker need a governess or nanny?

Brandon pushed the door open the rest of the way. Annie was sitting on the bed, the boys curled up around her as she sang to them. Elizabeth stood on the rug, back straight, head high, eyes flashing, with Clyde Parker in front of her, bandy legs splayed and thumbs hooked in his gun belt. From what Brandon could see of his face, it was turning red.

"No consideration should be needed," he blustered. "You won't get a better offer than mine, missy."

Elizabeth looked more calm. "Thank you for coming, Mr. Parker. I won't detain you."

He huffed, then turned on his heel. His brows rose a

moment when he sighted Brandon, but then he jerked his head back toward Elizabeth.

"Pastor, you tell this woman she ought to stop all this considerin' and just marry me."

Chapter Eight

Of all the nerve! Elizabeth could hardly speak. Truly, it was no wonder Mr. Parker hadn't remarried if all his proposals involved ordering his prospective bride to the altar.

Brandon's brows shot up as if he was just as shocked. Then he made the effort to school his face, brows coming down, mouth tightening and chin rising.

"I'm not sure Miss Dumont realizes the honor you're doing her," he told the rancher.

What! Elizabeth gritted her teeth. Surely Brandon couldn't take the fellow seriously.

"She doesn't," Parker complained. "I left my stock to ride all the way in here, even put on my Sunday hat."

Brandon nodded at the dun-colored Stetson. "And a fine hat it is too. No, I'm sure she hasn't given proper weight to your proposal. After all, even though you are considerably older than she is, with less education and a gruff manner, you are one of the town's most noted misanthropes."

Elizabeth was fairly sure Mr. Parker had no idea what the term meant, for he puffed out his chest. "Quite right!" He paused, brows gathering like storm clouds. "Wait. What did you just call me?"

Brandon smiled. "My brother, Bo, always says you can call a man anything, just don't call him late to supper."

Parker blinked.

Brandon turned smoothly to Elizabeth. "And speaking of supper, I believe it must be time for the triplets to eat. We would not want to keep you from your duty, Miss Dumont. After all, the Lone Star Cowboy League is paying good money for your time."

"Quite right, Mr. Stillwater," Elizabeth said, fighting to keep her face solemn. "And I take my responsibilities seriously."

"Commendable." He turned to Annie, who was watching from the bed with the babies, and gave her a nod. "Miss Hill. Please give my regards to your family, whom I hope you will be seeing soon. Come along, Parker. I'd like your advice on the children's home. It's vitally important that we trim the cost without sacrificing quality." He took the rancher's arm and led him from the room, but just before he closed the door, he sent Elizabeth a wink and a grin.

Well!

Annie heaved a sigh. "It must be nice having someone fight for you instead of fighting around you."

Elizabeth shook her head. How did he do that, smile at a ridiculous situation and get his own way at the same time? Very likely Mr. Parker was listening to him talk about the children's home only to give in on some point the rancher had once held dear. And Mr. Parker would probably thank Brandon for it!

"You don't always have to fight," she told Annie,

going to the bed and picking up Eli, who grinned at her with the same amount of mischief in his eyes. "Sometimes, you just have to stand your ground."

"And sometimes you have to walk away," Annie insisted. Theo latched on to her finger and tried to put it in his mouth. Annie pulled back with a giggle.

"I think Pastor Stillwater was right. We better feed these hungry little birds."

It was easy for Elizabeth to forget her offers—employment in far-off San Francisco or marriage to crotchety Clyde Parker—while she and Annie fed the triplets, cleaned them up and kept them busy until bedtime. And it was nice having someone to help her change just as she helped Annie change into a spare nightgown. But as Elizabeth lay on the bed, listening to Annie's and the boys' soft breathing, her mind kept going over her options.

Despite Brandon's comments, she thought San Francisco could be a good place to start over. From what she'd read in the newspapers and novels, an upper class was growing, building fine houses, chartering civic improvements. People like that often employed governesses, so that she might be assured of ongoing situations. But it meant moving farther away from anything she'd known, living with strangers just when she was starting to feel comfortable in Little Horn.

Then there was Clyde Parker. Mrs. Arundel had said he had a fine ranch, so he likely could provide for a wife. If Elizabeth married him, she wouldn't have to leave Little Horn. But he had such a domineering manner. She could see him insisting that she act a certain way, think a certain way. She'd be trading her freedom for a mess of porridge.

And both choices meant she could never adopt the triplets, for Parker had made it clear he had little use for children. Given his age, she could well find herself a lonely widow in the not-too-distant future. She shuddered at the image.

Staring up into the dark of the room, she opened her heart.

Lord, Brandon was right to say that we should pray about what You would have us do. But for so long, I haven't felt as if You were listening. And if You are listening, I don't hear Your answer. What should I do? Was the letter from San Francisco Your way of nudging me farther West? Or am I to make my way here somehow?

From their side of the room came a sigh from one of the boys, and she heard shifting as if one rolled closer to another in the crib. How fortunate they were to have siblings, someone to rely on in bad times and celebrate with in good. That was what she wanted in her life—friends, family, helpmates to cheer and comfort. She couldn't convince herself that either the work in San Francisco or marriage to Clyde Parker would bring her all that.

Annie seemed to have recovered some of her usual sunny outlook by the next morning, for she smiled and chatted with Elizabeth and the babies as they rose, breakfasted and dressed for the day. But she still cast a glance out the window from time to time with a heartfelt sigh.

"You could borrow a horse and ride out to talk to your mother," Elizabeth suggested as she gathered up some of the boys' clothing for the wash. "I know being apart from those you love is difficult."

Annie shook her head. "She made her decision, and now I've made mine. Besides, she's probably good and mad at me for not coming home for chores yesterday like she wanted." She cast Elizabeth a troubled glance. "Unless you'd like me to leave."

Elizabeth shook her head, but a knock on the door prevented her from urging the girl further. Annie hurried to answer, and Elizabeth saw Stella Fuller and Caroline McKay on the stoop.

The triplets immediately perked up, waving their hands or crawling toward the woman who had recently been their nanny. Eli's calls of "Lala" pierced the air. Caroline beamed at them, light brown hair shining nearly as brightly as her hazel eyes.

At Elizabeth's encouragement, Caroline went to sit on the bed, and Elizabeth brought her Theo, mindful of her arm still in a sling.

"Oh, how I've missed you," she said, giving the baby a hug.

Elizabeth bent and picked up Jasper to keep him from climbing up Caroline's dusky green skirts to her lap.

"I'll take one," Stella offered, dipping down to scoop up Eli. "They are so sweet I could eat them up with a spoon."

"Miss Dumont has the best job in the world," Annie said with another sigh, this time in obvious envy. Jasper reached for the girl, and Elizabeth let the little boy go into her arms.

"Best job, but not the best situation," Caroline said.

"You need something permanent, Elizabeth, if we are to keep you in Little Horn."

Elizabeth couldn't help but be warmed by the statement, and this from the woman who had married her groom. "I quite agree. I'd love to stay."

"I heard Clyde Parker proposed marriage," Stella put in, giving Eli a jiggle. He must have recognized the more censorious tone of her voice, for the baby frowned.

Caroline met Elizabeth's gaze, her mouth turned down in sympathy.

"Last night," Annie confirmed. "He told Miss Dumont she had to marry him."

Stella shook her head. "That's it. We need to promenade."

Caroline frowned. "Promenade? Where I come from, that generally involves a lady and a gentleman taking a turn about the room or garden together."

"That's the way my aunt used the term," Elizabeth told her.

Stella had other ideas. "Not here. You might have noticed, not too many folks have a house big enough to take a turn in, much less a fancy garden. Out West, if you want to promenade, you and your friends dress up in your best and sashay down the street together, see who takes notice."

Elizabeth felt her face heating to the point that Jasper reached up to touch her cheeks. "Oh, I couldn't."

"Don't see why not," Stella said. "The babies need air. Caroline and I are in our visiting clothes. If we go with you and Annie, no one in town should complain."

It wasn't the complaints of the townsfolk that concerned her. What would the members of the Lone Star

Cowboy League think if they heard she'd been parading around Little Horn with the triplets? And very likely the gentlemen taking notice would be no more suitable as husbands than Clyde Parker.

Caroline slid off the bed, earning her a grin from Theo. "It sounds like fun. Count me in."

Annie giggled, raising a smile on all the babies' faces. "I'll go, though I don't much care who notices now that I can't have Jamie."

"What's this?" Caroline asked, stepping closer to the girl. "What happened?"

"Did that fool father of his say something he shouldn't?" Stella demanded.

Annie hung her head. "It was Ma. She just can't get along with Mr. Coleman. And I can't live my life with them fighting over every little thing."

Caroline glanced at Elizabeth. "Surely there's something that can be done."

Elizabeth certainly hoped so. "Annie is staying with me for now while she thinks things over."

Stella nodded. "Good. And I say you should promenade too, Annie. It doesn't hurt to see if you have options."

Options, she said. Elizabeth could certainly use one. But displaying herself to the populace? That just seemed wrong. She'd told Annie that sometimes it was best to stand her ground. Perhaps it was time she took her own advice.

"Ladies," she said, glancing around at their determined faces, "I appreciate your concern, but I have a duty."

"To the triplets," Stella agreed, tucking Eli against

her and marching for the door. "And I'm taking this one promenading."

"Me too," Annie said, heading after her with Jasper.

Caroline shook her head. "You're outvoted, it seems. Come along, Elizabeth. Help me with Theo."

Left with little choice if she wished to keep up with her charges, Elizabeth went along.

As always, escaping the little room raised her spirits. It was a gloriously sunny day, and something tangy she couldn't name hung in the air. Carts and wagons rumbled past, on their way to various businesses in the heart of town, and ladies ventured out to hang wash and work gardens.

Stella headed a block over to Main Street and strolled up the sidewalk, her boots clacking on the wooden planks. Caroline, Annie and Elizabeth clustered around her. Elizabeth was a little concerned about how the people would react, but every lady they met stopped to exclaim over the boys, and the older men paused to chuck the babies under the chin or pat their shoulders. Jasper, Theo and Eli preened at the attention.

"Don't look now," Stella murmured as they came past the Arundel General Store, "but the gents are noticing too."

Elizabeth was almost afraid to see who might be watching them. Annie had no such concern, for she craned her neck.

"Oh, who's that?" she whispered to Caroline, who was closest. "The fellow with the hair black as midnight?"

Stella stopped as if to eye the goods displayed in the window of the general store. She nudged Elizabeth and nodded to the pane, which gave back a reflection of their faces and the street behind them.

Three cowboys had just ridden in. The one with the long black hair tipped his hat in their direction. She heard Annie giggle.

But the man who made Elizabeth catch her breath was the sandy-haired minister who was heading their way with a frown on his handsome face.

Brandon had to force the frown from his face at the sight of three cowboys admiring Elizabeth and her friends. He was supposed to be pleasant, congenial, welcoming. Besides, how could any man fail to appreciate her? Though she was wearing her more practical clothes today, her hair captured the sunlight and gave it back as flame.

But that didn't mean they had to stare as if they'd never seen a pretty girl before.

"Pastor!" Mrs. Fuller heralded, turning from admiring something in the window. "We were just taking the babies for a walk. Why don't you join us?"

He had a dozen things calling for his attention this morning, from renovating the Crenshaw house to determining the next course of Sunday school lessons. But suddenly he could think of nothing more important than spending time with Elizabeth.

And the triplets. Of course the triplets.

He smiled as he joined her and the others. "I'd be delighted." All too aware of the cowboys watching them, he offered Elizabeth his arm. "May I, Miss Dumont?"

She hesitated, and for a moment he thought she'd refuse. Was it pride or had he done something to offend her? Would they never come to a time when they could be easy in each other's company?

Then she placed her hand on his arm, and a jolt went through him. Perhaps being easy was overrated.

"See?" Mrs. Fuller said with a grin to Elizabeth. "You never know who you'll meet when you go promenading."

He wasn't sure why Elizabeth flamed or Caroline chuckled.

"You sure don't," Annie said, falling in behind them as they continued up the street. "Do you know that black-haired cowboy, Pastor?"

Brandon glanced back at the men, who had dismounted and were heading into the general store. "Kit Durango. He's new to Little Horn. He recently signed on at the Thorn ranch."

"Kit Durango." Elizabeth said the name as if fascinated. She shot him a grin. "Now, that sounds like a hero in a dime novel."

He ought to share her smile, but some part of him wanted to order Mr. Durango back on his horse and out of Little Horn.

"Oh, yes!" Annie enthused.

"He sounds like the villain to me," Brandon heard himself say. "I doubt he'll stay in Little Horn beyond roundup."

Annie sighed.

Elizabeth gave his arm a squeeze. "And how many cowboy dime novels have you read recently, Pastor?"

Her smile was so sweet he felt his lips turning up in response. "I don't have to read about the West anymore, Miss Dumont. I live in it."

She laughed, and he felt like the wittiest fellow in Texas.

He walked the ladies up Main Street and back to Second, where he left them at the boardinghouse. Saying goodbye to Elizabeth was harder each time he did it. That just meant he needed to find a way to prevent that goodbye from being permanent, and he thought he knew just how to start.

Mrs. Arundel held a weekly literary discussion in the sitting room of the parsonage. That was the reason his congregation had built him such a large house, after all, so they could make use of it. Now, just like every Thursday afternoon, he found five ladies seated on the mismatched furniture. They all perked up as he entered.

"Care to join us, Pastor?" Mrs. Crenshaw asked, sliding over on the crimson camelback sofa as if to make room for him.

"You know the rules," Mrs. Arundel scolded before he could respond. "Mr. Stillwater may only join in the discussion if he's read the book."

The deacon's wife deflated.

He wasn't sure what they were reading, but that wasn't the reason he'd come.

"Actually, ladies, I was hoping for your counsel," he said, taking a seat on a hard-back chair at the edge of the room and bracing his elbows on his knees. "A member of our congregation will shortly be unemployed, and I'd like to find her other work."

Mrs. Hickey, who had been watching him with narrowed eyes as if waiting for the least infraction, leaned forward. "Is it Mercy Green? I hear her restaurant might fail."

He'd heard no such thing. The place was busy every time he went in.

"I told her that green tomato preserve wouldn't go over well," Mrs. Arundel said with a knowing nod.

"Not Mrs. Green," Brandon assured them, hoping to squelch that rumor before it went too far. "Her restaurant is a mainstay in the community. I would not want to see it fail."

"Mrs. Tyson," Mrs. Crenshaw said with a sympathetic sigh. "She's been at loose ends since her sons left."

Did they have nothing to do all day but look for trouble? "Mrs. Tyson seems content serving in our charities," Brandon pointed out. "She's in no danger of leaving the area."

"Whoever it is," Mrs. Arundel said with a quelling look to the other ladies, "we'd be happy to help her secure gainful employment, Pastor."

Brandon nodded his thanks. "I'm hoping to find a position as a nanny or governess for Miss Dumont. You've met everyone around Little Horn. Surely you know a family in need."

Mrs. Hickey drew herself up, and Mrs. Arundel's face darkened.

"I cannot help you, Pastor," the wife of the general store owner said, chin coming up.

Mrs. Hickey nodded. "We could not possibly risk our reputations for a lady of questionable character."

"What?" Brandon could not have heard her correctly. Elizabeth? Disreputable?

"I heard she has visitors at the boardinghouse at all hours," Mrs. Crenshaw told him, wide-eyed as if shocked by such behavior.

"Visitors for the triplets," Brandon protested. "You ladies among them."

"She was discharged from her last post," Mrs. Hickey maintained, glancing around at the other women as if in support. Two nodded; two positively squirmed in discomfort.

"Because the children no longer required a governess," Brandon told them all. "Not from any fault of hers."

"Mr. David McKay refused to marry her," Mrs. Arundel informed him.

"Because he was in love with Caroline Murray," Brandon reminded them.

"And she refused to marry Clyde Parker," Mrs. Hickey said, crossing her arms over her skinny chest. "After I expressly introduced them."

"Would you marry Clyde Parker?" Brandon demanded.

They all blushed.

"That is neither here nor there," Mrs. Arundel said, affixing him with her sternest look. "There are sufficient stories about Miss Dumont that I in good conscience could not recommend her. I believe the best thing for Little Horn would be to put those babies in the orphanage and send her on her way, as soon as possible."

Chapter Nine

By Friday, it was clear to Elizabeth that something must be done for Annie. The girl still refused to speak to her mother, even though her brothers had driven into town to plead with her, going so far as to bring her another dress and her night things.

"Ma's real sorry," her brother Peter said. Like his mother, the twenty-year-old had short blond hair and a mulish cast to his face. "She wants you to come home."

"We all do," her brother Randal confirmed with a nod of his head, blinking pale blue eyes.

Her youngest brother, Pauly, hitched up his worn jeans. "Can't you just forget about those Colemans?"

"No," Annie told them, face hardening until she also reminded Elizabeth of her mother. "I may not be able to marry Jamie, but I'm not going to pretend he and his family are evil. If Ma wants to apologize, she can show me she's willing to forgive Mr. Coleman. And so can you."

Shoulders slumped, her brothers had nodded agreement and left.

Worse was her interaction with Jamie. Annie and

Elizabeth had taken to wheeling the triplets out for a walk every afternoon, and they'd come across Jamie each time so far. He always doffed his hat, gazed at Annie as if she were a longed-for Christmas present and murmured his best wishes. Annie would nod and walk past him as if he were no more than an unnamed acquaintance. The pain in the young man's eyes cut Elizabeth to the quick. Why did their parents have to be so hardheaded?

Of course, Annie was equally so, but Elizabeth didn't feel as if she could argue with the girl. After all, Elizabeth had been nearly as determined when she and Brandon had parted four years ago. At least Brandon had left the area, so she wasn't reminded of the pain every time she saw him. With Jamie and Annie both living in Little Horn, the hurt would only go deeper.

She was so concerned about the situation that she didn't notice until Saturday that her visitors had dwindled. Louisa stopped by for a chat when she was in town to see her family, Mrs. Tyson couldn't resist the boys and Stella Fuller still came over to encourage Elizabeth. But Mrs. Arundel, Mrs. Crenshaw and the others of their circle did not put in an appearance. Was some civic event keeping them busy?

Even Brandon called fewer times and stayed only long enough to play with the triplets a moment and encourage Annie to reconcile with her family. He seemed to be avoiding conversation with Elizabeth, and she missed the camaraderie that had been growing between them. If anything, he acted a bit harried, and she put it down to his involvement with renovating the children's home on top of everything else. Given the number of things on his shoulders, she chose not to bring up the matter of her new position.

But she couldn't help thinking about it as she and Annie went to church that Sunday. Brandon had two more days of his promised week to find her a situation. Annie had tried to interest her in the mysterious Kit Durango, but Elizabeth couldn't see a future with the handsome raven-haired cowboy. He certainly didn't need a governess, and Brandon was probably right that his vagabond life made a wife just as unlikely.

Not that she wanted a husband. Even becoming a mail-order bride had paled as an option. Perhaps it was her experience with David McKay, who had disappointed her by marrying another. Perhaps it was Clyde Parker's ham-fisted proposal. She was beginning to think that if she ever married, it would be because she was tremendously in love.

And that seemed highly unlikely.

Still, she and Annie drew a great deal of attention as they walked into church with the babies. Gentlemen tipped their hats; children smiled in greeting. Mrs. Tyson hurried over to offer her help.

"I was hoping to help too."

Jamie Coleman stepped up to them, and Annie paled. He was dressed in a somber black frock coat and trousers, his blond hair slicked back from his face. Elizabeth was glad Annie had agreed to borrow one of her dresses, an olive twill with black-and-white bows at the waist and a black-and-white tucker down the front. With her hair done up on top of her head and one of Elizabeth's hats perched on top, she looked every inch the lady.

"It's good to see you, Annie," Jamie said, turning his hat in his hands.

Elizabeth and Mrs. Tyson exchanged glances, but Annie's gaze was all for Jamie.

"You too," she murmured. "But it doesn't matter. Our love was never meant to be."

Elizabeth started, gaze darting to the pulpit. Brandon hadn't come out onto the altar yet, but she felt his presence nonetheless. She'd said the same thing to him, just days ago, had consoled herself with it for years. Why did she suddenly feel like rebelling against the very idea?

"Seems to me you two should make that decision together," Mrs. Tyson said with a gentle smile. She reached out and took Eli from Annie. "Why don't you sit next to each other in service and think about it?"

Elizabeth was a little surprised when Annie and Jamie meekly agreed and went to take their seats. Even Tug, a few rows up, watched them go with a nod of approval.

"You have the wisdom of Solomon," Elizabeth told the older woman as they moved to a pew at the back of the church.

"At least I didn't have to suggest cutting a baby in half," Mrs. Tyson said with a smile to Eli in her arms. "I just wish my boys were here. They should be marrying and having babies too. As it is, I don't know when I'll hear from them, much less see them again." She tugged down on Eli's shirt. "I guess I just miss having children around. I loved being a mother."

Elizabeth could understand. A hole was already forming in her heart at the thought of leaving the triplets behind.

"If your sons settle elsewhere, will you move to be near them?" she asked, putting Theo's bootie back on his foot where he'd pulled it off. He studiously set out to remove it once more.

"I hope it doesn't come to that." She smoothed her brown hair back from her round face. "Little Horn is my home. I just wish I could do more to contribute to the community. It seems so many are hurting."

"You have been a great help to me, Mrs. Tyson," Elizabeth assured her. "And I see how you help Pastor Stillwater around the church."

She held up one hand, and Eli reached up to grab her fingers. She smiled at the baby, then glanced at Elizabeth. "Whatever I've done, it's small recompense for the kindnesses shown to me. And call me Fannie, dear. I feel as if we're kindred spirits."

So did Elizabeth. "Then you must call me Elizabeth. And thank you."

Just then Mrs. Hickey made her way to the piano, and Elizabeth and her new friend stood with the others to sing the opening hymn.

Contentment threaded its way through her as Theo rested his head against one shoulder even as Jasper in her other arm bounced himself up and down in time to the music. In Fannie's arms, Eli seemed content to thrust his fist in his mouth and listen. All three babies were surprisingly good as the service progressed. Perhaps that was why Elizabeth had a moment to notice the looks being directed their way.

It started with Mrs. Hickey. As she rose from her seat at the piano and started back to her husband's side, her gaze brushed Elizabeth's, and the woman looked away, nose in the air. Had Elizabeth sung off-key? How would Mrs. Hickey have even noticed at the front of the church?

Elizabeth turned her head to the right and caught Mrs. Arundel scowling at her. Now what had she done? She had chosen to wear one of her nicer dresses, a narrow-skirted tan silk with black lace parting and trimming the overskirt, but she hadn't chosen it from pride. She had only been able to bring a few of her dresses to Little Horn, and some still harked back to her days in Cambridge high society.

She looked left instead and found two more women regarding her speculatively. They quickly buried their noses in the hymnal.

"Have I dirt on my chin?" she whispered to Fannie.

The older woman smiled. "No, but not even dirt could mar that pretty face."

As if to prove it, Theo reached up and patted her cheek.

Behind them, sunlight speared the church as the door opened. Elizabeth couldn't help glancing back to see who was entering late. Jo and Gil Satler stood uncertainly, hands clasped, as if afraid they'd be ordered from the building.

Elizabeth set Jasper and Theo on the pew next to Fannie and rose to beckon to the children. Jo hesitated, but Gil tugged her forward, and Elizabeth and Fannie made room for them in the pew.

The pair had tried to make themselves presentable. Their peaked faces had that damp clean look of a fresh scrubbing, and Gil's cowlick had been pressed down against his forehead. Both glanced around as if waiting to be expelled. Fannie offered them a smile in welcome.

"Would you like to help with the triplets?" Elizabeth whispered.

Jo nodded, dropping her gaze. Fannie gave her Jasper, who grinned so widely his new teeth sparkled.

Brandon came to the pulpit then, and everyone in the congregation quieted.

"Have you ever wondered what it takes to please God?" he asked.

Elizabeth drew in a breath. In truth, at times, she'd wondered what she'd done to displease Him that He'd left her life so shattered. She leaned forward to hear what Brandon had to say.

"We read in First Samuel that God chose David to be king over Israel because he was a man after God's own heart," he told them. "Very likely because even though David sinned, he never lost faith in God to save him, to bring good from bad."

Good from bad? Was that even possible?

Brandon leaned an elbow on the pulpit as if getting comfortable. "Now, David wasn't your average king. Oh, he dressed in fine robes and lived in a palace, and armies marched at his command. But you know what he did? He was so eager to praise his God that he stripped down to his shirtsleeves and danced in front of the whole town."

An image came to her mind, Brandon without his frock coat, leaping down Main. Elizabeth smiled.

"Can you imagine?" Brandon pressed, smiling himself. "Your leader, the man you counted on to protect the nation, skipping about like a jackrabbit in the spring. Some folks probably laughed out loud for the sheer joy of it."

Others around her were also smiling, as if they could picture it too.

Brandon's smile faded. "But some folks have a hard time seeing the good in a situation. His own wife called him a fool and accused him of showing off. That had to have hurt. Another man might have begged her pardon, tried to look more proper, put on the airs of the lord of the land." Brandon straightened and puffed out his chest. "What did David do? He said I will do more ridiculous things than this to please my God."

As Elizabeth watched, fascinated, he leaned forward once more, gaze sweeping the congregation.

"What would you be willing to do to please your God? Would you dance down Main Street? Would you see to the needs of a widow when your own ranch was struggling? Move away to become a mail-order bride to a lonely widower with a child who needed a mother? Take on the care of babies not your own even though you had no place to call home?"

Elizabeth stared at him. Was he talking about her? His gaze met hers now, determined.

"Some folks might call that ridiculous. A few seem to find it shameful. I call it commendable. And I am not ashamed to say that you will see me do even more ridiculous things than that if they please my God. What will you do?"

Brandon glanced around one last time at his congregation, letting the question hang in the air. His brother was nodding, CJ Thorn and Edmond McKay looked thoughtful and David McKay had a look on his face that told Brandon he would have a lot to do with the children's home in the next few days.

The ladies, however, seemed less moved. Several avoided his gaze, and Mrs. Arundel had her arms crossed over her chest. He'd let the Lord contend with them. He was only the messenger. He said what the Lord instructed, spoke from his heart and hoped he did some good.

And we know that all things work together for good to them that love God, to them who are the called according to His purpose.

He hung on to the verse as Mrs. Hickey came forward to play the closing hymn.

Often when he came down from the pulpit he found himself surrounded before he could even make his way to the door to bid his parishioners goodbye. Today, however, people seemed to be keeping their distance so that he was nearly at Elizabeth's side before a couple stepped in front of him. The husband was short and stocky, with a thatch of blond hair. His wife was thinner, with wispy brown hair curling around her pretty face. He recognized them as the Tinsdales who had a small farm to the south of town.

"Inspiring sermon, Pastor," the husband said. "Makes me wonder what more we could do to help the community."

Needs sprang immediately to mind—the renovations on the Crenshaw house, the repairs on the Hill and Coleman ranches. But Brandon took one look at the three children clinging to Mrs. Tinsdale's skirts and the baby in her arms and he knew a life they could change.

"Have you ever considered taking on a governess?" he asked. "Miss Dumont will be available soon."

The husband frowned, but his wife's eyes widened.

"A governess?" she asked. "Like to help with the

children?" She turned to her husband. "Oh, Clem, could we?"

Tinsdale's jaw worked a moment, then he took his wife's arm, careful not to jostle the sleeping baby. "We'll discuss the matter and get back to you, Pastor." He hustled his wife and children down the aisle.

And Brandon could only hope that the seed he'd sown would bear fruit.

In two days. That was all the time he had left to find a position for Elizabeth before she made a decision to take the offer in San Francisco. Feeling as if something pressed a fist into his back, he continued down the aisle.

He managed to reach Elizabeth's side just as Annie rejoined her. He'd noticed Annie and Jamie sitting together and had hoped that meant reconciliation was in the air for the young couple. But the way Annie clung to Elizabeth dimmed that hope.

"And how are our boys today?" he asked, bending to put his face at a level with the babies'. Eli gabbled at him as if telling him all about his adventures. Theo put out a hand, begging for a hug. Jasper, however, cuddled closer to Jo Satler, thumb going to his mouth. Even though the little girl avoided Brandon's gaze, the sight of her and her brother in church could only warm his heart.

"Someone needs a nap," Mrs. Tyson said, eyeing Jasper with a fond smile. She reached out to rub his back with her free hand, then frowned.

"I should get all three of them back to the boarding-house," Elizabeth said before Brandon could ask the reason for her concern. Elizabeth looked his way. "Thank you, Pastor, for that sermon. It explained a lot."

Had she noticed the dark looks aimed her way? He had. "I just hope it had the intended effect."

As if in answer, Mrs. Hickey sailed by, nose once more in the air.

Annie frowned at her. "Maybe one of the babies needs changing."

"Never mind her," Mrs. Tyson said. "Some people don't have enough excitement in their lives, so they feel compelled to cause some in someone else's life."

That was what Brandon was concerned about.

"What matters is the triplets," Elizabeth said, voice firm with her convictions. "If there's someone better suited to care for them, a family who wants to adopt them, then of course I'll step aside."

Brandon put a hand on her shoulder. "No one in Little Horn cares for Jasper, Theo and Eli as much as you do."

Except maybe the Satlers. Jo looked brokenhearted as she handed the baby to Elizabeth. Her little brother must have felt for her, for he patted her arm. Jo waved to the triplets as Elizabeth offered Brandon a smile and headed out the door with two of the babies while Annie took the third.

"I'm sure Miss Elizabeth appreciates your help," Brandon told the girl.

Jo's gaze remained on her shoes, where one big toe was poking through the cracked leather.

"She's nice," Gil declared. "We like helping the babies. They're orphans, like us."

"That's right," Brandon said with a smile. "Miss Elizabeth and I are orphans too. Us orphans should stick together."

Gil nodded, chin sticking out. "Come on, Jo. Let's see what else we can do."

Still avoiding Brandon's gaze, she followed her brother from the church.

Brandon sighed. The Satler siblings were clearly attached to the triplets. So was he. He had to admit that to himself as he continued down the aisle. He wanted to protect the boys, make sure they had good food and pleasant surroundings. More, he wanted to guide their steps, help them become the men they were capable of being. He wanted to be the father his father had never been.

But that meant he needed a wife.

His schedule would never allow raising the boys on his own. A pastor might be called on at any time, day or night. He couldn't take the boys with him, and he couldn't leave them alone. Nor could he hire a woman to live in without risking her reputation and his. And there was no one near enough to the parsonage who could take the triplets at a moment's notice.

Finding a wife, even in Little Horn, where the men tended to outnumber the women, should not be difficult. Ever since he'd started divinity school, he'd had women glance his way. If he wondered about the picture he presented, he had only to look at his brother, who had been Little Horn's most eligible bachelor until he'd wed Louisa. Several young ladies and more than one widow had let Brandon know they would not be adverse to having him court them.

The problem was that only one woman had ever made him dream of matrimony, and she was no longer interested in his courtship even if he had been able to bring himself to try again.

He made it to the door and bid his congregation good day. But his sermon must have ruffled more feathers than he'd intended, because for the first time in months he received no invitation to dinner. Mrs. Hickey went so far as to rescind her offer from the previous week, claiming an urgent need to reorganize her spice shelf. Mercy Green's café held little interest either, so he found himself alone in the parsonage.

It was a good, solid house, with two bedrooms and a study besides the parlor and a big kitchen, but there were moments it didn't feel like home. Perhaps it was the mismatched furniture, donated from ranches around the area. Perhaps it was the lacy doilies the ladies insisted he needed on every flat surface. Perhaps it was the unrelenting quiet after a busy day out in the community. Whatever the reason, he retreated to his study and pulled out the dime novel he hadn't been willing to confess he was reading.

He had just put his feet up on the desk, with the thought that Mrs. Hickey would be appalled to find him so, when someone rapped on the front door. He set aside the book, rose and shrugged into his coat, resigned to help whoever had come seeking him.

Annie stood on the stoop, face puckered.

"It's Jasper," she said without preamble. "He's come down sick. Elizabeth sent me to the doctor, but Doctor Clark's wife says he's out birthing a baby and isn't expected back until morning. Oh, Pastor, what should we do?"

Chapter Ten

Elizabeth sat on the bed, rocking Jasper back and forth as he fussed. Theo and Eli sat at her feet, toys forgotten around them and concern tightening their little faces. It felt like forever since she'd sent Annie for the doctor.

The door opened, and Annie rushed back into the room. Elizabeth looked up, but instead of Doctor Clark, Brandon followed the girl inside. His face was nearly as worried as the babies'.

"What's wrong?" he asked. His voice was kind, quiet, but she felt the tension under it.

"Mrs. Tyson mentioned she thought Jasper was too warm," she explained. "When he didn't want his supper, I thought maybe he was teething. But he's hotter now, and all he wants to do is to be held. Oh, Brandon, he acts as if he's in pain."

Jasper wiggled in her arms, then turned to reach for Brandon.

Brandon lifted him close, frown growing as he peered into Jasper's face. "What's the trouble, little man?"

In answer, Jasper sucked back a sob, lower lip trembling and one hand rubbing at his cheeks.

Eli crawled over to tug on Elizabeth's skirts, and she bent and picked him up. "Where's Doctor Clark?"

"Out birthing a new baby," Annie said with a pout, as if the good doctor was thoroughly in her bad graces for not being in town when she needed him.

"But I sent for Louisa," Brandon added, still watching Jasper. "She knows as much about babies as her father does. It might be an hour or two before she can reach us from Bo's ranch."

An hour or two? That seemed too long when she didn't know what was ailing the usually active little boy.

Annie must have felt the same way for she wrung her hands. "Isn't there anything we can do in the meantime?"

Elizabeth had felt the same helplessness when her aunt was ill, her uncle locked away for scandal. She hadn't given in to fear then, and she refused to give in to it now.

She drew in a breath, raised her head. "We can make all the boys more comfortable. Annie, take Theo and Eli up on the bed with you and play with them. Pastor Stillwater, hold Jasper while I make a compress."

Annie nodded, then went to gather the two babies in her arms while Elizabeth moved to the dresser. Someone had donated lavender water, if memory served—ah, yes! She took out a handkerchief and wet it with the aseptic, then let the material hang a moment in the air. Folding the handkerchief carefully, she brought it to place on Jasper's forehead.

The baby pulled back with a whimper, twisting in Brandon's arms.

"I know," Elizabeth soothed, repositioning the cloth.

"It feels odd, doesn't it? But it might help cool you off, sweetheart."

Under the white, lace-edged piece of linen, the baby's brown eyes looked huge and deep.

"Do you think he'd drink something?" Brandon murmured. "I could fetch fresh water."

"We couldn't get him to eat or drink," Elizabeth told him. "That's what made me wonder whether he was teething. Still, I'm not sure whether teething would bring on this kind of fever." She pulled off the handkerchief and laid her fingers against the baby's skin.

"Still too hot," she reported. "Help me take off his sweater."

"Ma says it's best to sweat out a fever," Annie put in from the bed. "She'd say stoke up the fire and pile on the blankets."

Elizabeth had heard the advice as well, but she just couldn't make herself believe it. "Cold water douses fire," she countered. "We just need to keep him as comfortable as we can until Louisa gets here."

Brandon nodded. "Whatever you need, Elizabeth. Tell me, and it's done."

Together, they stripped the baby to his diaper, then kept wiping him down with lavender water. Brandon left long enough to fill the porcelain pitcher with clean water from the pump in the boardinghouse kitchen. He even managed to get Jasper to take a few sips from a cup. But each time the baby swallowed, he grimaced, until he pushed the cup away and started crying.

From the bed, two more voices joined his.

Annie's eyes widened. "What do we do?"

Elizabeth was beginning to think Jasper was suffering from a sore throat, but there was nothing wrong with hers. "Caroline said singing comforted them," Elizabeth told her. She turned to Brandon. "Pastor, do you know a song?"

His brows shot up, but he nodded, and his warm baritone filled the room.

"Summer suns are glowing
over land and sea,
happy light is flowing
bountiful and free.
Everything rejoices
in the mellow rays,
all earth's thousand voices
swell the psalm of praise."

One by one, the babies quieted, watching him. Theo's thumb was in his mouth, and Eli leaned against Annie on the bed. In Elizabeth's arms, Jasper sighed and rested his head against her chest. Something stirred inside her, warm, soft. It whispered of hope, of peace.

Of love.

"We will never doubt thee," Brandon sang, gaze moving among the babies and coming to rest on Elizabeth, "though thou veil thy light: life is dark without thee; death with thee is bright. Light of Light! shine o'er us on our pilgrim way. Go thou still before us to the endless day."

With a yawn, Eli slid down onto the bed. Theo followed him, putting his back up against his brother's. Annie smoothed their hair with a smile.

"Thank you," Elizabeth murmured to Brandon.

He came close, laid a hand on Jasper's head. "Thank you, for caring for these little ones."

She did—oh, how she did! But she was coming to realize they weren't the only ones who had staked a claim on her heart.

She and Brandon took turns holding Jasper and walking him about the room. Every time they sat down with him, he started fussing, and Elizabeth was concerned he'd wake his brothers. As it was, she was surprised Annie could sleep. With Brandon in the room, the girl hadn't been able to change into her nightgown, yet somehow she looked comfortable curled up beside the boys on the big bed.

Elizabeth glanced out the window to find that evening had turned to night. A crescent moon was climbing over the humps of the hills. Jasper in his arms, Brandon came to join her.

"Where can Louisa be?" she murmured.

He rocked Jasper in his arms, face still soft. "Perhaps she didn't have an easy way to reach us. Bo might have had the wagon out on the range today for roundup. And likely she wouldn't come on horseback. She's not a practiced rider like Caroline."

Elizabeth could only hope nothing bad had happened on the way into town. "Shall I hold him?"

Brandon smiled down at the baby, whose eyes were at last drifting shut. "He's fine where he is."

She wasn't. Something pushed at her, gnawed at her. She moved to the dresser, rearranged the remaining fruits and vegetables in neat rows, then opened a drawer and counted the clean diapers.

"We'll have to find a way to wash soon," she murmured, straightening. "Mrs. Chambers takes away the dirty diapers, for which I am very thankful, but some of the boys' shirts need cleaning."

"Elizabeth," he murmured, nodding to the chair beside him.

She couldn't sit. "Have you noticed? The boys are outgrowing their clothing. I heard Mercy Green brought this set the ladies collected for them when the boys first arrived in Little Horn. Would people be willing to take up another collection? Or maybe Helen Carson and the quilting bee would be willing to sew new outfits for them if we could find someone to donate the material."

"Elizabeth," he said, moving closer.

She tapped her chin. "Mrs. Arundel might be persuaded to donate it. I'm sure I saw bolts of fabric in her husband's general store. And shoes! They'll be walking soon. I wonder..."

"Elizabeth." He stepped in front of her. "I know how hard it can be to see someone you love hurting. But wearing yourself out isn't going to help."

And that was what she was doing. She could feel it. Her feet and her back were protesting, and she'd been trying to shout them down with busyness. Her legs seemed to give out as she sank onto the chair.

"I hate this!" she hissed. "I want to do something. I felt the same way when Aunt Evangeline had her stroke. You knew her, Brandon. She was always so alive, so busy. She reminded me of a little bird, some part of her always bobbing. Uncle Hugh's scandal devastated her, inside and out. That terrible stroke left her confined to bed, and there was nothing I could do."

"You stayed with her, made sure she had care," Brandon said. "That must have brought her comfort."

"I like to think it did. She was everything I had. I

don't even remember my parents. When I was sick, when I was sad, the one who held me was Aunt Evangeline."

"And after her stroke, you held her." Brandon shifted the baby in his arms. "I wish I could have been there to help."

So did she.

Jasper raised his head and let out a whimper. Elizabeth opened her arms, and he came to her. Was he cooler than before? Or was she so desperate to feel improvement? How sick was he? Was his life in danger? Would Theo and Eli come down with it as well? Would she lose them all the way she'd lost her aunt?

Please, Lord, they're so little, so helpless. Show me how to care for them.

"They love you," Brandon said, watching her. "It's obvious in how they react to you. You bring them comfort as well."

He sounded awed, as if she'd done something amazing, and she felt humbled to think she might have made an impression on the three dear boys. "That's what you do for those you love," she said.

He nodded, and it struck her that he looked tired too. Fine lines feathered out around his silver eyes, and his smile dipped at the corners as if he was having a hard time keeping it up.

She had cared for her first charges, looked after her aunt and soothed the triplets. Why did it feel as if her greatest need was to comfort this man and him alone?

Brandon helped Elizabeth with Jasper as the night grew darker, the room cooler. Normally, Elizabeth and Jasper would be snuggled under covers. He couldn't help being concerned for them now, but he didn't want to leave her to locate where the boardinghouse owner kept wood for the fire.

He drew a blanket from the bed instead and wrapped it around both of them as Elizabeth sat in the chair with Jasper in her arms. She looked tired, her color faded in the candlelight, as if it took all her energy to manage that small smile. He remembered a night early on when Bo had spent time in a steam tent with Louisa and all three babies.

Where was Louisa? Why didn't she come to help? *Please, Lord, we need help.*

"You're good with them," Elizabeth murmured, smoothing a curl back from Jasper's forehead. The little boy's breath came out raspy. His eyes were closed, and drool pooled on his open lips. "Did you and your brother have little brothers or sisters?"

Brandon shook his head, leaning his hip against one corner of the bed. "It was always just the two of us, particularly after our mother died."

She rocked Jasper gently. "Did you lose your father too? You never mention him."

He hadn't mentioned much about his family, for good reason. Knowing she'd been raised by doting relatives, he hadn't been able to bring himself to share the pain that had been his youth at times.

But now, in the quiet of the little room, it felt as if those days were long ago, in the life of another little boy.

"My father was a busy man," he said, rubbing his hand along the smooth curve of the bedstead. "You might think we'd miss him. But Mother and Bo and I looked forward to the times he'd travel, because when he was home, he had a way of looking, of speaking, that said you were the most worthless person on the planet."

"Oh, Brandon," she murmured, eyes luminous. "I'm so sorry. Small wonder you wanted to leave Cambridge."

"We wanted to leave the moment Mother was buried," Brandon remembered. "Bo and I didn't plan to spend one more day with the man who'd made our lives miserable. But Father was sick, and we couldn't leave him. We hired a man to care for him during the day, but Bo and I saw to his needs until he died four years ago. Then we sold out, packed up and headed West. Bo liked what he saw around Little Horn, so here we are."

She stilled her rocking. "I always wondered why you didn't introduce me to your family. I thought you were ashamed of me."

Brandon straightened. "Ashamed of you? Never. You were everything good and bright in life, Elizabeth."

Her cheeks turned the color in the heart of a peach. "Thank you. When I look back, all I can think is how young and naive I was."

"And now you are old and wise," he teased.

Her smile hovered. "Perhaps not so old but definitely wiser."

Footsteps sounded on the stairs a moment before the knock on the door. Brandon strode to answer it.

Louisa hurried into the room. Her soft brown hair was falling loose of its pins, locks brushing the shoulders of her leather jacket, and her brown twill skirts were dusty.

"I'm sorry it took me so long to get here," she said, setting a valise on the floor. "Bo brought me to see the herd being rounded up, and Mr. Tyson had to ride out to find us. Then I had to go back to the house for my bag." She turned to Elizabeth. "What happened? How's Jasper?"

Elizabeth tried to rise, and Brandon moved to help her, hands braced under her elbows. For a moment, she stood in his arms, and he had to force himself to step away.

Cheeks pinking, she explained the situation to Louisa, who examined the baby and asked questions. Her no-nonsense attitude seemed to calm Elizabeth's fears. Brandon felt buoyed simply by her presence.

Thank You, Lord, for sending us aid.

"I think you're right," Louisa said, putting away the rod she'd used to push the baby's tongue aside and peer into his mouth. "His gums are swollen and red. He's teething."

Jasper scowled at her as if ready to scold her. She smoothed back his hair, and his look softened.

"Are you sure?" Elizabeth asked, glancing toward the bed, where Annie had woken and the other two babies still slumbered. "I wouldn't want his brothers to be exposed to something contagious."

Louisa made a face. "I wish medicine was more precise! It's possible the fever was caused by something more. He may be reacting to food he ate or he may have a cold coming on. But I'll tell you what, just to be on the safe side, we'll take the other two elsewhere for now. Pastor, can Annie bring them to the parsonage? I'll stay with her so propriety will be satisfied."

Brandon could only be relieved to hear that the boy would be fine. "Of course. I'll stay with Elizabeth and Jasper."

Elizabeth shook her head. "You can't. It wouldn't be proper."

It was on his tongue to argue, but he swallowed the words. She was right, of course. Some of the ladies in his congregation already had doubts about her. Even after his sermon today, he shouldn't fan the flames.

As if she expected him to disagree, she stepped forward. "Now that I know Jasper will be fine and the others are safe, I should be able to manage."

Brandon nodded. "Very well. But if you need anything, send someone from the boardinghouse for me. The parsonage is just across the street."

"I promise," Elizabeth agreed.

He didn't believe her. She'd said she'd been young and naive years ago. Now she seemed to have grown determined to do whatever she thought best, whether that meant helping her aunt or following her own path. It would take a lot for her to send someone for his aid.

He laid a hand against the silk of her cheek and watched her eyes widen.

"I mean it, Elizabeth. One word from you, and I will be at your side."

She nodded, causing her cheek to rub against his fingers. The touch brought back memories of holding hands, bringing her close, bending his head and pressing his lips to hers.

None of which was appropriate at the moment.

Brandon dropped his hand and stepped back. "Annie, let me help you and Louisa with the boys."

His sister-in-law had been regarding him with a frown, as if she could not understand him. Now her brow cleared, and she gathered up her things and headed for the door. Annie came behind her with a sleeping baby.

"I'll be sure to check on you and Jasper in the morning," Louisa promised Elizabeth.

The last sight Brandon had of Elizabeth was her weary smile as he shut the door.

Louisa encouraged Annie to go first down the stairs, then put a hand on Brandon's arm to stop him from following.

"You know I despise gossip," she murmured, "but Mrs. Hickey took it upon herself to warn Bo and me that you were in danger of succumbing to Miss Dumont's charms."

Brandon nearly lost his footing on the stair. "What!"

Louisa hurried after Annie, and he could only do the same. Most of the lights were out on Second Street, and clouds shrouded a crescent moon, but he could see Louisa's rueful look as they headed for the parsonage.

"Don't worry. Bo reminded her that you are a man of the cloth with a spotless reputation, and that Elizabeth is every bit a lady. To prove it, he told her a little about Elizabeth's life in Boston."

"And was she willing to listen to reason?" Brandon challenged. "I've already tried that route, to no avail, it seems."

"I'm sure it didn't help that Bo finished by telling her to mind her own business." Louisa spared a smile for her husband, then had to cover her mouth with one hand as she yawned. "Forgive me, Brandon. It's been a long day."

For all of them. Brandon couldn't help a glance back at the boardinghouse. He easily made out Elizabeth's room—it was the only one with the candle still glowing. A figure crossed the light, paused as if to look out into the night. He felt as if he could reach out and touch her, smooth the worries from her brow, lull her into the sleep she had so justly earned.

But what concerned him most was how much he longed to earn the right to hold her again.

Chapter Eleven

The next morning, Brandon threw on his clothes and hurried to the boardinghouse. Mrs. Causewell scowled at him, and he wasn't sure if it was because of his early arrival or his scruffy chin. She nonetheless opened wide the door and let him climb the stairs to Elizabeth's room.

Elizabeth answered his knock more quickly. Shadows darkened her eyes, but her smile was warm.

"He's much better this morning," she reported, gaze going to where Jasper was scrambling closer. The baby's eyes were on Brandon, and the joy on his face touched something inside him. Bending, he scooped Jasper up.

"And did you keep Elizabeth up all night?" he asked the baby.

"No!" Jasper proclaimed, displaying a bright white tooth on his lower gum. Then he went on to chatter at Brandon as if explaining everything that had happened.

Elizabeth covered a yawn. "I slept some. I'm just glad he's feeling better."

So was Brandon. He could only hope Elizabeth had a chance to nap with the babies later that day.

"He's lucky to have you," he murmured, gaze brushing hers.

Her cheeks darkened. "I'm lucky to have him. At least for a while longer."

He could not forget her sad look or comment as he went about his duties. After returning to the parsonage for a quick shave, he went to the Crenshaw house, where David, Edmund and Josiah McKay were adding a wall to turn an upstairs parlor into two bedrooms. While Edmund ferried the two-by-fours and planks his brother had donated up the stairs, Brandon worked with David and Josiah to nail the pieces in place. Within a few hours, they were ready to paint.

"We should expand the garden behind the house," David said as he and Brandon descended the stairs so David could fetch the paint and brushes. "That way we can grow some of the food and teach the children a little about farming as we originally planned."

"Sounds good," Brandon said, stepping out onto the stoop. Over the house next door, he could make out the roof of the boardinghouse. How were Elizabeth and Jasper getting on now? Had the baby's fever returned? When would Louisa agree to return the other two brothers from the parsonage? Would Elizabeth need more help with them after her restless night?

"And maybe pony rides on Christmas and Easter," David said.

Brandon frowned, turning to face him. "What?"

David chuckled. "Well, it's good to know I haven't bored you completely, Pastor."

Brandon smiled. "I'm not bored. And I can tell you the Lone Star Cowboy League won't pay for pony rides.

Sorry that my mind wandered. I have a few concerns I'm mulling over."

David sobered. "Ailing parishioners? Anything I can do to help?"

That was one thing Brandon admired about the community—how quickly people rose up to help one another. Why couldn't they find room in their hearts for Elizabeth?

"I'm concerned about Miss Dumont," he told David. "Apparently some people are questioning her reputation."

David grimaced. "That's at least partly my fault. I should never have invited her here, Pastor, but I thought I needed someone for Maggie. You know how things were. Turns out all Maggie and I needed was Caroline."

Brandon smiled at the tender way David said his wife's name. "I haven't helped matters," he admitted. "If the triplets need something, I help, day or night."

David shook his head. "Well, she won't have to put up with us for much longer. Once the children's home is ready and staffed, the triplets will have a permanent place, and she can find a position somewhere else."

That was what Brandon feared.

Perhaps that was why he borrowed David's horse and rode out to the Tinsdale farm that afternoon. It took him an hour to reach the spread to the south of town. He found a two-story farmhouse and wide barn nestled up against the hills. He thought Elizabeth would approve of the white shutters at the windows and the benches on the front porch just waiting for someone to sit and read. Then again, he supposed a governess didn't have much time to herself.

Mrs. Tinsdale was hanging wash on the line, the diapers and pinafores flapping in the breeze. She paused as he rode in, one hand pushing damp hair from her brow.

"How do, Pastor?" she asked, coming forward to take the reins of his horse so he could dismount. "What brings you out this way?"

Brandon swung down from the saddle and took the reins from her. Up close, he could see the dust dotting her nose and cheeks like freckles. Two children were peering out of the barn door, another from the window overlooking the front porch.

"I was just wondering whether you and Mr. Tinsdale had had a chance to think about hiring Miss Dumont," Brandon told her.

She clutched her apron closer even as she glanced toward the range. "I'm all for it, Pastor, I truly am. It's too far to send the boys to school, and some days it's all I can do to put dinner on the table what with looking out for all of them."

Brandon nodded. "Miss Dumont could teach your children to read and write and even play an instrument."

Mrs. Tinsdale sighed gustily. "Oh, wouldn't that be fine? I always wanted more music in the house. But Clem is against hiring her."

Brandon put on his best smile. "If it's a matter of money…"

She held up her hands. "No, no! Clem would be powerful mad if he thought I'd given you that idea. We do real well, and with roundup we'll have enough to pay her wages for a year."

Perfect! Elizabeth would be close enough to town that he'd see her at church and civic events and far enough away he wouldn't disturb her peace. "That's wonderful news. I'm sure Miss Dumont will be delighted."

Her face puckered. "But we can't hire her, Pastor. Clem says she isn't a proper lady."

Heat flamed up him. This again? Would nothing stop Constance Hickey?

"I assure you that Miss Dumont is a lady through and through," he insisted.

She shook her head as she released the apron. "I know Clem, Pastor. Once his mind is made up, it's done. I'm real sorry, but that's how it is."

He wanted to argue. He knew so many ways to show Elizabeth's education, her dedication, her character. He could paint a picture of a sweet-natured woman in need of a good home, encourage them to think of hiring her as their Christian duty. Yet he sensed Mrs. Tinsdale was right. Her husband would not change his mind, not after it had been poisoned against Elizabeth.

"Thank you, Mrs. Tinsdale," he said and remounted his borrowed horse to ride back to town.

But all the way home he kept hearing a clock ticking. It was Monday. He'd promised Elizabeth news by Tuesday night. He was running out of time, and the rumors made it impossible to achieve his goal.

Last night Elizabeth had said how much she hated feeling helpless. He understood. Whenever his father had lit into Brandon's mother or Bo, something inside Brandon had curled up tighter. He could not count the number of times he'd tried to intervene, smiling and cajoling, or how many times he'd earned a cuff or a curse for his trouble. One of the reasons he'd wanted to become a minister was that ministers had power. They championed the causes of the weak and unfortunate. They were called upon to be peacemakers. People listened when they spoke.

And they had a far greater ally listening to their prayers.

Help me, Lord! Do You want her to move away? I can't see Your plan in any of this.

That feeling of helplessness rubbed against him like a badly made saddle. Perhaps that was the reason he stormed into the parsonage, slamming the door behind him.

"Pastor?" Mrs. Tyson stuck her head out of the parlor as he passed, dust cloth in one hand. "Is everything all right?"

Her brown eyes were turned down in concern. The dear woman did not deserve his anger.

Brandon pasted on a smile. "Everything is fine, Mrs. Tyson. I forgot it was cleaning day. Anything I can do to help?"

"Yes," Mrs. Hickey said, popping out of his study. "You can come tell me where these books go. They were all over your office."

She made it sound as if he'd emptied the shelves and tossed their contents to the wind.

"I'm studying those books for their application to Sunday's sermon," he told her.

She wrinkled her nose. "Last Sunday's or next?"

Brandon bit back a sigh. "Just leave them on the desk, Mrs. Hickey. Or, better yet, just leave my study for me to tidy up."

She stiffened. "And shirk my duty? No such thing! Unlike some people in this town, I know my place."

Maybe it was the lack of sleep or those persistent feelings of helplessness, but his temper was threatening for the first time in a very long time.

"This is America, Mrs. Hickey," he informed her.

"The only 'place' anyone has is following the path God laid down of loving thy neighbor."

"Well, there's loving and then there's loving," she insisted. "I could tell you stories, Pastor."

Brandon stood taller, crossing his arms over his chest. "Please do. Who do you imagine is such a terrible person that I wouldn't have noticed?"

She opened her mouth, and he held up one hand. "And remember—let she who is without sin cast the first stone."

Mrs. Hickey closed her mouth. He could almost see the thoughts whirling behind her eyes as she weighed her choices: gratifying her gossipy nature or keeping quiet and being seen as a virtuous woman.

Nature, as he often found, won.

She took a few steps forward and lowered her voice. "I am very concerned for our community, Pastor. And the care of those three precious babies. Miss Dumont is not the woman you think her."

Brandon's jaw hardened. "On the contrary, Mrs. Hickey. Miss Dumont is exactly the lady I know her to be—bright, energetic, caring. An excellent example of Christian womanhood."

"*I* heard she only wants to marry above herself," Mrs. Hickey insisted. "And her uncle who raised her was just as greedy."

Bo had obviously filled her in on more than she should know. As Brandon had predicted, she'd taken threads of truth and woven them into a tapestry of lies.

"You are ill-informed," Brandon told her. "Miss Dumont's uncle was convicted of swindling his clients, but she is nothing like him. I will not have a member of my congregation treated poorly for the sins of another."

Mrs. Hickey drew herself up. "Well! You just wait. When those babies are in the orphanage, she'll show her true colors. She'll find a way to dig her claws into some wealthy rancher."

"No, she won't," Brandon said, matching her gaze for gaze. "Because if Elizabeth Dumont marries anyone in this town, it's going to be me."

The sharp intake of breath from Mrs. Tyson behind him told him he had just made a commitment. Mrs. Hickey's eyes widened as if she thought so too.

A shame the last person to hear about his intentions was the woman he had just named his bride.

The day had been going much better than Elizabeth had hoped. Though Jasper still rubbed his cheeks as if something hurt, he was willing to eat and drink, and he no longer lay about listlessly. Indeed, when she took him across the street to see Doctor Clark, the baby tugged at the stethoscope put to his chest and tried to wiggle off the table.

"Louisa was quite right," the gray-haired doctor told Elizabeth when she lifted Jasper back into her arms. "He appears to be teething. I can't find anything more wrong with him."

Elizabeth drew in a breath. "Then he isn't contagious."

Louisa's father smiled, reminding Elizabeth of her friend. "Not in the least. I checked Theo and Eli this morning, and they are fine. Louisa and Annie are ready to help you take them home."

The three women met outside the doctor's house. Jasper, Theo and Eli seemed overjoyed about being together again, calling each other "baby" and touching shoulders and hands while grinning. Louisa helped them carry the tots back to the boardinghouse and get them settled.

"Call whenever you need help," she told Elizabeth with a kind smile. "I'll come faster next time. I promise."

She and Elizabeth exchanged hugs before Louisa headed back home.

"I'm glad that's over," Annie said. "I feel like I haven't slept in days."

Elizabeth felt the same way. "When they nap today, so do we." She cast the girl a glance. "Unless you're ready to go home."

Annie lowered her gaze. "I don't know what to do. Jamie told me at church that his father is trying to make up to Ma, but Ma just won't bend."

Elizabeth sat on a chair, watching the boys tussle the worn stuffed animals Louisa had told her the Good Samaritan had given them. "Why does she dislike Mr. Coleman so much? You mentioned a ring, but surely that was years ago."

"Before I was born," Annie confirmed, perching on the bed. "But the story I was told was that Mr. Coleman's uncle and my grandfather had a falling-out over a diamond ring. Pa vowed it was stolen. Mr. Coleman says it was won fair and square." She made a face as if that was how little use she had for the trinket. "I don't know why they can't leave the past alone, but they just keep bickering, and now Jamie and I are ruined."

"You could leave the area," Elizabeth suggested, bending to keep Jasper from crawling over Theo. "Leave their squabbles behind."

Annie looked horrified. "But they're family!"

And family came first. She understood that. She

might have left Cambridge years ago, but she'd stayed for her aunt. Brandon and his brother might have struck out on their own after their mother had died, but they'd felt responsible for their father.

And she felt responsible for the triplets. If only there was some way she could stay in Little Horn and care for them!

She and Annie spent the rest of the morning changing and feeding the babies, then taking a quick nap when the boys did. A noise woke Elizabeth, and she jerked upright, only to find that Jasper was poking Eli in the nose and laughing. Thankfully, Eli was laughing too. She gave them their stuffed animals to play with and settled herself in for a long afternoon.

A knock on the door had her hopping to her feet. Annie glanced her way as if surprised by her sudden energy. She couldn't tell her it was because she hoped to see Brandon on the other side of the door.

Instead, Mrs. Arundel stood there, foot tapping under her long rust-colored skirts. The feather in her hat nodded a greeting. It was the only thing that looked welcoming.

"Good afternoon, Mrs. Arundel," Elizabeth said, opening the door wider. "Have you come to see the triplets?"

The lady drew a sheet of paper from her reticule. "No, indeed. I heard they were ailing in any event. I wrote a list of verses for you. You may already know them, but as a preacher's wife, you will be expected to quote the Bible on occasion."

Elizabeth accepted the piece of paper. "Thank you, Mrs. Arundel, but I have no plans to marry a preacher."

The lady drew herself up. "So Mrs. Hickey predicted, but I told her she was entirely mistaken about you. If your heart is set on a rancher, remember that silver does not become a lady." Head high, she picked up her skirts and swept down the stairs.

Elizabeth shook her head as she closed the door. "What was that about?"

Annie shrugged. "I don't know, but she obviously thinks she knows the good Book."

And quoted it entirely out of context. To what purpose? The way things stood between Elizabeth and Brandon, she was more likely to strike it rich in the gold fields of California than to marry a preacher.

She was merely thankful that it wasn't much longer before all the babies were rubbing their eyes and yawning again. Annie was doing the same. She helped the girl put the babies into their crib, and they all curled up to sleep. Annie stretched out on the bed. Elizabeth would gladly have joined them, but she felt as if something was prodding her again.

She picked up the stuffed animals the boys had left lying on the floor and put them away carefully. The things had obviously been used far beyond the few weeks the boys had been cuddling them. Had they belonged to the Good Samaritan's children? Were those children now grown, so they had no more use for the toys?

She frowned. Fannie's sons were grown and gone, and she said she missed being a mother. Could she be the Good Samaritan? She certainly loved the boys, and she had time to move about the area. But she wasn't afraid of letting anyone see her affections for the triplets. Why would she have to hide her gifts, her good deeds? Besides, Elizabeth couldn't see her sneaking out to the Windy Diamond just to fold clothes.

No, the Good Samaritan had to be someone else. What connection did the person have to the babies? Was it someone like her, with no hope of adopting them?

She sank back onto the chair, shoulders slumping. That was why she couldn't rest. She knew what she should do—take the job in California and get on with her life. But that wasn't where her heart lay.

In an attempt to focus her mind on something other than her yearnings, she picked up Mrs. Arundel's list and looked at it more closely.

Romans 8:28, And we know that all things work together for good to them that love God, to them who are the called according to His purpose.

That sounded like what Brandon had preached on. Funny how it kept coming up.

Revelation 21:4, And God shall wipe away all tears from their eyes; and there shall be no more death, neither sorrow, nor crying, neither shall there be any more pain: for the former things are passed away.

She could imagine a preacher's wife offering that in times of sorrow.

Ecclesiastes 9:4, For to him that is joined to all the living there is hope: for a living dog is better than a dead lion.

She couldn't imagine offering that to anyone ever!

The final one made her spine stiffen.

Ecclesiastes 5:10, He that loveth silver shall not be satisfied with silver; nor he that loveth abundance with increase: this is also vanity.

Suddenly she understood what Mrs. Arundel had meant.

Like Brandon in Cambridge, they thought she wanted to marry for money.

The paper shook in her hand, and she slapped it down on the arm of the chair. How dare they assume she was so greedy to put aside all scruples! What about her behavior could possibly have given them that impression? If she'd wanted a wealthy husband, she would have accepted Clyde Parker!

She was in such a stew she barely heard the tap on the door until it came again. Rising, she composed herself and went to answer it before the noise woke Annie or the triplets.

Brandon stood on the landing, hat in his hands. She had so longed to see him, but she couldn't seem to push Mrs. Arundel's unkind assumption from her mind. Perhaps she was still scowling, for he looked at her with concern written on his handsome face.

"I just wanted to check on you and the boys," he murmured.

Elizabeth glanced back into the room where Annie and the babies slept.

"They're resting," she said, stepping out onto the landing and shutting the door partway. "But Doctor Clark says Jasper will be fine. He isn't contagious."

She thought that would ease the tension in him, but he merely nodded as he turned his hat in his hands.

"That's good to hear. I also wanted to let you know that I may have found a solution to allow you to stay in Little Horn and care for Jasper, Theo and Eli."

The last frustrating moments disappeared like raindrops in the sun. "Oh, Brandon, that would be wonderful! Did the Lone Star Cowboy League decide I could run the children's home after all?"

"No." She could see him swallow. "And no one I can find wants a governess or nanny."

She frowned, hope dipping. "Then what?"

He drew in a breath as if making a decision. "Elizabeth, you should know that there are rumors going around about you."

She should have realized he'd hear them too. Everyone spoke to the pastor in Little Horn. She raised her head. "I caught a whiff of them this afternoon. It seems I value money over love."

He grimaced. "It's ridiculous."

She cocked her head. "You didn't think so four years ago."

"I was foolish," he replied, so quickly and firmly she could not doubt him. "You are a fine woman, Elizabeth, one who cares deeply for those she loves. I cannot stand by and watch your good name be slandered."

He raised his gaze to hers. "Elizabeth Dumont, will you marry me?"

Chapter Twelve

Elizabeth stared at Brandon, feeling as if the landing had tilted. She must have swayed with the sensation, for he reached out a hand to catch her arm.

"What did you say?" she asked.

He released her. "I asked you to marry me. I know Little Horn is a far cry from Boston or even San Francisco, but I can see that you genuinely care for Jasper, Theo and Eli. Just as important, they care for you. If we married, we could petition the Lone Star Cowboy League to adopt them." His voice softened until she could hear the yearning in it. "We could be a family."

A family. She could be mother to those three darling babies, see them grow into the fine men she was sure they could be. She could stay in Little Horn, deepen her friendships with Louisa, Caroline, Fannie, Annie and Stella. She would finally have a home to call her own.

All she had to do was give up on love.

For he hadn't offered that. He hadn't claimed any sort of affection for her. Even now, as he stood on the landing, she could see his struggle. He kept his pleasant smile, like a good minister, but those quicksilver eyes were dark, hurting. He was giving up on love too.

That was simply unacceptable. When Brandon had left her four years ago, she'd thought she'd never hand her heart to another. Her position as a governess had made it unlikely she might meet a suitable gentleman in any regard, and that thought had not troubled her overly much. She'd been willing to become a mail-order bride, with no promise of love, simply to escape the stifling confines of Cambridge.

But to enter into a marriage of convenience with Brandon? It seemed wrong, impossible, something likely to twist her into someone she didn't want to be.

She must have taken too long to answer, for his shoulders slumped.

"Have I offended you?" he murmured, face so worn she wanted to reach out and stroke the lines from beside his eyes.

"No, of course not." She brushed at her skirts, anything to keep her hands too busy to touch him. "It was very kind of you, Brandon, but we both know your heart wasn't in it."

His mouth quirked, more pain than smile now. "It seemed like the perfect plan for us both. I've come to care about the boys, but I'm not in a position to adopt them. A minister must be able to ride out at a moment's notice to see to the needs of the community. And it wouldn't be seemly to hire a nanny to live in the parsonage."

Something poked at her. "So of course you thought about marrying a nanny instead. How very economical."

He made a face. "Economy wasn't the reason I asked.

I was under the impression you wanted to stay in Little Horn with the boys."

She did. Outside her aunt's home, she had never felt so welcome anywhere, until those vicious rumors had started.

"And there are those rumors," he added as if he had heard her thoughts. "Constance Hickey knows about your uncle."

She fought a shiver. So the story was out. Some part of her was relieved. She'd felt as if she'd explained the situation a hundred times. Now she need only correct the rumors.

Rumors. Gossip. How easily they tainted a life. Though her uncle had been guilty of crimes against his clients, the gossip was what had driven everyone away from her and her aunt. Would it drive everyone away here too? If people in Little Horn thought her of poor character, she might well find it impossible to secure another position in the area.

And how would the people of Little Horn react if those rumors tarred their pastor with the same brush?

Heat flamed through her. "You're concerned about what people will say about us. You're worried for your reputation."

He colored. "My reputation will survive. I'm more concerned about yours."

She put her hands on her hips. "Oh, so now you agree that I'm some kind of fortune hunter?"

"No." He puffed out a breath. "Elizabeth, please. Consider my offer. I will make no demands of you. You and the boys would have a secure home, a place in the community. I can protect you. But if marrying me is unthinkable, even under those terms, I'll understand."

David McKay had offered her a similar arrangement, and she'd accepted. But this was Brandon. Brandon, who had once claimed her heart. Brandon, who had made her believe she might live her dreams of adventure.

Brandon, who had abandoned her when she needed him most.

"Frankly," she told him, "I don't know what to think. I'm willing to believe we've both grown since our days together in Cambridge. But a marriage of convenience? I had once hoped for more."

He nodded. "So had I. But we are different people now. I promise you all my support, all my respect. I hope more will grow with time."

Time. Might as well say chance. He was asking her to risk her future on him. How could she?

"All I can say," she told him, "is that I'll give the matter due consideration. Good day, Pastor."

He nodded again, face once more concerned, and she slipped into the room before she could give in to her feelings to console him.

Back to the door, she gazed at the sleeping babies. Jasper opened one eye and smiled at her before nodding off again. Her heart constricted.

How could she leave them?

How could she marry Brandon?

His offer was practical. It allowed her to stay in Little Horn, be the boys' mother. He had said he'd make no demands on her, that love might grow with time.

The problem was, she wanted it now.

She pressed her lips together to keep from crying. When had she decided that? Perhaps it had been growing since the moment she'd seen him in the chapel with David and Caroline. Perhaps some part of her had never let go of the love she'd felt for him. All she knew was that she wanted Brandon to love her, to gaze at her once more as if she were the most important person in his world. To feel the tender touch of his hand on hers, the sweet pressure of his lips. Anything else felt cheap, wrong.

Someone rapped on the door again, the sound furtive, hesitant. Elizabeth drew in a breath, steeling herself to tell Brandon not to badger her. She wasn't ready to answer him, wasn't ready to admit she still had feelings for him.

But when she opened the door, she found Jamie Coleman on the landing. The young man's face looked longer from his sorrow, his eyes dipping down and his blond hair hanging limp under his Stetson.

"Please, Miss Dumont, could I talk to Annie?"

Elizabeth glanced toward the bed. As if the girl had heard her beloved's voice, Annie opened her eyes and met Elizabeth's gaze.

Elizabeth stepped out of the way. "Won't you come in, Mr. Coleman?"

Jamie snatched off his hat and hurried in as if afraid she'd change her mind. Annie climbed off the bed. Elizabeth crossed to the crib to keep an eye on the triplets. Then she turned her back to give Jamie and Annie some privacy.

"How do you do, Miss Hill?" Jamie asked. The floor creaked as if he was shifting from foot to foot.

"Since when was I *Miss Hill*, Jamie Coleman?" Annie demanded.

Elizabeth fought a smile at the saucy tone in the girl's voice. Jasper opened his eyes as if he'd heard it too. Elizabeth put a finger to her lips, even though she didn't think the little boy knew what it meant. Jasper put his whole hand over his mouth.

"I never think of you as *Miss Hill* in my mind," Jamie assured Annie. "You'll always be my darling Annie."

Annie sighed. "And you're my dashing Jamie. But I just don't see how we can be together."

Jasper climbed to his feet in the crib, and Elizabeth reached down and picked him up before he could wake his brothers.

The rustle of cloth behind her told her Jamie and Annie had moved closer. "Your ma finally said she'd accept my pa's apology. They spent the morning working on the fences together."

A whole morning? That was progress.

"They did?" Annie asked. "Without shooting each other?"

She would have to bite her cheeks to keep from laughing at this rate. As if Jasper knew it, he wiggled against her, grinning.

"I promise you," Jamie vowed. "And your ma invited my pa to dinner tomorrow night."

"Oh, Jamie!" Annie's skirts whispered as she stepped closer yet to her beau. "Watch that she doesn't spit in the food."

Elizabeth cringed, and Jasper stilled.

"She won't," Jamie insisted. "I tell you, they're trying to make peace." He cleared his throat. "Please, Annie, won't you reconsider? I'm no kind of man without you beside me."

Elizabeth glanced back in time to see Annie throw herself into his arms.

Tears burned Elizabeth's eyes. That was what marriage was supposed to be—tender regard, warmth and kindness, hope for the future.

If only she could have that with Brandon.

Brandon spent that evening feeling as if he groped through fog. It hadn't been easy to propose marriage to Elizabeth. At times, he was certain it was selfish to subject any woman to the demands made of a pastor's wife. Only a deep and abiding love could withstand such pressure. He doubted whether he and Elizabeth would ever come to that place again. Still, he had thought she would see the practicality of his offer. It met her needs. It gave the boys a home. She'd been willing to marry David McKay under a similar arrangement. Apparently the problem was with him.

He hadn't been good enough to marry her back in Boston. Even though in Little Horn the town minister might be accounted a responsible, respectable position, he still wasn't good enough. And he had no idea how to change her mind.

With the matter hanging between them, he couldn't bring himself to call and check on the boys the next morning. Surely she would see it as harassment. Still, he kept glancing up at her window every time he looked out of the parsonage, but he caught no glimpse of her or the boys.

When Annie came by the parsonage that afternoon, he perked up, hoping she might be coming to tell him Elizabeth wanted to see him. Instead, she stood on the front step, beaming.

"Jamie says my mother and his father are getting

along," she told Brandon. "We might be able to get married after all!"

"That's very good news," Brandon replied, though a part of him would have liked news about his own wedding. "Will you be moving back home, then?"

Annie glanced at the boardinghouse. "Maybe. Miss Dumont is good with the babies. She doesn't need me all that much. She's self-reliant."

She said the words with such admiration. Brandon couldn't argue with her. Elizabeth did indeed seem to be able to take care of herself. Except where these rumors were concerned. But perhaps they wouldn't be enough to allow her to consider marrying him.

He tried to focus on his work. He went to the children's home, where David was just finishing a second coat of sunny yellow paint in the new bedroom.

"Good news," his friend told him. "Arundel is going to donate dishes for the house—a set of twenty. And Casper Magnuson's offered a wooden train set his boy outgrew."

So the people of Little Horn were once again stepping up to help.

"Very good news," Brandon said, fingering the handle of the brush sticking out of a can of paint.

"You don't sound pleased." David climbed down the ladder and set aside his brush. "What's wrong?"

What was wrong indeed? He wasn't sure he wanted to share his thoughts with his friend. He'd learned early on to school his face so his father never knew he'd scored. Now he made himself smile. "Nothing."

David didn't seem convinced. "Still worried about Elizabeth Dumont?"

He must be slipping. But he found it hard to keep

up his pleasant smile while David looked at him with such concern. "Not exactly." He released the brush. "I asked her to marry me."

David's brows shot up.

"It's a marriage of convenience," Brandon hurried to assure him. After all, marrying the woman David had originally intended to wed only a month after he'd decided against it had to look odd to the rancher. "She needs protection from these rumors, and I want to give the triplets a home."

David glanced around at the room. "More than this one, it seems."

Brandon felt his face coloring. "Well, we always hoped someone would adopt all three of them."

"That's true enough." David's look returned to him. "Is that the kind of marriage you want?"

"Certainly. It's practical."

David snorted as he bent to pick up his brush again. "There's nothing practical about marriage. Two people decide to trust each other with their deepest secrets, their most closely held dreams, their lives. It's all or nothing."

Brandon shook his head. "Said the man who brought out a mail-order bride."

"A mail-order bride you tried to talk me out of," David reminded him, starting up the ladder. "I wasn't ready to listen then. Now I can tell you the only reason to marry is because your life won't be right without the woman you love in it."

A high standard, one he'd once held himself. But he could see no other way to help Elizabeth and the triplets.

He and David worked in silence for a while, then

Brandon excused himself to return to the parsonage. The quiet there mocked him. Still, he had work to do. He was a minister. He'd felt the tug of a new sermon series on the Great Commandment and had only a few notes written as yet to support it. Mr. Tyson had brought over the plans for the Harvest Festival, and he needed to review them and provide input.

But no matter what he did, thoughts of Elizabeth intruded. What a poor pastor he would prove to be if he didn't get his feelings under control!

Of course, his brother noticed when he stopped by the parsonage that afternoon on his way to pick up some supplies from the lumberyard.

"What is it this time?" Bo asked as they walked down the corridor to Brandon's study. "Is the feud worsening between the Hills and the Colemans? The orphanage not coming along as fast as you wanted? I know that furrowed brow means trouble."

Brandon forced his face to relax as he took a seat behind his desk. Bo knew the place well enough to sit on the more comfortable chair across from him. Brandon reserved the hardest chairs for those who needed to think about their actions or who might wear out their welcome. Now sunlight slanted through the window, highlighting his brother's hair with gold. In his rough work shirt and Levi's, he looked comfortable, capable. Brandon felt a stab of envy.

He shoved it back. Bo had borne the worst of their father's taunts. He deserved to be happy, fulfilled.

"The Hills and the Colemans appear to be making peace," Brandon told him, leaning back in his chair. "I suspect Annie's ultimatum upset everyone. And David hopes to have the children's home ready before the Harvest Festival."

"That reminds me." Bo dug in his pocket and pulled out three rosy red apples to set on Brandon's desk. "These were on the front stoop."

Brandon shook his head. "You know those aren't for me. They're..."

"For the triplets," Bo finished. "I thought so too. It seems our Good Samaritan is still watching over them. Too bad we've never been able to catch the culprit in the act."

"And thank the person," Brandon agreed. "Did you notice anyone about as you came in just now?"

Bo shrugged. "This area of town is always busy, with the school, church, doctor's office and boarding-house so close. There must have been a dozen people around—the Tysons, Mrs. Johnson and her brood, Louisa's sister and brother-in-law among them."

"Any of them could be our Good Samaritan," Brandon mused.

"With the exception of Amy and Lawrence. Louisa's sister and brother-in-law came to town after the first good deeds showed up." Bo leaned back in his chair as well. "So, what's bothering you?"

Brandon shifted on the chair, reached out to rearrange the papers on his desk. His brother's look told him Bo knew he was delaying. He never could hide much from his brother. Might as well get on with it.

"I asked Elizabeth to marry me," he said.

Bo let out a whistle as he straightened. "Such a sacrifice, marrying a pretty gal who once adored you. I can see why you'd have second thoughts."

Brandon shook his head. "She never adored me. And

I don't have second thoughts. It was the right thing to do. Louisa told me you'd heard the rumors."

Bo's face darkened. "You know I don't stand for people putting other people down."

Neither of them did. They'd lived through enough of it to know the pain it could cause. "Elizabeth needs someone to protect her. Marrying me would give her standing in the community."

"Highly regarded minister that you are," Bo teased. "I guess congratulations are in order."

"Not yet. She refused to answer me."

Bo frowned. "She said no?"

"Not exactly," Brandon admitted. "She said she would consider the matter."

A smile tilted his brother's mouth. "And you're stewing because she didn't jump at the offer."

Put that way, it was a small wonder Elizabeth seemed to find him arrogant. Brandon made himself shrug. "Well, I had hoped for a warmer reception."

His brother laughed. "Just be glad I'm already married. You wouldn't want competition. After all, I am the better-looking one."

He regarded his identical twin. "Taller too."

"Don't forget more charming."

"And witty."

Bo grinned. "That's right. Given all that, it's a wonder she didn't laugh in your face."

Brandon sobered. "She did once."

Bo cocked his head. "So are you finally ready to tell me the details of what happened in Cambridge?"

Brandon studied his papers. "I courted her. I thought I was in love. I thought she loved me. But her family fell on hard times, and we fell apart. Now she says our love was never meant to be." He could not tell his brother how those words haunted him.

"And yet you asked her to marry you."

Brandon met his brother's gaze. "Because she needed my help."

Bo leaned forward. "That's how you counter Father's influence. You help people. There's no shame in that."

"Tell that to Elizabeth."

Bo rose and moved closer to the desk. "Maybe I will, if it comes to that. But I have a feeling she's going to say yes. Not many in her position would refuse a pastor."

Brandon grimaced as he rose as well. "I hope she doesn't agree because I'm the pastor here. As it is, I'm going to have to shield her from the town's expectations. I saw how the dean's wife had to turn herself inside out to meet all the demands on her time. I won't force that on Elizabeth."

"Not like Father forced things on Mother," Bo murmured.

Brandon nodded. "Remember how she tiptoed around, trying to make sure everything was exactly the way she thought he would want it?"

"Trying to make sure nothing set him off," Bo agreed. "But it didn't matter. She couldn't please him. No one could. Sometimes I wonder if he didn't want to be pleased. He was just looking for an excuse to despise us." His gaze went off across the room as if he was seeing their old home in Cambridge. "I used to fear I'd end up like that, but Louisa proved me wrong."

Brandon laid a hand on his brother's shoulder. "You're nothing like Father, Bo."

"So you told me," Bo said, gaze returning to his. "If I recall, your exact words were 'God is sufficient for our past.' If that's true for me, why not you and Elizabeth?"

Why not indeed? He'd certainly counseled people to trust God to forgive their circumstances. But in his case, he hadn't really done anything that required forgiveness. So why did he feel guilty?

"I just hope she agrees to my proposal, *despite* our past," he told his brother.

"I have a feeling she will," Bo said. "There's a strength in her. You can see it when she's caring for the triplets."

He'd sensed it as well. Back in Boston, she'd seemed more fragile, like a dainty figurine meant to be admired. She'd been more afraid to try new things then too. Was that old fear the reason she needed time to consider his proposal?

"It can't be easy coming to Little Horn," Brandon allowed, "living in a boardinghouse, trying to find the next position in a place where she knows no one."

"Yet she's managing," Bo pointed out. "She's good with the babies. Louisa even says so."

Praise indeed from the woman who had first taken the babies in.

Brandon leaned a hip on the desk. "I was hoping Elizabeth and I could petition the Lone Star Cowboy League to adopt the boys."

Bo shook his head, but Brandon could tell it was more in admiration than denial. "So you'll not only be getting a wife but a family. Those are big changes, brother. Are you sure it's what you want?"

David had asked him the same question. He hadn't

been sure how to answer then. Now an image swam up of him, Elizabeth and the triplets around the kitchen table, laughing together. Warmth wrapped around his heart.

"It's what I want," he told Bo. "Now I just have to hope it's what Elizabeth wants as well."

Chapter Thirteen

Elizabeth spent the next two days mulling over Brandon's proposal. Her whole life, it seemed to her, depended on her answer. She asked advice from Louisa, Caroline and Fannie Tyson, all of whom told her how much they admired Brandon, what a good man she would be marrying.

She had come to the conclusion they were right. Brandon was a fine minister and a caring man capable of providing for her and the triplets. But she still could not convince herself that marrying him was the right path.

She confessed her background with Brandon to Caroline one afternoon when she came to call on Elizabeth and the triplets. Annie was out helping Louisa at the doctor's office, so Elizabeth and Caroline sat across from each other on the floor while the babies crawled or scooted from one to the other. Caroline was at last out of her sling, though she was still careful with her arm as she helped with the babies.

"So you were in love," she said, holding up Theo's

hands to help him stand. "If it grew once, it could grow again."

Elizabeth drew in a breath. "That's the problem. What if the feelings we had for each other have faded? What if I'm dooming Brandon and me to a loveless marriage? Won't we grow to hate each other in time?"

Caroline smiled as Theo dropped back down on his behind and Eli took his place. "I think it's more likely you'll at least wind up friends. Especially if you're helping each other raise these three."

There was that. Brandon sincerely cared for the boys. But would raising the babies provide enough of a bond to make a good marriage?

Having wiggled his way between her and Caroline, Jasper pushed up from the floor and stood teetering. His gaze on Elizabeth, he took a halting step forward. She didn't dare say a word to break his focus, but pride soared inside her. Across from her Caroline pressed her fingers to her mouth. Oblivious to the reason for her awe, Eli copied her. Even Theo stopped his scooting to watch.

Jasper's face flushed with triumph as he took a second step. Elizabeth opened her arms, encouraging him. But his next step caught the edge of the braided rug, and down he went. His howl of protest set his brothers to crying as well.

Elizabeth scooped him up even as Caroline set about comforting Eli and Theo.

"There now, young man," Elizabeth told him, peering into his red face. "What a brave explorer you are! You watch, next time you'll be halfway across the room."

He sucked in a breath as if trying to regain his composure, but his trembling lower lip told Elizabeth he wasn't any too sure of the matter at the moment. As she sat on a chair with him on her lap, he looked around as if wondering what part of the room would rise up against him next.

"You'll be fine," Elizabeth assured him, rubbing her cheek against his hair. "Very soon, there won't be anything you can't do."

He turned in her arms, brown eyes gazing up so trustingly. "Mama."

Caroline gasped.

Elizabeth felt as if her bones had melted as she cuddled the little boy closer. "Oh, Jasper, I so want to be your mama. I want to stay with you and love you forever."

"There's your answer, then," Caroline murmured, and Elizabeth could see tears swimming in her eyes. "Marrying Brandon will allow you to stay with the boys, if that's what you really want, Elizabeth."

The need was fierce and strong, and it felt right and just. And she knew what answer she would give Brandon. When Annie returned from the doctor's office, Elizabeth sent the girl to invite him over that evening.

In the meantime, she tidied the room and swept the floor, to the chagrin of the triplets, who kept trying to catch the broom as she passed. Then she cleaned them up, smoothing down their dark hair and wiping off their soft chins. She was tucking a stray lock of hair back into the bun at the top of her head when she caught the boys watching her in the mirror. Jasper was frowning, Eli looked pensive and Theo was sucking his thumb. She had to remember they sensed her moods.

She turned to them with a smile. "I'm just a little nervous. Silly, eh?"

Their babbled response was surprisingly encouraging.

A short while later, Annie ushered Brandon into the room. He was dressed in his minister's coat and trousers, his shirt crisp, his boots polished. Elizabeth's brown skirts, spotted with applesauce from the boys' earlier feeding, felt wilted and worn. He didn't seem to notice as he squatted beside the babies on the rug.

"And how are my boys today?" he asked. Theo crawled up to him, and Brandon lifted him in his arms as he stood. The look on the little boy's face was almost as adoring as the one on Brandon's.

"They're doing fine," Annie told him when Elizabeth didn't speak. "Jasper took a step today, and Eli has a new tooth."

Brandon shook his head in evident awe. "They change every day."

"Every hour some days," Elizabeth countered. "And I don't want to miss a minute of it. So the answer to your proposal is yes, Brandon. I will marry you and be the boys' mother."

His smile was slow and soft, and something inside her rushed to meet it.

"Thank you, Elizabeth," he murmured. Careful of Theo in his arms, he bent his head toward hers.

He was going to kiss her. The same excitement she'd felt in Boston bubbled up inside her, and she closed her eyes in expectation. His lips brushed her cheek before retreating, yet she trembled. She opened her eyes to find him regarding her wide-eyed, as if the touch had awoken something inside him as well.

He took a step back from her. "I'll need to write to the pastor in Burnet," he said, all business. "See when he can come perform the ceremony. Do you have a preference?"

"As soon as possible," Elizabeth told him. Before she lost her nerve.

"I'll let you know when the day is set." He handed Theo to Annie. The baby pouted.

Jasper crawled up to Elizabeth and fisted his hands in her skirts to pull himself up. She bent and lifted him, hiding her blushing face behind his head.

"Ladies," she heard Brandon say, then Annie's "Good day to you, Pastor," as she saw him to the door.

Elizabeth knew that should have been her role, but she couldn't get her feet to move. She was getting married.

To Brandon.

"Oh, sweetheart," she whispered to Jasper, "I hope I made the right choice."

Jasper beamed at her. "Mama."

Elizabeth sighed. Maybe someday she would tire of hearing that word, but right now it sounded so sweet coming from the little boy.

Annie was beaming as well as she hurried back to her side. "Oh, Elizabeth, I'm so happy for you! Pastor Stillwater is a fine fellow, and you'll be a good pastor's wife."

A pastor's wife. Mrs. Arundel's list came to mind. Was that what Little Horn expected of the wife of its pastor, that she spout Bible verses at the least provocation? She'd considered how she felt and how Brandon might feel about their marriage. She hadn't thought about what it meant to marry a pastor. Elizabeth had known more pastoral students than pastors' wives!

"Why do you say that?" she asked Annie as the two settled down to play with the babies.

Annie blinked big blue eyes. "Why, you're smart! And you know how to talk to people. Plus you're sweet as can be."

She wasn't sure how she'd given the girl that impression. She thought she'd been more vinegar than honey since coming to Little Horn.

She pondered the idea that evening as she wrote to the family in San Francisco and declined their offer of employment, then discussed the upcoming wedding with Annie. Elizabeth's aunt had been involved in a number of such preparations for community members, but Little Horn wasn't Boston, and Elizabeth and Brandon weren't marrying for love. It would probably be best to have a quiet, private affair.

The ladies of Little Horn thought otherwise.

They descended upon her the day after she'd agreed to Brandon's proposal. As Annie and the babies stayed on the bed, six women crowded the room in the boarding-house and clustered around Elizabeth with determined looks. She wasn't sure why Mrs. Hickey was among their number, but the gossipy pianist seemed content merely to glower. Still, Elizabeth knew that not even handing around the babies would save her from their attentions this time.

"We are here to arrange your wedding," Mrs. Arundel announced.

"I couldn't impose," Elizabeth started, but the woman held up a meaty hand.

"It is no imposition," she intoned, feather in her hat bobbing its agreement. "It is our duty. I told Mr. Arundel the moment he sent the telegram for Pastor Stillwater that nothing would stop me from making sure you two were married properly."

What other way was there to marry, particularly when she was marrying a minister?

"It's very kind," she tried again. "But…"

"Helen," Mrs. Arundel barked.

Helen Carson stepped forward with a motherly smile. Fading blond hair framed a pleasant face made kind by the wrinkles fanning out beside her blue eyes. "If you'll let me take your measurements, the ladies of the quilting bee would be delighted to sew you a wedding gown."

"How thoughtful," Elizabeth said, truly touched, "but there's no need to go to such trouble."

"Nonsense," Mrs. Arundel said. "We cannot have you marrying our pastor in rags."

If her aunt had still been alive, she would have had some choice words to say about calling the expensive dresses she'd had made for Elizabeth into question.

"Mrs. Fuller," the lady continued as Helen took out a tape measure and began wrapping it around Elizabeth's waist.

Stella grinned at Elizabeth as she stepped forward. "My roses are gone, but I have foxglove and lilies coming on, and I know where to get some green eyes and rose mallow. We can gather some up for your bouquet and can put a vase or two around the church for color."

Mrs. Arundel nodded her approval. "Mrs. Green."

Mrs. Carson nudged Elizabeth to stretch out her arm for measuring as Mercy Green took Stella's place in front. "I'll have apple, peach and blackberry pie for the reception. Pastor likes apple, and his brother is partial to peach."

Elizabeth noticed no one asked her preference, but she couldn't complain. Blackberry was her favorite.

"The general store will donate cider," Mrs. Arundel added. "And the church has plates and cutlery."

"And I'll bake a wedding cake," Fannie promised, face flushed with excitement Elizabeth wished she could feel.

"We'll have the usual gentlemen play for the reception," Mrs. Arundel put in.

A reception with music? Perhaps things were getting a bit out of hand.

"We needn't do anything so fancy," Elizabeth protested.

Mrs. Arundel ignored her, tapping her chin with one finger. "We'll invite the whole town, of course. And all the outlying farms and ranches."

Mrs. Hickey, who had been mercifully silent until now, spoke up at last. "*All* the farms and ranches?"

"All of them," Stella insisted. "Those cowboys deserve a party, same as the next person."

Mrs. Hickey sniffed. "I simply thought that, as a pastor's wife, Miss Dumont might care who she associated with."

They all looked to her. There was no easy answer. If she included everyone, she ran up the cost and the effort. If she excluded the cowboys, she was no better than Mrs. Hickey.

"If we intend this as a community celebration," she said, "it would be wrong to keep some members of the community away."

Mrs. Hickey deflated, but Mrs. Arundel nodded again. "Quite right. We are all God's children."

"But no dancing," Mrs. Hickey insisted. "I don't hold with a pastor cavorting."

Annie frowned at her. "But your husband calls the dances."

"There will be dancing," Mrs. Arundel decreed before Mrs. Hickey could answer her. "And Pastor Stillwater can decide whether it's seemly for him and his bride to take part."

They all nodded at that, and it struck Elizabeth again how easily they all deferred to his judgment. Would they expect her to do the same? As the pastor's wife, was it her role to make everyone happy?

Was she ready to take on that role?

Brandon wasn't entirely surprised to find the ladies of his congregation planning an elaborate wedding. In general, Little Horn was blessed with bighearted people, and they loved any excuse for a community get-together. What did surprise him was how little of the event was in his and Elizabeth's control.

"The wedding gown, food, music and decor are all arranged," Mrs. Arundel told him scarcely two days after Elizabeth had accepted his proposal.

There was no question in his mind how the lady knew he and Elizabeth were getting married. The telegraph ran out of the Arundel General Store, and her husband had sent the message to Mr. Milner in Burnet seeking the other minister's help.

"Have you determined what the minister should say as well?" Brandon inquired with a polite smile.

If she heard any sarcasm in his question, she ignored it. "A reminder of the wedding at Cana should suffice. Or perhaps the creation of Eve. The Book of Common Prayer may have recommendations. I could look if you like."

"I think we can safely leave that in Mr. Milner's hands," Brandon said.

She nodded, feather twitching in her hat. "I merely wished to ensure you had a ring. We have several at the store."

She looked at him pointedly. No doubt she expected him to assure her that he would be delighted to purchase a ring from her fine store, but he had something else in mind.

"I have my mother's ring," Brandon told her.

He thought she might protest that the rings at her store were far superior, but she smiled. "How suitable. The product of one happy marriage blessing another."

He refused to tell her how wrong she was. His parents' marriage has been anything but happy. Still, his mother had been so loving, so kind, he knew she'd want Elizabeth to have the ring. It was certainly finer than anything a country parson could offer.

Yet he could not help but wonder after Mrs. Arundel left him to the peace of his study. Bo had sworn off marrying so he would never perpetuate the hurtful family they'd known. Brandon had followed their mother's way instead—loving service, care for those less fortunate. Would she have been pleased he'd offered for Elizabeth, or had he taken his beliefs too far? Should he have held marriage sacred to love?

He drew out his Bible, thumbed through the pages, so worn now that the edges were curling, the lettering smudged in places. After his mother had died, this book had offered solace. When his father had called him worthless, the Bible had whispered he was truly loved. He knew what it said about marriage. Husbands and wives were to cleave together, stand united against the difficulties life brought, rejoicing in the good.

Could he do that with Elizabeth?

Could he do that with anyone but Elizabeth?

She was the only one who had ever stirred his heart beyond the affection a pastor owed a member of his congregation. He had never thought to marry her for convenience's sake rather than love, but he could not be sorry for his offer. As her husband, he could protect and provide for her, ensure she lacked for nothing. He felt as if he owed her that at least.

And so he found himself standing at the foot of the altar rather than its head two weeks later on a sunny September day when Mr. Milner came to read the vows.

The church was filled to overflowing. His usual congregation came to wish their minister and his bride well. The others came from curiosity or the promise of food and entertainment. He spotted Jo and Gil Satler in the back row, eyes wide and faces scrubbed clean. Even Dorothy Hill, he noted, was sitting near the back, beside Tug Coleman of all people. Annie and Jamie sat on either side, the girl glancing about as if memorizing every detail for her own wedding. Perhaps that was a good sign.

Bo and Louisa were in the front row, beaming at him, with Jasper in Louisa's arms and Eli in Bo's. Beside them, Caroline held Theo while Maggie made faces at the tot, and David gave Brandon a nod of encouragement. Lula May looked dreamy-eyed on Edmund's arm, and CJ and Molly Thorn smiled at each other as if remembering their own wedding a year ago.

Then Mrs. Hickey wiggled into place before the

piano, and music wove through the building. Elizabeth appeared at the end of the aisle.

Helen Carson and the ladies of the quilting bee had done themselves proud. The graceful cream-colored gown was embroidered all along its hem with red roses on twining green vines, rose buds on the puffy short sleeves and vines edging the modest fitted bodice. Her hair was piled up high, and pearl combs fixed in place a veil that draped her shoulders. He felt as if he could see the blue-green of her eyes even from this distance as the crowd rose and she started down the aisle toward him.

His bride.

His wife.

It was a good thing he wasn't preaching today, because his tongue seemed to be stuck to the roof of his mouth, and all he could do was drink her in.

She walked alone, having no father, uncle or brother to give her away, yet Brandon thought each step was brave and sure. What had he ever done to deserve such a wonderful responsibility, such bright hope?

Whatever happens, thank You, Lord.

As she drew abreast of him, he took her hand and held it tight. Her smile was soft.

"Dearly beloved," Mr. Milner began. A slight man with flyaway white hair, he managed to convey seriousness and delight at the same time. "We are gathered together here in the sight of God to join together this man and this woman in holy matrimony, which is commended by St. Paul to be honorable among all men and therefore is not by any to be entered into inadvisably or lightly."

Brandon had said those words more than a dozen

times himself, yet never had they pierced his heart so surely. He wasn't entering into this lightly. He entered marriage knowing that he and Elizabeth would have to work hard to make a family. There was no doubt in his mind she was up to the challenge.

Was he?

Chapter Fourteen

Elizabeth could hardly believe she was married as she wandered through the reception in the field between the church and parsonage on Brandon's arm. Much as she had wondered at all the help she'd received, she could not wonder at the results. Her beautiful dress whispered about her ankles as she crossed the grass. The walls of the church and parsonage were draped in red-and-white bunting that vied with the wildflowers for attention, and the tables were groaning under the pies and the wedding cake.

The local cowboys, including Kit Durango, were polite and humble, standing off by themselves as their employers talked and danced, but Elizabeth could see some of the young ladies casting glances in their direction and thought it was only a matter of time before someone asked one to dance as well.

"Congratulations," Fannie said, coming up to them with Jasper in her arms. The little boy reached for Elizabeth, and she took him and cuddled him a moment.

Annie and her mother had also offered to care for the triplets during the reception, and Elizabeth could see them now, moving through the crowd and stopping to let folks visit with the boys. The quilting bee had also sewn new shirts for the boys, a soft blue with a rosebud embroidered on the collar. It was almost as if they had been the groomsmen.

"Thank you," Brandon said to Fannie, bending his head to make a face at Jasper. The baby crowed in delight.

"So, are you all settled into your new home?" the older woman asked.

Reluctantly, Elizabeth handed her back the baby before he could christen the wedding dress. "I believe so. I understand Mr. Arundel and Mr. Crenshaw are moving my things and the boys' over to the parsonage this afternoon."

Brandon smiled and nodded, minister's face firmly in place. Then he took Elizabeth's arm and continued their stroll about the area.

"I can see I'm a terrible husband already," he said, nodding to a couple who had raised their cups of cider in toast.

"What do you mean?" Elizabeth asked, smiling at a family they were passing.

"If we were still in Boston, I would have whisked you away for a romantic honeymoon. New York, Paris." He wiggled his brows. "The mighty metropolis of Burnet."

She giggled. "The parsonage will do. I know you have responsibilities. So do I."

"The boys," he agreed. "I'll do my best to make sure no one interferes with that responsibility, Elizabeth."

She wasn't sure what he meant. Would the Lone Star Cowboy League suddenly take even more interest in the triplets now that she'd married Brandon? Or should she expect more visitors because she was in the parsonage?

Caroline sashayed up to them just then and batted her lashes. "Shouldn't the bride and groom be having fun at their own reception?"

"I'm having just about as much fun as I can tolerate," Brandon said, face solemn.

She shook her head, smile broad. "Don't you tease me, Pastor. You need to dance."

Elizabeth remembered the argument in her room about whether a pastor should frolic. Very likely Brandon wouldn't feel comfortable. Some of the country dances did seem to involve a lot of hopping about.

"It's probably not wise," she told Caroline, glancing about to find Mrs. Hickey watching them avidly.

Brandon gazed down at Elizabeth. "Would you care to dance, Elizabeth?"

Her gaze went to the couples, who were just finishing a set. The ladies were laughing, the men patting each other on the back for their efforts. Wouldn't it be delightful to just let go for a time?

"Does the minister's wife dance?" she asked Brandon.

He bent closer, until his breath brushed her ear. "My wife can do as she pleases. I see that smile on your face. Let's dance."

Before she could argue, he pulled her into the group.

Mr. Hickey grinned at them as they took their place at the head of the line. His wife might wonder about the advisability, but he certainly had no qualms. Neither did anyone else. They nodded and called greetings before Bo stepped forward, guitar in hand.

"What will you have, Pastor?"

Brandon eyed Elizabeth. "Something sweet, for my sweetheart."

Several ladies sighed.

Elizabeth wanted to sigh as well. The look in his eyes was so tender, so endearing, that the silver warmed. If only she could believe the love it promised.

"A waltz, then," Bo ordered, and he struck up the chord. The other musicians followed suit.

Brandon swept her into his arms. They had never attended a ball together in Boston, him being a divinity school student, but the feeling of his arms around her brought back memories of stolen kisses and murmured promises. He twirled her about the grass, the skirts of her wedding gown belling out about her. She knew other people were dancing too, but all she could see was Brandon's smile, all she could hear was her heart pounding.

All she could feel was hope.

Laughter woke her from the dream.

"Your timing's off, brother," Bo called. "The music ended four beats ago."

Brandon's cheeks were pinking as he drew her to a halt.

"Sufficient unto the day are the worries thereof," Brandon told their audience. "And so are the joys."

To applause, he took her arm and walked with her away from the dancing area.

Elizabeth had barely caught her breath when Mrs. Arundel sailed up to them.

"Tolerable reception," she pronounced. "And I was pleased to see you dance, Pastor. Some people need such a good example." She glanced to where Mrs. Hickey was glaring at them. The lady had obviously counted that dance as one more mark against Elizabeth, but she found she couldn't care.

"Though perhaps you should take the opportunity to speak to the cowhands," Mrs. Arundel continued with a look to Brandon. "We must convince them to change their ways."

As the riders had been uniformly polite and restrained, Elizabeth couldn't see what needed correcting.

"I'll be sure to invite them to services," Brandon promised the lady.

She raised a graying brow. "Well, there's no need to go that far." She turned to Elizabeth. "I will see you at the literary tea on Thursday. Do bring someone to manage the babies so they don't interrupt."

She sailed off without waiting for a response.

"Literary tea?" Elizabeth asked Brandon.

"Several of the ladies meet in the parsonage parlor to discuss books," he explained. "I'll see if I can convince them to try another location."

"That might be better considering the babies," Elizabeth agreed. "I'm not sure they're up to a literary tea. But you won't turn away Mr. Durango and his friends, will you?"

His true smile appeared. "Have a soft spot in your heart for cowboys? Never fear. Everyone is welcome in God's house, Mrs. Stillwater."

Mrs. Stillwater. She couldn't accustom herself to the name, for all she'd once dreamed of making it her own. She heard it more than a dozen times before they quit the reception and took the boys inside the parsonage, leaving the congregation to set things to rights.

Elizabeth hadn't visited the parsonage in Little Horn yet. Given her past association with Brandon, it had seemed intrusive to say the least. Now she couldn't help glancing around as they entered through the front door, Jasper in her arms and Eli and Theo in his.

"It isn't anything grand," Brandon said. "The good people of Little Horn designed this house with the needs of the community in mind." He settled the babies more closely and nodded to the wall of the entry hall. "Brass hooks for the hats, coats and gun belts of visitors and an iron boot scraper to knock the mud off their feet."

Jasper was leaning toward one of the brass hooks on the paneled wall. Elizabeth turned him for the doorway on the right. "And in here?"

"A parlor big enough to hold the ladies' literary tea," Brandon said, leading the way into the room. "Or a meeting of the Lone Star Cowboy League, should they need it."

It was a large space, with two windows looking out on the street and a wood-framed hearth with an iron arm to hold a teakettle.

But surely Brandon had not been asked about the decor, for the wallpaper was a rosy color with fanciful cream medallions, and the braided rug was done in rose, pink and cream. Porcelain figurines and carved wooden animals decorated most surfaces, resting on lacy doilies. Though the room boasted six chairs, a camelback sofa and two sturdy wood benches, they were all different styles and sizes, from the delicate bentwood chair with the needlepoint seat to the solid armchair upholstered in brown leather.

"Donations," Brandon said, taking a step to the left to keep Eli from grabbing a tassel on the rosy drapes. "Every family who could manage it offered something to the house, from the furniture to the paintings to the dishes and linens. We're a generous bunch in Little Horn."

So she could see. But for all the chaos of color and shape, it felt as if each part, each piece of the house had been settled in place with love.

He nodded to the door opposite the windows. "The kitchen's through there, with a door onto the field. The ladies used the kitchen for the reception, so it's probably best not to disturb them as they clean it up." He headed back toward the entry hall. "Let me show you the rest of the house."

Three more doors led off the hallway to the left. He led her to the end one. "This is my bedroom. If you need me, please come in."

She'd most likely knock. He might be her husband in the eyes of the law and the church, but they both knew theirs was a marriage of convenience. As if determined to be open and aboveboard, he juggled Eli to one side and managed to swing wide the door.

A solid-wood four-poster bed, draped with a patchwork quilt, sat along the center of one wall. Pillows were piled against the simple headboard. A tall dresser stood on the wall next to the window, and a solid armchair rested by the fire, a book open on the table beside it. She could imagine Brandon taking his rest there, far from the demands of his position.

How often would he retreat to it now that she and the triplets had come to live in the parsonage?

Why did his bedroom seem smaller than usual, as if he'd somehow outgrown it? Brandon turned from it and started back down the corridor, Elizabeth beside him. "There's a second bedroom at the front of the house.

It was meant as a guest room for grieving families. It's large enough for you and the boys."

"That should be fine," she murmured.

He paused before the next door down the hall. Of all the rooms in the parsonage, this was his alone, and he found himself eager for her approval.

"My study," he said, opening the door.

She wandered in, glancing about. Mrs. Hickey and the others had been in recently, so everything was neat and tidy, which probably meant he'd be hunting for his sermon notes come morning. Would Elizabeth be impressed with the number of books on the tall case by the window? His diploma hanging on the wall?

"What an interesting desk," she said, moving closer to the polished wood as Jasper shifted in her arms to keep Brandon in sight. Her fingers touched the wide plank surface, skimmed the finials that made up one side. "Who donated it?"

"No one," he told her. "I made it."

She glanced his way, brows up. "Why, Brandon, I had no idea you were so skilled at carpentry."

His face heated. "It was something I picked up from Russell Maynard, the man who taught Bo about ranching. He had a real love for carpentry. He used to say he could hear the wood talking to him, telling him what it longed to be. I saw this pine at Josiah McKay's yard and it said 'make me a desk.'"

She smiled as if she could imagine it. She had always been able to see the potential in people. He hoped it wasn't such a stretch to apply the principle to something inanimate like a plank of wood. Just saying his thoughts aloud made them seem foolish.

"You fulfilled its wish," she assured him, and suddenly it didn't seem so foolish after all. "Have you made other pieces?"

"A few," he admitted. Eli and Theo started squirming, and he jiggled them up and down to amuse them. "I like to whittle. It clears my mind."

"Those animals in the parlor," she said, smile forming. "They're yours?"

He nodded. "But I haven't had much time lately."

She turned from the desk. "Well, perhaps I can help there."

He didn't see how. Three babies would surely keep her plenty busy, and helping her with them would add more tasks to his overflowing list. But he couldn't mind. Already the parsonage felt less silent, less empty.

Almost like a home.

"Things will let up soon," he promised, stepping out of the doorway to allow her to pass. "I just have to help David finish the children's home and make sure everyone gets through roundup."

"Roundup?" She frowned as she passed him, Jasper staring at him from her arms. "Does the minister have to help with roundup?"

"Everyone helps with roundup," he told her, following her down the hallway for the room at the front of the house. "I usually go to Bo's Big Rock Ranch and do what I can, and the church sponsors a watering station near the rail for cowboys and their horses. And when it's all over, there's the Harvest Festival."

"You should have taken a wife sooner," she teased.

"The wife I wanted didn't come West with me." As soon as he said the words, he wanted to call them back. He'd said he'd make no demands on her, and that included emotional demands. He shouldn't remind her of what he'd thought they shared.

"How odd," she said, reaching for the doorknob. "I heard you took up with Florence before you left. I would have thought she would follow you anywhere."

Florence? Why would he have asked Florence to marry him? He'd never thought of her as more than a sister. But then, his heart had been too broken when he'd left Cambridge to consider marrying anyone.

"This will be your room with the boys," he said instead, reaching past her to push open the door.

She moved into the room, away from him, and suddenly he felt as if she'd gone miles. Perhaps it was the stiff back, the high head. He knew he shouldn't have mentioned their past, but she hadn't bridled when he'd talked about Boston earlier.

Now she glanced around as if noticing the wide bed with her trunk at the foot, the high dresser, the crib and the boys' cart in the corner. Three blocks of wood, cleaned and sanded, sat on the bed, as if waiting for the babies. He couldn't see George or Amos putting them there. So who else had been in the room? With so many people coming and going at the reception, anyone might have dropped in unnoticed.

"We can make do," Elizabeth said. She bent to set Jasper on the rug, then eyed Theo and Eli.

He knew dismissal when he saw it. He bent and set the boys down. As he straightened, he saw that Elizabeth was pulling the doilies and knickknacks off the furniture.

"Here," she said, handing them to him. "We'll need to remove them from everywhere else in the house as well. Baby love can be hard on porcelain and lace."

So he would imagine. He juggled the pile even as Jasper started crawling toward the trunk, his brothers hard on his heels.

"Good night, Brandon," she said pointedly, and he had no choice but to quit the room and head for his own.

Sleep was a long time coming, so it felt as if he'd barely closed his eyes when he heard a baby cry.

Brandon bolted upright, heart pounding. By the time he'd thrown on his trousers, two voices were wailing. He dashed down the hallway and pushed open the door even as the third joined in.

Elizabeth, wrapped in a flowered dressing gown, hair falling around her shoulders like fire, had just lit the lamp and was attempting to calm them. "It's all right! You're safe." She glanced at Brandon in evident appeal.

He strode into the room. "Easy there, my boys. What's all the fuss?"

He picked up Jasper, who blinked big brown eyes, round cheeks shining with tears.

"I think it's the strange surroundings," Elizabeth offered, patting Theo's and Eli's backs as they sat up in the crib. Both babies had trembling lower lips and gazed at Brandon accusingly, as if he was somehow to blame for the situation.

In a way, he supposed he was. But he couldn't regret having brought them here from the boardinghouse.

"It probably doesn't help that they're all piled on top of each other like a pack of puppies," Brandon reasoned.

"When one wakes, they all do," she agreed. "But they seem to take comfort sleeping next to each other."

"I'll make them their own beds," he said. "We can line them all up along the wall so they can see each other. Until then, maybe I should take Jasper with me."

"He's the most likely to wake," she warned him. "And the hardest to get back to sleep."

"All the more reason to separate him from the others." He met the baby's gaze. "What do you think, little man? Want to come sleep with the pastor?"

Jasper patted his shoulder. "Papa."

Brandon stared at the baby, warmth washing over him. He looked to Elizabeth in awe. "Did you hear that? He called me his father."

"And so you are." Elizabeth rose, smile watery. "I can't think of anyone more dedicated. Thank you, Brandon. For everything." She came and pressed a kiss to his cheek.

Longing rose up inside him, fierce, strong. She and the babies were his to protect, his to provide for.

His to love?

Chapter Fifteen

Over the next few days, Elizabeth and the babies settled into a routine. They were up with the sun, then fed and dressed for the day. Brandon usually fended for himself for breakfast, making coffee and eating some of the baked goods that had been left for him. Then he was out of the house and going about his duties as a pastor, visiting sick or hurting parishioners, meeting with various groups and helping to renovate the children's home.

Elizabeth kept the triplets busy while she did chores. After her narrow governess's quarters in Cambridge and the boardinghouse in Little Horn, it was a delight to have a whole house to live in again. With the kitchen door open, she could let the boys explore the parlor, having removed all the dainty figurines and doilies, while she started something on the stove. Or she could prop the cart up in the yard while she hung the wash. The fully stocked parsonage kitchen made cooking, washing and cleaning so much easier.

But, she quickly learned, such conveniences came at a price. She had already determined that Brandon's

congregation doted on him. Now she saw that that admiration meant they rarely left him alone.

Whenever he was at home, men came to seek his
advice about some situation. They'd sit with him in
his study, the murmur of their deep voices reaching
her where she played with the boys in the parlor. They
joined him in the yard as he oiled the boys' cart to fix
the squeak and began building their new beds. Seeing
their pastor in his shirtsleeves did not seem to trouble
the men. Indeed, many pitched in to help, as did Gil
Satler, who seemed to be very good with woodworking.

Women came to request Brandon's participation in
some event and often to include Elizabeth and the triplets in the invitation. They brought food and firewood
and lamp oil. They offered to help with the triplets, so
Elizabeth often found she had an extra pair of hands
or two, usually from Annie, Fannie or the Satler siblings. Each morning, Mr. Arundel delivered the newspaper from Austin. Each afternoon, one of the local
farmers left fresh milk or eggs. And one evening she
found a full bushel of peaches waiting for her on the
kitchen table.

The Good Samaritans were also in evidence. Who
else would leave the little can of kindling on the back
stoop every day? Louisa told her that she'd had the
same thing happen when she'd been caring for the triplets. And the pile of wood blocks, each one sanded,
was growing, to the point where the babies used them
to build teetering towers on the rose-colored rug in
the parlor.

Still, she was surprised to hear voices in the hallway
the first Thursday when she came inside from the yard.
Annie was playing with the boys so Elizabeth could

deal with the peaches. Knowing Brandon was out, she went to investigate.

Mrs. Arundel was just fluffing up her puffy lavender sleeves. Four other women crowded around her.

"Pastor Stillwater suggested we meet somewhere else for our literary tea," she informed Elizabeth. "That would be entirely inconvenient." Without waiting for a response, she swept into the parlor, twill skirts knocking the blocks aside, and took her place on the largest chair while Mrs. Crenshaw, Mrs. Hickey, Mrs. Bachmeier and Mrs. Henley found their places around her and looked expectantly at Elizabeth.

"Tea?" Mrs. Arundel prompted as Elizabeth hurried to gather up the blocks.

She was supposed to serve the tea? Who had served them before she'd arrived?

"Pastor Stillwater must not have told her," Mrs. Bachmeier murmured to Mrs. Henley.

She certainly didn't want to make Brandon look bad. So she hugged the blocks to her chest and hurried to brew some tea. She found them all waiting for her as she carried in a tray with a teapot and the dainty bluebell-painted porcelain cups someone had no doubt donated. She poured and handed the cups around, reserving the most-battered one for herself.

"We are reading *Pride and Prejudice*," Mrs. Arundel informed her, book open on her ample lap. "And we are on page 34. I don't suppose you have read the book."

"Yes, quite some time ago and several times since. I believe Brandon even has a copy." She went to the shelf and pulled it down, then returned to her seat, prepared to acquit herself admirably. "How are you liking it so far?"

"I believe this Darcy fellow to be entirely short-sighted," Mrs. Arundel declared. "He will come to a bad end. You mark my words."

"Perhaps he just needs the love of a good woman," Mrs. Crenshaw put in dreamily.

"Or to reform a bad one," Mrs. Hickey said with a look to Elizabeth.

She refused to acknowledge the comment. "I believe you will find him a different sort of gentleman in the end, one much misunderstood but entirely worthy."

Mrs. Crenshaw gasped, hands going to her mouth. What had she done now?

"We are not allowed to read ahead," Mrs. Hickey scolded her.

Mrs. Arundel held up a hand. "No harm done. Mrs. Stillwater offered a point worth remembering."

Fire flashing in her eyes, Mrs. Hickey seemed far from mollified. She set down her teacup. "I wonder, what did you plan to serve with the tea today, Mrs. Stillwater?"

All gazes swung eagerly to hers. Elizabeth gave the ladies her best smile but feared it was as chipped as the cup in her hands. "I wasn't aware I was expected to bake for your meeting."

Mrs. Crenshaw offered a commiserating smile, but Mrs. Hickey shook her head, eyes narrowing, and Elizabeth had no doubt the entire town would soon hear of the deficiencies in the pastor's new wife.

"Normally, one of us would supply the victuals," Mrs. Arundel acknowledged. "But now that you are here, that role clearly falls on you. Speak to your husband about your other duties. If he is too busy, I would be happy to instruct you."

"No need," Elizabeth assured her, seething. "I'm certain Brandon and I can come to an understanding about my role. Now, I'll leave you to your important discussions while I go check on the boys."

She made sure that effort took sufficiently long that she only had time to say farewell as the ladies were leaving. She could only be glad that Brandon was busy on the children's home so that she did not see him until dinner. By then she'd had time to cool her temper. She couldn't help noticing as she prepared the meal, however, that the preserves and baked goods on the shelves were dwindling. Very likely the citizens of Little Horn considered it her duty to bake and can for Brandon now.

"Is there some book I should read?" she asked him that night. "Some canon that spells out the duties of the minister's wife in Little Horn?"

He smiled in obvious sympathy as he handed Jasper a slice of cooked carrot to chew on. He had arranged the three high chairs around the table so that Elizabeth and Brandon could each reach the boys as needed.

Now that she had a kitchen, she'd all but eliminated the need for hand-feeding. Instead of relying on the canned foods, she could cook things the boys could eat for themselves. Elizabeth made sure to cut the food into tiny cubes for each so they could eat with their fingers, and she kept wooden spoons on hand to entertain them if they finished before she and Brandon did.

Now she caught Jasper trying to imitate the look on Brandon's face as her husband said, "I'm sorry, Elizabeth. The members of my congregation have no right to order you about."

"They aren't ordering me exactly, but there are clearly expectations." She raised her voice over the tapping of Eli's spoon on the table. "And I'm certainly willing to contribute to the community. Aunt Evangeline managed a far more complicated social calendar while raising me. I can manage, if I know what I have to deal with."

He shook his head as he dug into his chicken pot pie. "You focus on the boys. I'll make sure you aren't troubled further."

Elizabeth frowned. Did he think her so lacking or so fragile? Once, perhaps, back when she'd had servants and wealth to support her. But she'd grown in the last four years, had had to fend for herself and see to Aunt Evangeline's care. He would find her made of firmer stuff now.

And so would the rest of Little Horn.

Brandon couldn't help thinking about the situation as he finished the peach pie Elizabeth had baked, the sweet dessert every bit as good as his mother's. Elizabeth was a capable, competent woman, but she shouldn't have to deal with these demands on her time. Very likely she could contend with his overly helpful congregation, but that need he'd felt to protect her was only growing stronger. So, he redoubled his efforts to shield Elizabeth from the people of Little Horn.

Unfortunately, it wasn't easy. Requests popped up like gophers: unexpected, annoying and often leaving messes behind. When the committee helping him plan the Harvest Festival intimated that Elizabeth would bake all the pies this year, he directed them to Mercy Green. When the school board added Elizabeth to their committee without asking her first, he suggested they invite Lula May McKay instead. When the Society for the Destitute and Downtrodden wanted to elect Elizabeth its new president, he took the role himself.

He refused dinner engagements with the excuse of the triplets, claimed to be too busy for tea in the parsonage. He attempted once more to move Mrs. Arundel's literary group, this time to the café, and was roundly berated for his lack of sensitivity before the lady took herself off in a huff.

He would not back down. He'd seen what Louisa had gone through to manage the triplets and knew David had had to hire a nanny when he'd been in charge of their care. It was clearly a full-time job. The boys had to be fed and changed and dressed, multiple times a day. Moving about as they were now, they got into everything. Even though Elizabeth had rid the parsonage of anything fragile, the triplets still managed to leave smudges on the chair legs and drool on the carpet. He was constantly having to move things out of reach.

And then there were the chores that came with running a household, washing and cooking and cleaning. The ladies of the town had largely performed those functions when he was a bachelor. Now that he was married, they seemed to feel that those tasks should fall on Elizabeth as well.

And so he tried to help. He started with the washing. He'd seen his mother do it. How difficult could it be to clean a few shirts? He heated water on the stove, then lugged it out to a tub in the yard, shaved in soap and added the clothes. Elizabeth and the boys had been out for a walk. They returned in time to see him standing in his shirtsleeves, stirring the mess.

"This is hot work," he told her, wiping his forehead with one hand.

"It can be," she agreed, careful to keep the triplets away from the pungent steam. "Let me get the boys settled, and I'll come help."

"No need," Brandon assured her, giving the shirts an extra swirl. "I can do this."

As a result, his best white shirt was now a pale pink.

"It's generally best to separate the whites from the brights," Elizabeth advised him with a smile when she helped him hang the clothes to dry. "I'd be happy to show you next time."

She was similarly kind when he attempted to cook dinner one night. She chewed the burnt chicken so carefully he could hardly hear it crackle in her mouth. Even the boys refused to eat the watery mashed potatoes, gazing at him with sad eyes as if feeling his failure.

"I'm sorry, Elizabeth," he told her, letting his fork fall. "You deserve better."

She put her hand on his on the table, the touch warm. "I know any number of women who would be envious my husband thought to step in and help. The trouble isn't your effort, Brandon, it's the focus. Do what you do best, and leave me to what I do best."

That was when she told him she was planning a dinner party.

He felt as if ants were marching across his skin. "Perhaps that's not the best idea. We are newly married, after all, still learning our way. And we have the boys to contend with."

She cocked her head. "Are you afraid I'll embarrass you?"

"No, never," he promised her. "But I'm not sure you understand the dynamics of Little Horn society."

Her smile was tight. "I understand the dynamics better than you think. Leave everything to me."

He couldn't refuse her, even when she handed him the guest list.

"Dorothy Hill and Tug Coleman at the same table?" Brandon shook his head as he scanned down the list. "And Kit Durango?"

Elizabeth smiled at him. "Trust me."

He did. Truly he did. Unfortunately, some in his congregation had more trouble.

He and Elizabeth attended their first church service as husband and wife that Sunday. He felt a little concerned leaving her in the pew with the boys, even with Mrs. Tyson and Annie to help her. Who knew how many requests she'd have to fend off? As it was, his gaze kept finding hers as he delivered his sermon. When the service ended, people surrounded her, and he pushed his way into the crowd, ready to defend her.

Mrs. Arundel was already plowing into a lecture. "About this dinner you are giving, Mrs. Stillwater, you must include Edmund and Lula May McKay. They are one of our first families. Mr. Arundel and I would be glad to sit down beside them."

"Thank you for the suggestion," Elizabeth said, handing her Jasper. "But the invitations have already been sent. And may I just say that I am so grateful that you and your husband run such a superior store. Why, I found everything I need for my table there, and I would not hesitate to recommend it to my dearest friends."

The oddest sound came from Mrs. Arundel's throat as she beamed, and for a moment Brandon thought she was purring. Jasper must have approved, for he made the same noise.

"I haven't received an invitation," Mrs. Hickey said, scowling at Elizabeth.

"Certainly not," Elizabeth agreed, handing her Theo. "Why, when you come to my table, it will be a momentous occasion indeed, Mrs. Hickey, as rare as a snowflake in summer."

Mrs. Hickey's nose went into the air. "Indeed." Theo patted her shoulder as if he quite agreed.

"You seem to have found your footing as the pastor's wife," Brandon marveled as she retrieved the babies.

"Perhaps not yet, Mr. Stillwater," she said, looking determined as he walked her and Annie to the door. "But I'm working on it."

She was indeed. By Tuesday night, the day set for the dinner, the entire parsonage gleamed. Besides the feuding couple and the cowboy, Elizabeth had invited the Crenshaws, Bo and Louisa, and David and Caroline. With Annie watching the triplets in the bedroom, their guests were able to sit down to the table nearly a dozen strong. Brandon could see Dorothy and Tug glancing about at the others in confusion, and Kit Durango kept tugging at the throat of his dress shirt as if none too comfortable in such company.

But Elizabeth, ah, Elizabeth, was in rare form. She'd donned one of the dresses from Cambridge, the dun-colored one with the black lace. Though her aunt would have considered it a day dress, here in Little Horn it was nothing less than high fashion. With her hair bound up in the pearl combs from their wedding, she was the most beautiful woman in the room.

And the most confident.

"Thank you all so much for joining us," she said from the foot of the table, her gaze brushing Brandon's at the head. "My family loved to throw parties for those they admired. I'm honored you'd come to our table as we start the tradition here in Little Horn."

Now Dorothy Hill was squirming. "Not sure how I ended up here," she muttered to Mrs. Crenshaw on her left.

"You raised a family alone," Mrs. Crenshaw responded. "I say that's admirable."

"So do I," Tug said on her right. "But I told you that before. You're a fine woman, Dorothy Hill, and Mrs. Stillwater was right in inviting you to join us."

Brandon turned his gaze away from the remarkable sight of the indomitable Dorothy blushing to find Elizabeth lifting her glass to him in toast. He could only offer her a toast in return.

"I understand there was a wildfire here not that long ago," Elizabeth ventured as they all dug into the roast and mashed potatoes she'd served. "I imagine that's a difficult situation on the range. However did you cope, Mr. Durango?"

Kit hastily swallowed as everyone looked his way. "Well," he said, toying with his fork as if considering using it to protect himself, "first we had to keep the cattle calm. Then we had to move them to safety, out of the path of the blaze."

Bo nodded. "That's the tricky part. Never can tell which way a fire will run."

"That's true enough," Tug put it. "Why, if Dorothy

and her boys hadn't pitched in, we might have lost everything."

"You and yours fought that fire right beside us," she reminded him. "Kept it from destroying our house too."

"I've never seen neighbors so ready to help each other," Elizabeth told them. "I think you're all to be commended." She raised her glass again. "Here's to the people of Little Horn, our friends and family."

"To friends and family," Tug agreed, raising his glass as he smiled at Dorothy.

And so the evening continued, with merriment and good conversation. Brandon had never enjoyed himself more. The others seemed to feel the same way.

"Best time I've had in years," David told him as he said good-night to Brandon. Caroline was standing in the doorway to the boys' room, giving each of her favorite fellows a hug and kiss as Louisa waited her turn. "Who would have thought this crew would get along, much less enjoy each other's company?"

"Only Elizabeth," Bo said, clapping Brandon on the back. "You've got some wife there, brother."

He could only agree. Especially when she came to join him at the door to send the cowboy on his way.

"Much obliged, ma'am," Kit said, deep brown eyes warm. "Though I'm still not sure why you included me."

"You are the new breed of gentlemen paving a way on the frontier," she told him. "Everyone I know admires a good cowhand." She leaned closer. "And now that you've visited my house, Mr. Durango, I hope to see you and your friends in God's house on occasion."

He nodded as he settled his hat on his head. "We'll be there, ma'am, if I have to rope and hog-tie the rest of them to their saddles."

Brandon shook his head as he shut the door behind them. "What did you do?"

"What my aunt taught me to do," she said, beaming. "Bring people together."

She'd done more than that. She was a light of hope, a woman of encouragement. Everyone in the room had felt it. Their smiles and compliments were proof enough of that.

"You are amazing," he murmured.

It seemed the most logical thing in the world to bend his head and kiss her.

But there was nothing logical about the way his heart reacted. He wanted to cradle her close, never let her go. She smelled of peach pie and clean linen, and her kiss made him feel strong, sure. It was as if holding her, encouraging her, protecting her was what he had been born to do.

Could it be he was falling in love all over again, with his own wife?

Chapter Sixteen

The evening had gone exactly as Elizabeth had hoped, with good food, interesting company and congenial conversation. But Brandon's kiss wiped it all from her mind. The soft, sweet pressure, the warmth of his arms stealing around her waist, brought back memories, memories that quickly faded in comparison with the joy she felt now. He had changed for the better; she had changed for the better. Together, they were nothing short of magnificent.

He drew back with a sigh. "Elizabeth, forgive me, I…"

She put her finger to his lips to seal them, but the touch only reminded her of what they'd just shared. "No. No apologies. No misunderstandings. You kissed me, and I kissed you back. Let's just leave it at that."

He nodded, and a part of her was disappointed. What was wrong with her? What did she want him to say? She certainly didn't want to start an argument over a kiss!

"I'm going to change and clean up the kitchen," she said, backing for her room, where she could hear

Annie settling the boys for bed. "I'll see you in the morning, Brandon."

He caught her arm. "Let me help."

The image of him standing beside her, drying as she washed, was a pretty one, but he was already too much on her mind, and she feared he was making his way into her heart. She wasn't ready. Not yet. Not until she was sure.

"I'll be fine," she said. "As soon as I've changed, you can help Annie with the boys."

She pulled away before he could disagree.

But that night after she turned in she couldn't help wondering about her reaction. Brandon's kiss had likely been meant as no more than a kindness, thanks for what she'd achieved that night with her first dinner party. He alone of anyone in Little Horn knew what such a night meant to her, how it honored her aunt's memory. She thought Aunt Evangeline would be proud of her. She was certainly pleased with the results.

But that kiss? Oh, my. How would she ever get to sleep thinking of it?

She was simply thankful she had helpers the next morning, for she kept forgetting little things like setting out the sugar bowl for Brandon's coffee and removing the porridge from the stove before it boiled over. Today her assistants were the Satler siblings. She'd found them waiting on the back step when she opened the door to let in some of the cool morning air. Jo and Gil helped her feed the triplets and make coffee for Brandon, who stepped in a short while later and stuck out his lower lip as if impressed with the tidy picture they presented.

"I have to go to the children's home this morning,"

he told Elizabeth after his first sip of the coffee. He moved his cinnamon roll a few inches to the left to keep Jasper from grabbing it. "The building is nearly done, and David wants me to stop by and give it my blessing."

Jo perked up. Did she know she and Gil were two of the children for whom the home was intended? Elizabeth slipped an arm about the girl's shoulders as Eli and Theo gabbled at Gil.

"Perhaps we all should go. I'm sure Jo and Gil would like to see where they'll be living soon."

"Would I!" Gil slipped off the chair and hung on Brandon's arm, chatting away about what they might see. Jo clung to Elizabeth, head down and one hand stroking Eli's dark curls.

Poor child! Brandon had told Elizabeth a little about the siblings. She knew Mrs. Satler had loved and protected her children until death had parted them. Now they were alone, with people who didn't seem to know how to care for them. Small wonder the girl didn't trust anyone enough to speak.

"Give us a little time," Elizabeth told Brandon, "and we'll all come with you. That is, if you're willing to push the cart."

"Watch me," Brandon said with a grin that set something inside her to fluttering.

A short time later, they all left the parsonage together. Gil ran ahead, but Jo stayed close to Elizabeth, her flowered cotton skirts brushing the olive twill of Elizabeth's.

Elizabeth couldn't help noticing that the boys were more tightly packed in the cart than when she had first begun caring for them more than a month ago. Jasper was wiggling his shoulders as if trying to spread out.

Eli was waving his hands as if hoping to escape, and Theo in the middle had a puckered face as he must have felt the pinch on both sides. Each of them had grown in weight and height, and they'd only get bigger from here. She mentioned as much to Brandon.

"I'll stop by Josiah McKay's lumberyard later," he promised her with a wink. "Maybe he has some wood that's hankering to be a wagon."

Elizabeth smiled, remembering his story about the desk.

Gil was frowning. "Does wood want to be a wagon?"

"I don't see why not," Brandon said, shoving the cart over a rut in the street. "The Bible says the rocks will cry out to praise our God. I'd think a tree could be a lot more vocal."

Gil eyed him a moment, then shook his head. "I think you're joshing."

"Maybe about the tree," Brandon allowed. "But not about making the boys a wagon." He grinned at Elizabeth. "A feller has to have some way of earning himself a place in a lady's affections."

Was that why he was being so helpful? Did he think he had to earn a way into her heart? She didn't like the thought that she might have given him that impression.

"Why?" Gil asked, skipping along beside them.

Jo glanced up as if she was keen on the answer as well, and Elizabeth eyed Brandon.

"Well," Brandon said as even the triplets gazed up at him in question, "when you care about someone, you want to do nice things for them."

That was true enough. She wanted to help him with all his responsibilities in Little Horn.

Gil nodded. "Like we do for the babies. Jo says they ain't got kin to take them in."

So the girl talked to her brother at least.

"That's right," Brandon said with a smile to Jo, who looked away. "You help Mrs. Stillwater around the parsonage because you care about the triplets."

"And cuz she's pretty and nice," Gil said with a shy smile to Elizabeth.

She returned his smile as Brandon glanced her way. "She certainly is."

Her cheeks heated in a blush. "Thank you, gentlemen. I'm very glad for your help, both of you. But, Gil, school will be starting soon, and you promised me you would go."

Gil's smile faded. "Don't much like school. Teacher says I don't talk right." He suddenly brightened. "But at least I talk!"

Jo hunched in on herself.

Elizabeth squared her shoulders. "Jo will talk when she's ready, and I'm sure it will be worth the wait."

The look the girl cast her was equal parts thanks and admiration. Very likely Elizabeth was gazing at Brandon the same way. She was just glad they reached the house then, so they all had something else to talk about.

The Crenshaw home had been turned into a marvel of modern ministry, and Elizabeth couldn't help smiling as Brandon escorted them through the rooms. He was so excited, eyes shining and face animated, that she was reminded of the dreams they'd shared once.

"This is where everyone will gather for meals," he said, leading them through a formal dining room with a table big enough to seat a dozen or more. "And there's space for playing checkers or doing homework."

Gil had been grinning until Brandon mentioned homework. Now a scowl shadowed his lean face. Elizabeth knew from experience it could be hard for an active little boy to sit still and pay attention to lessons. Very likely the triplets would have the same challenge.

Though the rooms were large and open as she'd suggested, with plenty of light from the wide windows, she'd left the cart in the entryway. Now Brandon carried Jasper, she had Theo and Jo had Eli. The baby kept staring at the girl's face as if trying to see inside her. Jo gazed back just as solemnly.

"Above," Brandon was saying, starting up the stairs for the second floor, "we have bedrooms for boys and girls as well as the houseparents."

"My own room? Yeehaw!" Gil squeezed past Brandon and dashed up the stairs as if he couldn't wait to see.

Four large rooms opened off a center landing. One room, Elizabeth could see, had been outfitted as a nursery, with cribs and a rocking chair as well as a low dresser with a flat top for changing infants. Gil was more interested in the room with a wooden train set in the middle. Already he was running the engine around the circuit, making rumbling noises.

Jo looked troubled as she gazed in that room and then the one next to it. Brandon had said the boys and the girls would sleep in different rooms. Very likely she hadn't been separated from Gil even by a wall before.

"I always wanted sisters," Elizabeth mused, watching her. "How nice to have them in the same room."

Jo stroked Eli's back thoughtfully.

Gil left the engine and came skidding out into the hall. "Who's going to be our ma and pa?"

Jo looked to Elizabeth.

"We don't know just yet," Brandon answered. "But it will be someone who has experience with children and loves them."

"Like Mrs. Elizabeth," Gil proclaimed. "You can be our ma."

Elizabeth smiled at him. "I'm honored, Gil, but I need to stay in the parsonage with Pastor."

His face fell.

Elizabeth glanced at Brandon. "But I know someone who would be perfect: Fannie and her husband. They miss their sons so much, she's been wonderful with the triplets and she wants to do more for the community."

"She's nice," Gil agreed. He hopped over to Jo and peered into Eli's face. "What do you think, little feller?"

Eli reached for Gil. "Baby!"

Gil recoiled. "I ain't no baby! You're the baby!"

Elizabeth stepped between them as Eli's face clouded. "He calls his brothers baby, Gil. I think that means he likes you as much as them."

Gil nodded, shoulders coming down. "Well, that's all right, then. Come on, Jo. You got to see the girls' room. You'll like it. It's yeller."

She handed Eli to Elizabeth, and the two siblings wandered into the room to the left.

"Nicely done," Brandon said, moving closer. "And the Tysons are a good suggestion. I'll speak to them. David and I will present the final plans to the Lone Star Cowboy League at a special session tomorrow. If they agree and the Tysons are willing, we could open the house Sunday."

She glanced around, imagining children running

up and down the stairs, laughing over dinner, sleeping safely in the beds. "Oh, Brandon, it's perfect. I know this house will be a blessing to dozens of children over the years. It will be a place to call home."

He took a step closer, and the triplets reached out to hold hands, pulling him and Elizabeth together.

"I want the parsonage to be home too, Elizabeth," he murmured. "I was waiting for the right time, and I think this is it. When I meet with the league, I'd like to ask their permission for us to adopt the boys."

The thought was as warm as the babies in her arms. "Oh, yes, Brandon. Do you think they'll agree?"

His smile was pleased. "I don't see why not. I think they're satisfied with my service in Little Horn."

She was certain of it. Still, doubts poked at her. "What about those rumors? What if they think I won't be a good mother in the long-term?"

He shook his head. "Anyone with eyes and sense can tell you're a wonderful mother, Elizabeth. I couldn't ask for a better partner in ministry. I don't foresee any problems with our petition."

She could only hope he was right.

David was coming in the front door as they descended the stairs. Jasper, Theo and Eli crowed a welcome.

"So, what do you think?" he asked, glancing around at them all.

Elizabeth smiled at Jo and Gil, expecting the boy to share his excitement for his new home. Instead, he took Jo's hand and edged around David.

"Gil?" Elizabeth asked.

"We best go," he said. "Mrs. Johnson will be looking for us." The pair darted out the door.

"You must be a good influence on them, Elizabeth,"

David said, watching them go. "I've never seen Gil so concerned about his foster family."

Before she could demur, he turned to face her again. "Well, do you approve of the place?"

"Wholeheartedly," Elizabeth assured him. "You all have done a marvelous job. I'm sure the Lone Star Cowboy League will be pleased."

"No!" Jasper shouted.

"Here, now, young man," Brandon said as David chuckled. "This is a fine establishment. You wait and see—everyone in town will be praising it."

David's smile faded. "Well, everyone but a certain thief."

Brandon frowned, jiggling Jasper and Theo up and down. In Elizabeth's arms, Eli frowned too.

"Thief?" Brandon asked. "Has something been stolen?"

"Nothing important," David assured him. "I spotted some of the leftover scraps of wood missing a while ago, but I thought maybe someone had just gathered it up thinking it could go for firewood. But we're missing sandpaper too, and that's more costly."

Elizabeth cocked her head. So did Eli. "I don't know a great deal about carpentry," she allowed, "but scraps of wood and sandpaper remind me of the blocks that have been appearing at the parsonage on a regular basis."

Brandon nodded. "Could be."

David shook his head. "The Good Samaritan at work. If that's the explanation for our missing things, I won't worry. I just wish the person had lent us a hand while we were working on this place. We might have been done even sooner."

Brandon chuckled, but all three boys were beginning to fuss.

"We should go," Elizabeth said. "Rest assured the children's home is perfect, David."

He colored. "Thank you. And thanks again for including Caroline and me in your dinner party last night. It's the talk of the town."

"We'll have another soon," she promised.

"We will?" Brandon teased as they made their way back to the parsonage. "What do you have planned, Mrs. Stillwater?"

"Nothing less than complete capitulation, Mr. Stillwater," she told him.

Indeed, over the next couple of days it seemed to her that her dinner party had finally cleared her way into the hearts of Little Horn, for the visitors and gifts to the parsonage increased again, and not just because of the triplets. Stella asked Elizabeth's advice about raising boys, as her younger brother Charlie had been acting up. Helen Carson invited Elizabeth to join the quilting bee, promising to have young ladies present to watch the triplets. Even Mrs. Hickey unbent enough to ask her recipe for the butter brickle she'd served at the most recent literary tea.

Still, she was nervous the afternoon the league members started showing up at the door. Because it was a special session, Brandon had offered them the use of the parsonage.

She greeted David and his brother Edmund and chatted a moment with Lula May before seeing her and CJ Thorn into the parlor with the others. Clyde Parker snatched off his hat at the sight of her and mumbled something before scooting past to find a seat. She offered them coffee and cookies, but when Lula May nodded, she knew it was time to make herself scarce. She stepped out into the hallway and closed the door.

Please, Lord, help them to see Your plan, for the home and the boys.

Even with her prayer, she sincerely considered putting her ear to the door to hear what they would say about Brandon's proposal.

A sharp rap on the front door made her wonder whether a league member had come late. But when she answered, she found Dorothy Hill standing on the stoop. The Hill matriarch had been friendly to Elizabeth since the dinner party, but she came into the parsonage now and glanced around as if suddenly finding herself in a foreign country.

"The Lone Star Cowboy League is meeting in the parlor," Elizabeth told her. "And Caroline and Louisa have taken the boys over to the Clarks' for a visit. But you're welcome to chat with me in the kitchen."

Dorothy's face brightened. "I'd like that."

Elizabeth led her down the hallway and through the other door to the kitchen. She hadn't had much chance to clean up after breakfast, so she set about putting the dishes in the sink to soak and wiping down the table.

"I understand many of the families donated things to make the parsonage special," she said, following Dorothy's look at the cups and saucers on the sideboard. "Is one of these yours?"

She shook her head, mouth tightening. "What we own we need, and I don't have much time for fancy work."

Elizabeth nodded as she went to wring out the washcloth. "I don't have much time for crocheting or tatting either. The boys keep me plenty busy. That's why I'm so thankful for you and your daughter, Fannie and the Satler children. You've all been a big help."

"Folks hereabouts can be real neighborly, just as you said the other night," she allowed as she sank onto one of the hard-backed kitchen chairs. "That's why I came. It's about our neighbors, the Colemans."

Elizabeth refused to hear more complaints, from either of the feuding families. "Mr. Coleman is so good with the triplets," she said, going to pour some lemonade for her visitor instead.

Dorothy dropped her gaze to the table. "Tug Coleman isn't the man I thought him. He's a hard worker, and he's kind to everyone."

"So I've noticed," Elizabeth encouraged her, setting the glass in front of her.

Dorothy looked up and met her gaze. "I like him. I wasn't supposed to like him."

She sounded so dismayed that Elizabeth moved one of the boys' high chairs aside so she could sit next to the woman. "I know what you mean. When I arrived in Little Horn, I was prepared to dislike a certain gentleman, but he won me over."

Dorothy eyed her. "What did you do?"

Elizabeth smiled. "I married him."

Dorothy reared back, then a slow smile formed. "Well, I'll be." Her smile vanished. "But that doesn't mean I'm meant to marry Tug."

"Certainly not," Elizabeth agreed. "But perhaps it means Annie and Jamie might marry."

She nodded. "That's what I hope. I just needed to talk about it with someone who wasn't directly involved."

"I understand, and I'll keep our discussion in confidence."

Dorothy picked up the lemonade and took a good swig. "So," she said after she'd swallowed, "you and the Pastor fixing to have more babies?"

Heat flushed up her. "We haven't discussed the matter."

"Doesn't seem like something that needs discussion," Dorothy declared. "I'd say the triplets would like a little brother or sister by and by."

Elizabeth could see it now. A little girl with Brandon's silky hair. A little boy with his quicksilver eyes. But having more children who looked like Brandon surely meant opening her heart all the way.

Was she ready to give their love another try?

Chapter Seventeen

Inside the parlor, Brandon watched as the members of the Lone Star Cowboy League took their places. Once again, his brother's posture was all support. While the older men settled themselves in a corner of the room, Brandon approached Lula May.

"Madam President, would it sway the discussion if I offered you a gift first?"

Her blue eyes twinkled. "That depends on what you're offering, Pastor."

Brandon slipped the wooden instrument he'd made from inside his coat. "I thought you could use this. And that bookcase beside you is plenty sturdy to stand up under it."

Lula May took the gavel from him, weighed the polished wood in her hand. "I like it. This could come in real handy." She flashed him a smile that told him Edmund was one fortunate fellow. "Thank you, Pastor."

He nodded and retreated to the chair closest to the door.

Lula May brought the gavel down on the bookcase, and every man in the room jumped.

She beamed. "Good afternoon, gentlemen. As you can see, I have a new way to get you to pay attention at meetings."

"Who gave her that?" Casper Magnuson grumbled to his cohort.

"The first order of business," she continued while Brandon hid a smile, "is the status of the new children's home. David?"

David rose. "I'm pleased to report that the renovations are complete, and Pastor Stillwater has confirmed we are ready to open."

"At less than the budget originally requested," Brandon felt compelled to put in with a look around David to Casper and his crew.

Abe Sawyer and Gabe Dooley nodded their thanks.

"So when do we intend to move in the young'uns?" Clyde Parker demanded.

"We'd like to have a formal christening this Sunday after services," David told him.

Magnuson cocked his head. "And how much is that going to cost?"

"Nothing," David said with a grin. "My brothers and I will pay for the cider for toasting, and the Arundel General Store has agreed to provide the cups."

"Sounds all well and good," Abe Sawyer allowed, "but who's going to manage the house?"

"The Tysons," Brandon put in when David looked his way. "They are solid members of the community, and they have a special place in their hearts for children. They're planning on putting their farm up for sale and moving into the children's home this week, if you all approve."

"Why wouldn't we?" Bo demanded with a look of challenge to the older ranchers.

"I think it all sounds marvelous," Lula May agreed, glancing around the room as if daring any of the men to disagree with her. "All in favor?"

"Aye!"

The unanimous cry set Brandon's pulse to pounding. Bo and several of the other men rose to shake his hand or David's as the rest chorused their good wishes.

Lula May let them whoop it up a bit before bringing her gavel down on the bookcase again.

"We have one more order of business," she said as they quieted. "Pastor Stillwater has another proposal for us."

Magnuson crossed his arms over his barrel chest. "I'm not prepared to spend another cent."

"This won't cost you anything either," Brandon promised, rising. He glanced around at the assembled ranchers, and a tremor went through him. Why? He knew each one. Most were friends. All attended services on Sunday. They'd heard him preach on any number of occasions, knew that he had advocated for civic causes before.

But this time it was personal.

He cleared his throat. "Gentlemen, Madam President, my wife, Elizabeth, and I would like your permission to adopt the triplets."

"What?" Magnuson surged to his feet. "Why didn't you ask sooner? We might have saved the expense of building that fancy orphanage."

"The triplets aren't the only orphans in the county," David reminded him.

"Indeed," Brandon agreed. "I've already had requests to place five children, including the Satler siblings. I didn't expect to keep the boys, but Elizabeth and I have come to love the triplets as our own. We promise to raise them up in a loving Christian home, to help them become contributing members of society. As it was the league that took responsibility for them when they were abandoned, we come to you for your permission."

"I say yes, of course," David put in. "They couldn't ask for finer parents."

Brandon nodded his thanks.

"I suppose it would be all right," Parker grumbled.

Brandon inclined his head.

"But what about kin?" Sawyer protested. "We thought we had some before. We published ads hither and yon. Someone might still come for them."

"It's been nearly three months," Lula May pointed out, wrinkling her nose. "If my kin were missing, I'd have found them a lot sooner than this."

"But we don't know where the mother came from," Sawyer argued. "It could take a while for the news to reach her family and for them to get here. I say we wait. There's room in the orphanage."

Disappointment bit at Brandon, but he kept his smile pleasant. "No need to move the boys. Elizabeth and I can continue to care for them until the league is satisfied no one else will come forward." He glanced at Magnuson, who had leaned forward. "At no charge to the league, of course."

Magnuson leaned back.

"And just how long do you expect Brandon and Elizabeth to wait?" Bo demanded of Sawyer.

As all gazes swung his way, the rancher seemed to

shrink. Then he raised his chin. "Six months," he said. "Six months from the day we found them."

"That would be mid-December," Lula May calculated. "Let's say December fifteenth, so they can be settled before Christmas. All in favor?"

"Aye," most of the men chorused.

"Opposed?"

Brandon glanced at Magnuson, but the big rancher shrugged.

Lula May banged her gavel. "Motion carries. If no kin come forward by December fifteenth, Pastor and Mrs. Stillwater can adopt the triplets. And we'll gather up new clothes and toys for them when they do."

"Now, wait a minute," Magnuson started, but Lula May pointed her gavel at him, fixing him in his seat.

"Can't be easy raising three boys the same age," she reminded him. "There are no hand-me-downs when they're all the same size."

"He's the one who asked to take on the burden," Magnuson protested, though weakly.

"Elizabeth and I are prepared to take care of the boys," Brandon assured them all.

But it seemed they'd have to wait to become a family officially. He didn't like the thought of explaining that to Elizabeth.

After Dorothy Hill left, Elizabeth paced about the kitchen, straightening dishes on the shelves, inventorying the preserves, polishing the kitchen table. No matter how swiftly she moved or how hard she tried to think of something else, she was all too aware of the men and Lula May on the other side of the door. Brandon had seemed so certain the Lone Star Cowboy

League would agree to his proposal to adopt Jasper, Theo and Eli. What if he was wrong?

Would they lose the boys after all? Would she have to watch them go to the children's home, knowing they were just across the street but so far out of reach?

Would Brandon regret he'd married her if they couldn't adopt the boys?

Oh, but she was just borrowing trouble!

She heard the voices grow louder for a time, but they sounded happy, and she let herself hope. Everyone so respected Brandon. How could they refuse his request? Very likely he'd be coming through that door any moment to tell her the boys were theirs to love and keep forever.

Then it grew quiet again, punctuated by one loud "What!" She shivered and forced herself to go out into the field and gather some wildflowers to brighten the kitchen table. But even the sunshine and the sound of birdcall couldn't calm her thoughts.

At times, she thought she saw something in Brandon's eyes that said he cared more for her than their marriage of convenience would imply. That kiss would seem to prove it. She knew her heart was leaning in his direction. But was she just mistaken, as she'd been in Cambridge? Was she building castles in the air?

A movement at the corner of the lawn caught her eye. Was that the hem of a skirt just disappearing around the corner? Had she discovered the Good Samaritan? She clutched her flowers close with one hand, lifted her skirts with the other and dashed off in pursuit. This time she would catch their well-wisher!

She rounded the corner and ran right into Constance Hickey.

The pianist recoiled even as Elizabeth's flowers flew in all directions. Elizabeth caught her balance and sucked in a breath. Mrs. Hickey, the Good Samaritan? It couldn't be! She glanced around the woman, but the only other people on the street were Gil and Jo Satler, showing Mrs. Johnson the children's home.

"Mrs. Stillwater."

Elizabeth's gaze returned to Mrs. Hickey. The lady's mouth was tight and her eyes narrowed. Oh, what had she done now, upset some closely held Little Horn tradition?

"Mrs. Hickey," she greeted her, bending to pick up her flowers. "What brings you to our door on this lovely day?"

"What are the Lone Star Cowboy League members doing in the parsonage?" she demanded, as if Elizabeth was harboring fugitives of the law.

"Meeting to approve the children's home," Elizabeth told her, straightening.

Mrs. Hickey brightened. "Oh, is there some problem with the orphanage?"

Must she find something to complain about in every situation? From the moment Elizabeth had met her, Mrs. Hickey had been on the lookout for trouble. Was it gossip she wanted or something more? Perhaps it was time she found the challenges she sought.

Elizabeth leaned closer and dropped her voice. "Yes, there's a terrible problem. I'm sure I don't know how we'll deal with it."

Mrs. Hickey's eyes widened. "Do tell."

Elizabeth heaved a sigh. "Well, since you ask, and seeing how you are such a pillar of the community, I'm sure I can confide in you."

Mrs. Hickey's head bobbed up and down so fast Elizabeth wondered she didn't get dizzy. "Yes, yes, of course. I am a lady of discretion."

Or not. "All those orphans will need someone to love them, someone to encourage them," Elizabeth told her. "They'll have houseparents, of course, but I fear no two people can give so much. I only wish I knew someone of good character and impeccable taste who could organize a ladies' auxiliary, a group of dedicated women to support those dear children."

Mrs. Hickey straightened, eyes narrowing once more, and Elizabeth sent up a prayer that she had judged the woman's need correctly.

"I'll do it," she declared. "I'll charter a ladies' auxiliary for the orphanage. I know everyone in town. People listen to me."

"Oh, Mrs. Hickey, thank you!" Elizabeth put a hand on her arm.

"It will take a great deal of effort," Mrs. Hickey said. "But I don't mind. If there's anything I hate, it's being idle."

Thank You, Lord!

"I'm not good at that either," Elizabeth admitted. "I'd much rather keep busy. Dare I ask you to do me the honor of attending our next dinner party? I'm sure everyone will want to hear your plans for helping our dear children."

Mrs. Hickey's smile was soft, melting the frown that habitually sat on her narrow face. "I would be the one honored, Mrs. Stillwater. I'll let you know when the auxiliary is set to meet. I hope you'll have time to join us."

"I will make time," Elizabeth promised her.

With a nod, Mrs. Hickey strode off, skirts flapping and steps determined.

"What do you know, Lord?" Elizabeth murmured. "All she needed was a purpose."

She shook her head in wonder as she went to pick a few more flowers for her bouquet.

She returned to the kitchen to find Brandon sitting at the table, hands spread on the worn surface. She was ready to tell him what had happened with Mrs. Hickey when she remembered the meeting and all that was at stake. It had obviously not gone well. Once more lines drew down around his eyes, and his smile looked strained. Stomach knotting, she set the flowers on the sideboard and went to join him.

"What happened?" she asked as she took her seat. "Did Casper Magnuson find fault with the children's home?"

He drew in a breath. "No. The league agreed unanimously to open the home this Sunday."

"But something didn't go the way you wanted," she pressed, afraid to hear the answer.

He raised his brows. "What makes you say that?"

Elizabeth shook her head. "You have the most polite smile, pleasant even. But it commits to nothing. I know it stands you in good stead with your congregation, but I've come to realize it generally means you are trying to hide how you really feel."

He sighed, shifting on the chair as if the seat had become uncomfortable. "I suppose it started with my father. The less you did to set him off, the better. Now it seems there are too many times when a minister must be circumspect. But you have every right to know how I'm feeling. I didn't like how the meeting ended." He met her gaze, the silver of his eyes clouded. "The league wants to wait before letting us adopt the triplets."

Now it was all she could do to keep her face pleasant. "Oh? Why? Please tell me those wretched rumors had nothing to do with the decision."

"No one mentioned the rumors," he said, so firmly she pitied anyone who did mention them in his presence. "They're still hoping that relatives will turn up."

Elizabeth frowned. "How likely is that? It's been months."

Brandon spread his hands. "It's possible the family didn't receive word right away and then had to wait through roundup and harvest before starting out."

Disappointment was like a blade in her heart. "So even though rumors spread like wildfire in Little Horn, they move like molasses everywhere else?"

He smiled at that. "Apparently so." His smile faded as quickly as it had come. "I'm sorry, Elizabeth."

Every part of him showed that sorrow, from the downturn of his lips to the slump of his shoulders. Though her own heart was hurting, she only wanted to reach out, to reassure him.

"Don't worry," she said, laying a hand on his. "It will come out right."

His head came up. "How can you say that? I thought you wanted us to be a family."

"I do," she promised him. "I'm disappointed, of course, but I understand the league's reasoning. If loving relatives are searching for the boys, we'd want to give them every opportunity to find them." She made herself smile. "So, the children's home was approved to open. That's good news."

"Now who's putting on a pleasant face?" he asked, his smile returning.

Elizabeth raised her chin. "I am. Quite determinedly and unapologetically. I learned during the scandal with my uncle that it was better to move forward than stay stuck in what might have been."

"I admire you for that. I still wonder sometimes how different life would be now if we hadn't had our misunderstanding."

She dropped her gaze to her lap. "I've asked myself the same question. I'm not sure in the end we would have been happy, regardless. Either you would have stayed in Cambridge, become the dull, pedantic minister they were all grooming you to be, or I would have come West with you and Bo and shriveled under the challenges."

He shook his head. "I have never seen you shrivel, Elizabeth."

Hadn't he? Perhaps friendship was as blind as love. "I look back, and I see so many times I could have done more, could have been more, but I stepped back from the precipice. If I had been stronger, I wouldn't have needed Florence as an intermediary. I could have reached out to you directly. But the scandal and Aunt Evangeline's stroke nearly buried me. It took a while for me to find my feet again."

"And then you came to Little Horn," he marveled.

She felt her smile broadening. "And then I came to Little Horn and found adventure aplenty. Feuding families, secret Good Samaritans…"

"Demanding parishioners," he added.

"Interesting parishioners," she countered. "With

stories and characters worth knowing. I'm thankful I came."

"I will always be thankful that David answered your advertisement. Did he tell you I was the one who pointed it out to him when it was reprinted in the Austin newspaper? I never dreamed you were on the other end."

Funny how that had worked out.

"So, what now?" she asked.

"Now we wait," Brandon answered. His fingers flexed under hers, a caress against her palm.

"And pray," Elizabeth said. "That the triplets will finally have a family."

And please, Lord, let that family be ours!

Chapter Eighteen

That Sunday, Elizabeth joined everyone in Little Horn and the surrounding areas to dedicate the new children's home. Clouds scudded across the sky as a cool breeze played with the ladies' skirts and set the gentlemen's hats to tilting. The crowd was so large it fanned out halfway across the street and bellied ten deep in front of the table where Mercy Green was ladling out the cider the McKays had donated under a banner advertising the Arundel General Store. Mrs. Hickey was busy recruiting for the newly organized Children's Home Ladies' Auxiliary, moving from lady to lady with great determination. Annie and her mother helped Elizabeth with the triplets, and the three were able to move toward the front of the crowd, where they could see all the activities.

A sharp noise sounded from the front steps, where Lula May was making good use of the gavel Brandon had made for her. The diminutive strawberry-blonde raised a hand to turn all eyes her way.

"Thank you for coming," she called, glancing at the men and women who thronged around her. "As president of the Lone Star Cowboy League, I just want to thank everyone who had a hand in making this day possible. I think we agree how important it is to care for all of Little Horn's citizens, young and old. First, let's have a round of applause for Amos and Susan Crenshaw for donating this fine house for the children."

In Elizabeth's arms, Jasper clapped his hands as the people around him did the same.

"And we owe a debt of gratitude to David McKay, who brought up the idea and never let us forget it." She smiled fondly at her brother-in-law as he stepped up beside her.

"There's a reason for that," he said, glancing out at their audience. "As many of you know, after our parents died, my brothers and I were separated and farmed out to relatives, some of whom struggled to raise us. This house means that no child in Little Horn will ever feel unwanted or unloved again, that each will have a chance to become part of our community."

Someone let up a cheer, and Edmund put his fingers in his mouth and whistled in support.

David stepped down to rousing applause, cheeks turning red.

"This is a good thing they did," Dorothy murmured beside Elizabeth, and she could only nod in agreement, her heart was so full.

"Finally, we want to thank Fannie and Frederick Tyson," Lula May was saying as the couple came forward, faces pink and beaming. "They'll be serving as mother and father to these little ones."

Elizabeth was sure tears were shining in Fannie's eyes as she accepted the keys to the house from Lula May. But she had to admit she had never felt more proud than when Lula May invited Brandon to offer the blessing.

He stepped up beside the lady, breeze ruffling his sandy hair. His gaze swept the crowd and seemed to rest on her. Elizabeth smiled encouragement, though she knew he likely didn't need it. He had been born to be a minister.

"Papa!" Jasper yelled from her arms.

Brandon's smile widened as the crowd chuckled. "Actually, I was going to say Heavenly Father," he said. The crowd quieted, bowed their heads.

"Dear Lord," he continued. "As we gather before You today, our thoughts are on those who have no earthly father or mother to guide and comfort. You said to let the little ones come to You and never hinder them, for such is the Kingdom of Heaven. So we dedicate this home for orphans in Your name. May all who enter learn the power of Your love and find their place in Your Kingdom and the family of those who love You. Amen."

The crowd rumbled with the answered "Amen."

Elizabeth glanced around. Caroline was kissing David on the cheek, while their daughter, Maggie, jumped up and down in excitement. Gil was pulling Louisa into the house to show it off, with Bo right behind them. Beside Elizabeth, Dorothy was holding up Theo while Tug made faces at him, setting both the little boy and the widow to giggling. Even Mrs. Hickey looked happy for a change, talking with Mrs. Arundel as they praised Mrs. Crenshaw's generosity in donating the house, making that lady stammer her thanks.

It was a family, just as Brandon had said, a great big contentious, loving family.

You could be part of it, if you'd just open your heart.

Elizabeth sucked in a breath at the thought. She'd felt as if she'd grown after the scandal, forced to make her own way in the world. She had congratulated herself on leaving the scared little girl behind. But that scared little girl was still hiding down inside her, whispering of all the bad things that could happen if she truly moved forward.

People in Little Horn might not like her.

The triplets might be taken from her.

Brandon might not return her love.

For so long, she'd felt as if God had been distant, unheeding to her prayers. Yet here, now, she felt His presence hovering. Perhaps He'd been with her all along, taking the bad and turning it into something good, just as Brandon had said in his sermon. She had too often focused on the bad, when so much good had come from moving to Little Horn.

Caroline, Louisa, Fannie, Annie and Stella had become friends. Mrs. Arundel and Mrs. Hickey were coming to respect her. Because she'd married Brandon, she could be a mother, if not for the triplets, then for other children in need. She might even have Brandon's children to love if she opened herself up to the feelings she had for him.

She'd accepted Brandon's offer of a marriage of convenience, knowing that he didn't love her. In truth, she'd been afraid to tell him her feelings for him were still strong. She'd been afraid he'd disappoint her again, fail to support her when she needed it most. Why had she doubted him? He'd proved himself to her over and over—his kindness, his readiness to provide for and guide the triplets, his willingness to help even in the unpleasant tasks or those for which he had little skill. He was a good husband, a good father. She wanted to be his wife, in every sense of that word. United in love over the triplets, surely they could unite as husband and wife. It was all the adventure she could want.

Now she just had to find a way to tell him.

In the midst of shaking Casper Magnuson's beefy hand, Brandon glanced at Elizabeth and nearly forgot what he was saying. She was gazing at him with such a glow about her that he might have thought the sun had broken through the clouds on the gray September Sunday. What had brought such a look to her face? As if she saw his interest, she blushed and crooked her finger at him.

"Excuse me," he said, interrupting Magnuson's diatribe about the excessive cost of raising a child. As the rancher frowned, Brandon headed for Elizabeth.

Tug moved to intercept him. "Mighty fine prayer, Pastor."

"Thank you," Brandon said, trying to ease around him.

The man shifted, blocking Brandon's way and his view of Elizabeth. "I've been meaning to ask you something. The Bible talks a lot about being kind to widows and orphans. I can see that this house will help the orphans, but what about the widows?"

Brandon caught himself putting on his polite smile and nearly grinned. Elizabeth was right. He did tend to default to noncommittal. He made himself look interested instead.

"Widows, Tug? Do we have widows in need of a home?"

The rancher pulled at his collar. "Well, maybe not a home, but there's something to be said for congenial company, a helpmate at your side as the days of life wind on."

He had no idea Tug could be so poetic. "That sounds more like a husband to me."

"Well, yeah." Tug visibly swallowed. "That is, I was wondering what you thought about Dorothy Hill."

Despite himself, Brandon felt his brows jerk up. "What do *you* think of Dorothy Hill?"

Tug dropped his gaze as if to watch his shuffling feet. "She's a whole lot more tolerable than I expected."

He could not be saying what Brandon thought he was saying. "I'm glad to hear you're getting along."

"We get on fine," Tug assured him, raising his gaze once more. "In fact, there's just one problem." He cleared his throat. "I found the ring."

"The ring." It took a moment for the words to sink in, then Brandon grabbed his arm. "*The ring?* You had it the whole time?"

Tug nodded, face twisting in obvious misery. "I promise you, Pastor, I didn't realize it, but she was going on and on about it, and when she described it, I knew it was in my mother's jewelry box." He heaved a sigh. "What am I gonna do, Pastor? I was starting to hope I might ask Dorothy to be my wife. We could let Annie and Jamie marry. But if she finds out I have that ring, she'll never speak to a Coleman again."

Brandon put a hand on his shoulder. "Believe me, Tug. If you don't tell her, and she finds out some other way, it could inflict a wound that will never heal. Explain that you didn't realize it was the ring in question and give it to her."

Tug nodded slowly. "I suppose that's the best way to do it."

Brandon dropped his hand. "I'll be praying for you."

"Thank you, Pastor." He ambled off, shoulders slumped, and Brandon could only hope Tug would heed his warning.

He glanced around again and found that Elizabeth had moved since he'd last sighted her. She was now over at the cider table, where Mercy Green was offering her a cup to share with Jasper, who was in Elizabeth's arms. Her gaze had been on the baby, but she glanced up as if she felt Brandon watching and gave him such a smile he thought his heart might leap from his chest. Determined to reach her this time, he started out once more.

Seven hands shaken and six congratulations later, he finally succeeded. Elizabeth gazed up at him, blue-green eyes shining. He wanted to take her in his arms, offer her his heart. He couldn't say what had changed between them, but he knew that it had. Against all odds, against all circumstances, they had found a way back to each other. He and Elizabeth could be a family, held together by three precious little boys.

As if he couldn't wait either, Jasper reached out and grabbed Brandon's lapel, tugging him closer.

Thank You, Lord!

Mrs. Crenshaw, who was standing nearby, smiled. "There you go, Pastor. Your favorite boy."

"All the boys are my favorite," Brandon assured her, accepting Jasper from Elizabeth as the baby started blowing cider bubbles. Jasper immediately squirmed to be let down, but Brandon didn't dare turn him loose in the crowd. As it was, all he wanted to do was talk to Elizabeth.

Mrs. Crenshaw turned to accept her own cup of cider from Mrs. Green, and Elizabeth edged closer.

Brandon swallowed, the words drying up in his throat. She was so beautiful—her hair bright and shiny, her figure shown to advantage in her peach-colored gown. His heart swelled so much it seemed to be blocking his tongue.

"Wonderful turnout," she ventured.

He nodded. What was wrong with him? Where was his voice? He was a trained orator. He'd given coherent sermons to hundreds of people. Why couldn't he confess his feelings to his own wife?

Because she wasn't really his wife, not yet. And once again, this was personal.

"I'm sorry I had to interrupt you," she murmured, smoothing down Jasper's hair. "But I realized something just now, and I had to tell you."

His heart was pounding so loudly he couldn't hear the crowd around them. "Oh?"

Her smile was soft. "Yes, Brandon, you see…"

"Pastor?"

The unfamiliar voice came from behind him. It couldn't have been more ill-timed. For once in his life, he wanted to tell the person to go away and leave him alone. But he knew his duty.

So did Elizabeth. She offered him a commiserating smile and nodded for him to respond.

With a sigh, Brandon put on his polite smile and turned to find a man and a woman standing hesitantly among the crowd. They were a fine-looking couple, the man tall and dark-haired with a solid chin, the woman shorter and well-proportioned with huge blue eyes. Both seemed to be dressed in their Sunday best, from the man's black coat and trousers to the lady's sunny yellow taffeta and flowered hat. The woman's gaze lit on Jasper in Brandon's arms, and she gave a gasp.

"Look, honey," she cried, fingers pleating a lace-edged handkerchief. "It's them as I live and breathe."

The man's lower lip trembled, but he raised his chin as if to keep anyone from seeing his emotion. "You're right, sweetheart. I was beginning to think this day would never come."

Elizabeth pressed against Brandon's side, as if wishing she could snatch Jasper away. He felt the same way. But the baby was leaning in his arms, showing every inclination of wanting to leap toward the newcomers. Nearby, Eli let out a happy crow from Annie's arms, and even Theo waved a fist from her mother's.

"Oh, the precious darlings," the woman cooed. "How we've missed you!"

Dread settled like a rock in Brandon's gut. "Do you know our boys?"

The man puffed out his chest, setting his pocket watch to glinting. "I should say we do. I'm John Brown, and this is my wife, Nancy. These are Jasper, Eli and Theo, sons of my wife's cousin Harriet. And we've come to take them home."

Chapter Nineteen

Take the triplets home? Elizabeth took a step away from the couple to steady herself. She wanted to gather the boys close, carry them away from these strangers who claimed kinship.

She was their mother.

Brandon seemed to be having similar problems, for he couldn't even manage his polite face.

"You're related to the triplets?" he repeated as if he wasn't sure he'd heard right.

The lady nodded, tears streaming down her cheeks. She was a pretty woman, with a soft face and full lips, and Elizabeth wanted to dislike her on sight but couldn't quite muster it.

"My cousin Harriet birthed these three dear boys shortly before her husband died," Mrs. Brown said with a brave sniff. "I'm sure they were such a comfort to her in those dark days." She blew her nose daintily in her handkerchief.

"Nice gal," her husband agreed. "They lived a ways north from us, but after we heard she had taken ill, we went to see how we could help, only to find that she'd left the farm and taken the babies."

"We've been searching for them ever since," the wife confirmed. "We knew she was sick, but…" She shuddered and dabbed at her cheeks.

"Now, then, darling." Mr. Brown patted her shoulder. "Our journey's finally at an end. We found the boys, and we'll do right by them." He dropped his hand. "Somehow."

Was there some reason they couldn't take the boys? Elizabeth met Brandon's gaze, watched his eyes narrow as if in determination.

"If raising the boys is a hardship," he told the couple, "perhaps we could help."

The wife's eyes widened. "Oh, I couldn't see them raised in an orphanage."

"Though I'm sure your new facility is a fine one, Pastor," her husband hurried to add.

"Jasper, Theo and Eli won't be raised in a children's home," Elizabeth told them. "My husband the pastor and I would like to adopt them."

Mrs. Brown's lower lip trembled, reminding Elizabeth of the boys when they had been denied. "Oh, how sweet of you, to take our boys into your own home."

"Mighty kind," her husband agreed. "But I know Harriet would want them raised by kin."

Mrs. Brown sniffed. "If only she'd waited for us to arrive. We could have helped her, maybe even found her a doctor who could cure her." She leaned closer to Elizabeth, the scent of roses hanging about her, and lowered her voice. "I blame that terrible sickness. It affected her mind. Why else would she leave her boys to strangers?"

And how could Elizabeth give her boys to strangers?

"It is a tragedy," Brandon said, and Elizabeth could see him stand taller, his minister's face sliding into place.

No! she wanted to shout. *Don't play peacemaker! Fight for our boys!*

"But you understand we'll have to confirm your claims," he continued. "Loving the triplets as you do, you wouldn't want us to hand them over to anyone who came calling."

"Of course not," Mr. Brown said with a nod. "You check all you like, Pastor. You'll find everything above-board. But be quick, if you can. The missus and I need to get back to the spread for harvest. We've been gone too long as it is."

Brandon handed Jasper to Elizabeth, his fingers brushing her arm. She tried to meet his gaze, desperate to get his attention. She needed his support now, his strength.

His gaze was tormented, like silver twisted by the fire. "I'm sorry," he murmured, before turning to Mr. Brown. "If you'll come this way, I'll introduce you to the head of the Lone Star Cowboy League and our sheriff."

"You'll be all right, dear?" Mr. Brown asked his wife.

Elizabeth wouldn't. Not if Brandon let them take the boys.

Mrs. Brown was smiling at Jasper. "I'll be fine now that I know our boys are safe."

With one last look to Elizabeth, Brandon led Mr. Brown off through the crowd.

And once more, she stood alone with her fears.

No, not alone. Even though Brandon was now at the other side of the crowd, conversing with Lula May, Edmund, Stella and Sheriff Fuller, he hadn't truly left her. She had to believe in him, believe that he would do what was best for the boys. She'd said she'd let the babies go with family. Her needs were not as important as theirs.

"May I hold him?" Mrs. Brown asked.

She wanted to refuse, but she knew that was wrong. She turned to offer Jasper to the woman.

But Jasper clung to Elizabeth, refusing to move, and buried his head in her shoulder. Did he sense her concerns? Or did he sense something wrong with Mrs. Brown?

The lady in question dropped her arms, face melting. "Oh, my poor dear. He's forgotten who I am."

Elizabeth supposed it was possible. "Three months must feel like forever to a baby."

She nodded. "They change so fast. Look how big they've grown! Are they walking yet?"

"Almost." Elizabeth swallowed the lump that was forming in her throat. If the boys went with the Browns, she'd never see them walk, listen to them recite their lessons or help them find a trade or profession. It sounded as if the Browns had come a distance. She might never see the triplets again.

She must have done a good job at hiding her feelings, for Mrs. Brown warbled, "Oh, the darlings! I can't wait to get them home, show them all the horsies." She leaned forward and chucked Jasper under the chin. "You like horsies, don't you, Eli?"

Jasper scowled. Did he realize she'd mistaken him for his brother? Brandon seemed to be the only one besides Elizabeth, Louisa and Caroline who could tell them apart easily.

"No," he said.

Mrs. Brown recoiled.

"It's his favorite word," Elizabeth explained. "I'm sure he'll love horses when he's a little older."

"No, no, no," Jasper chanted, bouncing in Elizabeth's arms to emphasize the point.

Mrs. Brown's smile seemed a little tight. "How sweet. Well, I'm sure we'll find something that will satisfy him. Babies just love me."

Jasper blew bubbles at her.

"Have you found a place to stay in town?" Elizabeth asked above the noise.

Mrs. Brown took her eyes off the sputtering baby. "We just got in on the morning train, and the nice fellow at the station directed us to the orphanage." Her face clouded. "But I'm not sure where we'll stay if Pastor Stillwater can't confirm our claims quickly. We don't have enough money for a fancy hotel."

"Little Horn doesn't have a fancy hotel," Elizabeth told her. "Or any hotel for that matter. There is a boardinghouse just down the street."

"I hope we're not here long enough to need a boardinghouse." She rubbed at the sleeve of her yellow gown. "I worry about the farm. We have very helpful neighbors, but it's not the same as being there yourself."

Annie came back just then, Theo fussing in her arms. Her mother was right behind with a stormy-faced Eli.

"I think they're getting tired," Dorothy told Elizabeth.

Jasper was squirming as well.

"We should get them home," Elizabeth said, then nearly took the word back. It seemed their home was far away.

"Their mother used to sing to them," Mrs. Brown put in helpfully. "Have you tried that?" She hummed a snatch of a song Elizabeth didn't recognize, but all three babies stilled to listen.

"Lala?" Eli asked with a frown.

No wonder they had enjoyed Caroline's singing and Brandon's song when Jasper was sick. The sound must remind them of their mother.

Mrs. Brown stopped humming. "That's right, sweetheart. La, la, la. That's what your mother used to sing to you. She had such a sweet voice." She glanced around at Elizabeth and the other ladies. "And no one knows where she went?"

Annie and Dorothy were staring at her as they must have realized the woman had known the babies' mother.

"No," Elizabeth said. "But we never knew her name until now, so we could only make general queries."

"The note she left said she'd gone home to meet her Maker," Annie supplied.

Mrs. Brown gasped. "Oh, no! But she never came home. Oh, I can't bear the thought of poor Harriet, alone and dying." Tears started down her face again.

In unison, Jasper, Theo and Eli broke into wails. Annie, Dorothy and Elizabeth jiggled and cooed at them while Mrs. Brown wrung her hands and looked dismayed.

"I'm sure my husband will know how to contact you," Elizabeth said over the tumult. "Excuse us now.

The boys need a nap. Dorothy, hand me Eli, and allow me to borrow Annie a moment."

Dorothy nodded as she complied, and Elizabeth and Annie hurried away from the crowd without another look at Mrs. Brown. Elizabeth might have to give up her boys, but not yet, not now. They were hers to comfort, hers to hold.

Please, Lord, help Brandon learn the truth, and help me learn to live with it.

Her quick steps seemed to calm the boys, for they quieted away from the crowd.

"Was that lady related to the triplets?" Annie asked, scurrying along beside her.

"So she claimed," Elizabeth said, reaching the yard of the parsonage. "Brandon is having the sheriff check to be sure."

"You don't think someone would lie about that," Annie said, clearly shocked by the very idea.

It did seem far-fetched that a couple would come all this way to claim three babies who would be a challenge to raise. What benefit could there be for the Browns? At some point, the boys would be good helpers around the farm, but not for many years to come. And the couple had known the boys' names, even if Mrs. Brown found them hard to tell apart.

"I doubt they're lying," Elizabeth said as they paused on the stoop so she could open the door. "But it doesn't hurt to confirm their claims. We want the best for our boys."

Annie rubbed her nose against Theo's, earning herself a watery smile. "Yes, we do." She glanced at Elizabeth. "But you'll pardon me for thinking you and Pastor Stillwater are the best. You love them."

She did, and she knew Brandon did. She had just decided they might make a real family. What would Brandon do if the triplets were taken away? How could God make something good come from this?

After hearing Mr. Brown's story, Lula May called an emergency meeting of the Lone Star Cowboy League. Most of the members had come into town for services and to open the children's home, so it was relatively easy to alert them to the meeting. Still, Brandon didn't get back to the parsonage until just before the meeting was due to start in the church.

He found Elizabeth in the parlor, one of the boys' shirts unheeded in her lap, the missing button dangling from a thread in her hand.

"They're napping," she reported, clearly trying to rally. "What did Sheriff Fuller say?"

"He sent a telegram to Fredonia, where the Browns say they are from. The telegraph operator there sent back word that there is a Brown farm a ways outside town. It's remote enough that they wouldn't have heard about the boys easily and would have needed time to get here. So, that part of the story seems to be true. Jeb is sending out inquiries about Harriet Smith."

Her fingers pleated the shirt. "Must we give them up, then?"

Brandon went to sit on the chair next to hers, a dainty affair that shuddered under his weight. "I don't know, Elizabeth. I talked some more with Mr. Brown. Their area was hard hit by the drought too. Their farm is struggling. Perhaps I can convince them to leave the boys with us."

"I suggested as much to Mrs. Brown." Her voice

caught, and she drew in a breath before continuing. "She seemed to feel compelled to keep them."

He laid a hand on hers, finding it cold, stiff, with none of her usual energy. "Let me try, Elizabeth. For the boys' sake, and ours."

She raised her head. "I know you'll do what's right, Brandon. I believe in you."

Those last four words lifted a weight from his heart. There was so much more he wanted to say to her, so much he hoped to hear her say, but if he was to make his case to keep their boys, he had to go now. He rose, pressed a kiss against her hair and went to the church, where the league had agreed to meet so as not to disturb the triplets.

"I told you they had kin!" Abe Sawyer was crowing as Brandon entered. The ranchers were clustered in pews near the front, and it didn't escape Brandon's notice that Bo, David, Edmund and CJ were on one side of the aisle while Magnuson and his cronies were on the other. Lula May was standing at the pulpit, fingers toying with her gavel.

"Seems it was just a matter of time before they showed up," Clyde Parker agreed as Brandon took his seat behind David and Bo.

"Yes, well, it's best to be certain," Lula May said with a nod to Brandon. "It seems we're all here. Let's get this meeting started." She brought the gavel down on the pulpit.

The men must have become accustomed to the sound, for they settled into place under her watchful gaze.

"As you probably heard," she said, "a Mr. and Mrs. Brown arrived in town today, claiming to be related to the triplets. It seems the boys' mother was a widow named Harriet Smith, who was cousin to Mrs. Brown. The Browns want our permission to take the triplets home to their farm outside Fredonia."

Magnuson stood. "Permission granted. Meeting adjourned."

Lula May pointed her gavel at him. "Sit down, Casper. There's more to the story."

"There always is," he grumbled, but he resumed his seat.

"Jeb," Lula May said with a nod to the sheriff. "You want to share the particulars?"

Sheriff Fuller rose. Though he wasn't yet thirty, he had a practical approach to life that Brandon generally found refreshing. Now he explained the results of the inquiries he'd been able to make so far.

"But I haven't learned anything more about Harriet Smith," he concluded. "The telegrams that have been returned all state no one's heard of her."

Abe Sawyer shrugged. "So she was a quiet thing, probably kept to herself. There's no crime in that."

"You ever try to hide three babies?" Lula May countered. "I said it when Bo found the babies, and I'll say it again. Someone knows something."

Bo nodded.

"Yes," Magnuson insisted. "The Browns. That's why they came to Little Horn." He glanced around at the others, brow furrowing. "We have a golden opportunity to give those boys a home with family. I don't see why you folks are hesitating."

"Pastor?" Lula May asked.

Brandon rose to his feet, feeling heavy. "Mr. and Mrs. Brown are struggling financially. Even though they will receive the reward the league promised for information about the mother, Mr. Brown asked whether the league could help pay for the boys' care."

"What?" Magnuson was on his feet again. "Do they think we're made of money?"

Lula May struck the pulpit so hard Brandon thought he heard wood splinter. "You plant yourself in that pew, Casper, or so help me I'll throw you out of this meeting."

Magnuson sank onto the pew with a scowl.

As Brandon sat, Bo looked back at him, face troubled.

David rose and glanced around. "I can't believe what I'm hearing. We accepted responsibility for those children. We built a home for them and others like them. Pastor and his wife were willing to adopt them. Now we're just going to hand them over to the first people who claim interest?"

"They're kin, McKay," CJ put in.

Brandon remembered how the rancher and his wife had adopted his twin nieces when CJ's widowed brother Ned had disappeared.

Edmund heaved himself to his feet, towering over most of the other men in the room. "Sometimes kin isn't best to raise a child."

David nodded. "We know that to our sorrow. I say we tell the Browns the boys have a home here in Little Horn, with people who love them." He looked to Brandon, who smiled his thanks.

Jeb cleared his throat. "I know I'm not a member of the league, Madam President, but..."

Lula May nodded. "Go ahead, Sheriff."

"It isn't legal," Jeb said. "You can't keep children from kin, even if kin doesn't amount to a hill of beans."

Bo met Brandon's gaze again, and Brandon knew his brother was remembering their father.

"If the Browns protest and take the matter to a judge," Jeb continued, "I'll have to see they get the triplets."

David fell back into his seat, and Edmund sank down more slowly.

"There has to be something we can do," he insisted.

Brandon pushed himself up again. "There is. I'd like to try to convince Mr. Brown to leave the boys in my and Elizabeth's care."

David looked to Lula May. "I motion we let Pastor try."

Lula May raised her gavel.

"And I motion," Abe Sawyer put in, "that if the pastor fails, we pay the Browns two hundred dollars a year to care for the boys till they're grown."

"Two hundred dollars!" Magnuson exploded. "My boy didn't take nearly that much."

"There are three of them," Sawyer reminded him.

"But they're babies," Parker protested. "How much can they eat?"

"You'd be surprised," David told him across the aisle. "Why, when Maggie was little…"

Lula May's whistle pierced the air, and the ranchers quieted. "Anyone else want to motion?"

Magnuson shifted on the pew, setting it to groaning, but said nothing.

"All right, then. I have a motion that Pastor Stillwater will talk to the Browns about the triplets staying in Little Horn as his sons. If the Browns refuse, we'll offer them two hundred dollars a year to raise the boys. All in favor?"

"Aye," most chorused.

Lula May glared at Magnuson.

He threw up his hands. "Oh, all right. Aye. But I'm counting on you to be persuasive, Pastor."

Brandon could only pray he would be. For without the babies, would Elizabeth want to stay with him as his wife?

Chapter Twenty

The Tysons had offered to let Mr. and Mrs. Brown stay at the children's home for the night to save them the cost of room and board, so Brandon went there as soon as the league meeting ended. Mr. Tyson must have seen the strain on him, for he laid a hand on Brandon's shoulder before leading him into the parlor. The cheering crowds had left, and the children's home was already in full operation. The Browns were sitting with Jo and Gil, listening to Mrs. Tyson read from *Twenty Thousand Leagues Under the Sea*. The intent way Jo sat and Gil's wide eyes brought back memories of Brandon and Bo at their mother's side as she read to them from similar adventures.

Please, Lord, I want to read to the triplets like this. I want to share adventures with Jasper, Theo and Eli until they're old enough to want their own.

Mr. Brown sighted Brandon in the doorway and slapped his hands down on the chair's arms. "Well, Pastor? What did the league say?"

Mrs. Tyson stopped in midsentence, and every gaze swung to Brandon.

"The league is pleased to hear the triplets have family," Brandon assured him. "But I'd like to talk to you and Mrs. Brown privately, if I may, about the boys' future."

Mrs. Tyson set the book aside and rose. "Come with me, Jo and Gil. We should check on dinner."

Her husband went through the door to the kitchen as Gil hopped to his feet. Jo followed more slowly, frowning at the Browns. Brandon waited until the door had closed behind her before going to sit near Mr. Brown and his wife.

"Your desire to raise the triplets is commendable," he told the couple. "Taking on three babies is challenging for anyone, now even more so because of the drought."

The couple exchanged glances.

"We know, Pastor," the husband said. "That's why I asked if the league could help."

"Oh, honey, no!" his wife protested. "We can't ask these kind people for money. They've already done so much for our boys."

His face hardened. "Don't you think I know that? It wasn't easy asking for charity. But I don't know how else we can afford it."

Brandon leaned forward. "My wife and I want to help. We've come to love the boys as our own. As Elizabeth mentioned, we'd like to adopt them, raise them in the parsonage. You could visit whenever you like, and we'd bring them to you as often as we could."

Mr. Brown nodded slowly, and hope surged through Brandon.

"Your wife is awful sweet, Pastor," Mrs. Brown said. "And I know Harriet would be pleased to have the boys raised in such a fine Christian home. But I don't hardly see how I can part with them. My mother and aunt are gone, and now it seems I've lost dear Harriet too. The boys are all the family I have." Her lips were trembling, eyes tearing, and she sniffed courageously, as if trying to be strong.

"There, now," Mr. Brown said, face softening. "It's all right, sugar. We came here for the boys. We won't leave without them. I'm sorry, Pastor, but that's just how it is."

How could he argue? If he and Bo had been babies when their mother had died, he would have wished for such compassionate relatives to step in and claim them rather than their cruel father. Jasper, Theo and Eli were fortunate to have so many people who loved them.

"Very well," Brandon said. "But if you change your mind, please let me know."

"We will," Mr. Brown promised. Mrs. Brown nodded agreement.

Brandon stood. "Elizabeth and I will have the boys ready to go in the morning. And the Lone Star Cowboy League is prepared to provide two hundred dollars a year for the boys' care."

Mrs. Brown pressed her fingers to her lips. "Oh, Pastor, it's an answer to a prayer."

"Mighty generous of you," her husband agreed. "And don't you worry, Pastor. We'll raise those boys to attend church and tithe regularly. You and your wife can rest assured they'll be well cared for."

So it seemed. But Brandon's biggest worry at the moment was how to explain to Elizabeth that he'd lost them their sons.

* * *

Elizabeth knew she should start dinner, but she had no interest in food and she was fairly sure Brandon would feel the same way. Still, she made herself rise and go to the kitchen.

Three cups of cider sat on the table, and she recognized the vessels from the opening of the children's home. It seemed their secret Good Samaritan had thought of the boys even now. Would the person mourn when the triplets left Little Horn?

She shouldn't think that way. She had to have faith in Brandon. But what if she'd been right? What if she and Brandon, and now the triplets, were never meant to be a family?

She sank onto one of the kitchen chairs.

Oh, Lord, I was beginning to believe You've been with me all along, helping me through the difficult times. But this situation feels wrong. I want to rejoice that Jasper, Theo and Eli will have a family, but I wanted to be their mother, Brandon their father. How can we let them go?

A timid tap sounded at the door. Very likely someone had come seeking Brandon's help. Wiping away the tears that had started down her cheeks, she went to the door.

Jo Satler stood trembling on the back stoop. Tears sparkled on her lean face.

Elizabeth's heart sank. "Oh, Jo, what's wrong? Did you hear the boys are leaving Little Horn?"

Jo nodded. She squeezed past Elizabeth into the kitchen, gaze darting all around as if she feared the babies had been taken already.

Elizabeth caught her shoulders before she could

dash into the hall. "It's all right. They're still here. They're just napping."

The girl slumped in her grip.

Elizabeth pulled her close for a hug. "I don't want to lose them either. But Brandon is going to talk to Mr. Brown, ask him to let the boys stay here."

Jo shook her head so violently she yanked herself out of Elizabeth's arms.

Oh, no! "Were you there?" she guessed.

Jo nodded again, avoiding Elizabeth's gaze as if feeling guilty about eavesdropping.

"And Mr. Brown refused?" Elizabeth pressed.

Once more she nodded.

Elizabeth sat down hard. "Oh, Jo. Now I know why you were crying. I think I'll join you." She pressed her knuckles to her lips as the sobs rose inside her. She'd known Jasper, Theo and Eli such a short time, but they were written on her heart. And her heart was breaking.

Jo came closer, laid her head on Elizabeth's shoulder.

"Don't let them go," she whispered. "Those people ain't their kin."

Elizabeth bit her lip to keep from gasping, afraid she'd frighten the girl back into silence. Instead, she rubbed Jo's back in encouragement.

"Sheriff Fuller checked their hometown," Elizabeth told her. "The people there said they were from that area."

"They're lying," Jo insisted, still in that hoarse whisper of a voice rarely used. "The boys' ma was Betty Lane, not Harriet Smith."

Elizabeth frowned. "How do you know that?"

"I heard her." She pulled back to look Elizabeth in

the eyes for the first time, her little face scrunched up in sorrow. "I was there when she left the babies."

"You were at the fair?" Elizabeth couldn't believe it.

Jo's eyes widened. "I didn't do anything wrong! I was just looking at the pies, I promise. And then this lady came in with the babies. She was real nice to me, promised not to tell I had been peeking. She told me to take care of the boys, and I did. Me and Gil, we watched over them. We left them presents. We helped their new mothers. We were their friends."

The Good Samaritans! "And you're sure her name was Betty Lane?" Elizabeth said, watching her.

Jo nodded. "Betty Lane, from West Falls way. That's why you can't let the babies go with those other people, Mrs. Elizabeth. They're liars. And I'm afraid what they'll do with Jasper, Theo and Eli."

Brandon took his time returning to the parsonage. Ever since he was a child, he'd prided himself on his ability to play the peacemaker. He'd intervened between his father and Bo, solved problems with other students at the divinity school and helped people leave their fears behind and grow in their faith. He felt deep down that having him and Elizabeth raise the triplets was the right thing, that sending them away was a mistake. But he'd failed to convince the Browns.

"I can't wait to get them home," Mrs. Brown had kept repeating as she and her husband had walked him to the door of the children's home.

All he could think about was how empty his home would be without them.

And Elizabeth. How could he admit that he'd failed her again? Back in Cambridge, he was beginning to believe, they had been misled. Florence had seemed a conscientious friend at the time, eager to comfort Brandon after Elizabeth's supposed betrayal. He could still see her face, eyes shining with unshed tears, as she promised she would do anything to help. Could she have been hinting at a proposal? She'd certainly been angry when he'd told her he was heading to Texas with his brother.

"What about St. Matthew's?" she'd exclaimed. "I thought you were going to be the curate. I would have been happy there."

At the time, he'd thought she'd meant she'd have been happy if she had been a minister offered the position. Now he couldn't help wondering if she had hoped to join the congregation of the prestigious church as his wife.

He couldn't very well say that to Elizabeth. It was all conjecture, and not very kind conjecture, about a woman she'd considered a friend. And it made him seem arrogant in the extreme to think a woman would go to such trouble to catch his eye.

So, to Elizabeth, it would appear that he had failed her not once, but twice, and both times when so much was at stake. But what else could he do? Whether he liked it or not, the Browns were family. He was just the local minister. By law and in the eyes of the church, the Browns held precedence.

Even if no one would love those boys more than him and Elizabeth.

He was crossing in front of the general store when Mrs. Arundel and Mrs. Hickey stepped out of the door. Brandon nearly groaned aloud. *Not now, Lord. I don't know if I can be pleasant at the moment.*

He tried to detour around them, but Mrs. Arundel inclined her head, the feather in her hat making a little bow. "Pastor. I understand we've found the babies' family."

Of course, her husband would have read every telegram Jeb had sent.

"It appears so," Brandon said. "Now, if you will excuse me, ladies…"

Mrs. Hickey sniffed. "Who are these people? Do we know they're good Christians?"

"Good enough that they'd travel a great distance seeking three lost boys," Brandon informed her, hearing the testiness in his own voice.

"They're like the Good Shepherd who sought after His sheep," Mrs. Arundel said. "Still, Pastor, I am very disappointed in you."

Oh, but she'd picked the wrong day to argue with him.

"I can understand why," Brandon told her. "I am coming to see that I am a very disappointing fellow."

He had the satisfaction of seeing both sets of brows go up.

"I came to Texas," he told the ladies of his congregation, "because the girl I loved broke my heart, but when she arrived on my doorstep, did I welcome her back? Did I forgive and forget as the Good Book advises? No. I allowed myself to pretend I didn't know her, to listen politely while women who should be glad to know her judged and vilified her. I let her into my house, but I didn't let her into my heart."

He bent and met their gazes in turn, watching their eyes widen. "Do you know why, ladies? Because I was taught to keep my heart well hidden. All my life

I tried to earn my father's love. I thought if I did well enough in school, if I excelled at sports, if I had talented, popular friends, he would approve of me. He never did. Each unkind word felt like a lash. So I retreated. It took me years to see God as the loving Father, not the Almighty Judge. And yet I keep expecting to be judged and found wanting, by Elizabeth, by my congregation. No more."

He straightened. "I am your minister, and I am a man. I make mistakes, and I am thankful every day that my God is big enough to forgive them. Now I intend to forgive myself and go tell my wife that I love her and she is the only one for me."

Mrs. Arundel drew herself up. "All I can say, Pastor, is it's about time."

Brandon stared at her.

Mrs. Hickey nodded. "She is a lovely lady, and you are a dear man. And I'll gladly speak to anyone who claims otherwise."

Words failed him. Thankfully, self-preservation did not. He fled while he could, with their well-wishes ringing in his ears.

Only You, Father, could have made that happen. Thank You! Now, please, give me the words to tell Elizabeth how I feel.

He heard voices as he entered the parsonage and resigned himself to dealing with another crisis before he could speak to Elizabeth. He found her in the kitchen with Jo, and it took him a moment to realize the second voice he'd heard was the girl's. He paused in the doorway, afraid to interrupt. But Elizabeth must have sensed him, for she turned. Her bright smile lifted his heart.

"See who came to talk with me?" she asked. "And, oh, Brandon, but she has something important to say."

Brandon smiled at the girl, who ducked her head.

"I'd love to hear it," he encouraged her.

Jo raised her head, glanced between him and Elizabeth, then squared her shoulders.

"Mr. and Mrs. Brown are lying," she rasped out. "They aren't kin."

Brandon's gaze snapped to Elizabeth. She rose with a nod.

"We can't let the triplets go, Brandon. They aren't related to the boys, and Jo can prove it. She spoke with the real mother at the fair."

Could it be true? Thanksgiving rose inside him, nearly lifted him off his feet. He pulled Elizabeth into his arms, held her against his heart for a moment. Praise came swift and easy in a single word.

Hallelujah!

When he released Elizabeth, she beamed up at him, and he could see tears on her cinnamon-colored lashes. Brandon knew he owed his thanks to another as well. He crouched beside Jo's chair.

"Thank you, sweetheart. This is just what I need to save our boys. Do you think you could tell Sheriff Fuller what you told Elizabeth?"

Jo shrank in on herself.

Elizabeth turned to put an arm about the girl's shoulders. "It's all right. Sheriff Fuller won't hurt you."

Jo's lower lip trembled, and tears pooled in her eyes.

Elizabeth gave her a hug. "Don't worry, Jo. You don't have to say a word. You gave us enough information that we'll know how to trip up the Browns."

Brandon nodded. "We'll do it in the morning, when

they come for the boys. I'll go now to explain the situation to Jeb and ask him to be here just in case things get difficult. Jo, let's get you back to the children's home before the Tysons worry. Don't say anything to the Browns. You leave that to me and Elizabeth."

And he could hardly wait.

Chapter Twenty-One

Elizabeth doubted she would sleep that night. The triplets woke hungry and quarrelsome, and she spent the next couple of hours feeding and changing them, then cajoling them into a better humor. As if he feared someone might come for them if he stepped away, Brandon stayed by her side the entire time. He knew just what to do to put a smile on Theo's face, could wrangle Jasper out of and into a diaper faster than anyone she knew. As she settled them into bed for the night, he bent to kiss each boy on the forehead.

"Never doubt, boys," he murmured, "your first mama loved you and your Mama and Papa Stillwater love you too, no matter what." He glanced at Elizabeth as if seeking consensus.

"No matter what," she promised the boys.

"How about a song?" he asked the triplets, who wiggled under his gaze as if they couldn't wait.

"Sleep, my child, and peace attend thee, all through the night," Brandon started.

"Guardian angels God will send thee,
All through the night.

Soft the drowsy hours are creeping.
Hill and vale in slumber sleeping,
We our loving vigil keeping.
All through the night."

Elizabeth knew the song. The nanny at her first position had sung it to the children there. She joined Brandon on the second verse. But as the third verse drew close, Brandon touched her hand, and she quieted to hear him. His gaze was all for her.

"Love, to thee my thoughts are turning.
All through the night.
All for thee my heart is yearning,
All through the night.
Though sad fate our lives did sever.
Parting did not last forever.
There's a hope that leaves me never,
All through the night."

Tears were starting in her eyes, and she looked away. His finger touched her chin, drew her gaze back to his. In his silver eyes, she saw the answers she'd been seeking. He bent his head and kissed her, the touch soft, sweet, so very precious.

Eli crowed, and Jasper clapped his hands as they parted. Even Theo was beaming at them.

"That's enough from you for tonight," Elizabeth told them, feeling her cheeks heating. "Good night, boys."

"Sleep well," Brandon agreed, and he slipped her hand into his and led her out into the hallway.

She thought he might speak of love then, but it seemed his concerns about the situation echoed hers.

"Maybe it would be best if you and the boys head out to Bo's ranch tomorrow morning," he suggested, fingers laced with hers. "If the Browns prove difficult, I don't want you to see it."

Elizabeth offered him a determined smile. "I'll ask Fannie to watch the boys in their room, but I intend to be at your side when you confront those villains. To think they could make off with our boys. The charlatans!"

Brandon gave her hand a squeeze. "We don't know their motivation. Some families long for children. Perhaps Mrs. Brown is barren."

"Many orphans need homes," Elizabeth protested. "Some much closer than Little Horn to Fredonia, if that's where the Browns really came from. Why travel all the way here? Something's very wrong."

"And we're going to make it right," Brandon promised. "But there's something else that must be made right, Elizabeth." He gazed down at their joined hands, then up into her eyes, his face turning solemn. "I failed you in Cambridge. I wasn't there when you needed me. That will never happen again."

The last corner of the shell around her heart chipped off. "And I judged you harshly. Forgive me. You are a fine man, Brandon, and I know I can count on you."

"Until my dying day," he vowed. "Elizabeth, I love you. I always have. I don't know if you can find it in your heart to consider changing our agreement…"

In answer, she stood on her tiptoes and kissed him.

She felt his lips turn up in a smile a moment before his arms came around her, pressing her close. She reveled in the feel of being loved, protected and cherished. For so long she'd wondered where she should go, what she should do. Now she knew. All her life had led her to Brandon.

And she would never leave.

Morning came early, it seemed. Concerned about the boys, she had stayed with them through the night, Brandon dozing on a chair in the corner. She'd watched his lashes sweep down over his quicksilver eyes, listened to the sound of his breathing as his chest rose and fell. Her husband. Her love. Joy made it difficult to sleep.

She felt as if she'd barely closed her eyes before a giggle from Eli woke her. He was sitting up in the bed Brandon had made for him, chanting "baby, mama." As she climbed from bed, Jasper and Theo joined him, sitting up and bouncing as if they couldn't wait to get up and get going.

"Everything all right?" Brandon asked, words almost eclipsed by his yawn as he stretched long legs and rose.

"Everything is perfect," Elizabeth said, smiling at him. He came and pecked her on the cheek before lifting up Jasper and Eli and carrying them out of the room to change while she dressed and changed Theo. The baby's brown eyes followed her as she drew out the triplets' clothes. Funny how only a few hours ago she'd thought this might be the last morning with her boys.

A shiver went through her, but she shook it off. She had faith in Brandon. God hadn't brought them through so much to abandon them now. They would not lose their boys.

Jo and Gil showed up at the door bright and early, and, while Elizabeth fixed breakfast, Brandon sent the boy back to the children's home to ask Fannie to join the Browns when they came. For once, Jo declined to eat with the babies, and Elizabeth wondered whether she was worried about the outcome of the meeting. Then she realized that Jo's face was clean, her hair combed and her movements relaxed. She even whispered things in the boys' ears, setting them to grinning. Very likely she'd been sufficiently fed for the first time in a long time. Fannie's loving care was already having an impact.

Elizabeth took Fannie aside when she arrived with the Browns. "Would you watch the boys with Jo and Gil?" she whispered.

Fannie nodded, face lined with sorrow. "I'm so sorry the triplets will be leaving you, Elizabeth."

"Don't fret," Elizabeth told her. "God works all things to the good for those who love Him and are called unto His purposes." She clapped her hand to her cheek. "Oh, my! I used Mrs. Arundel's list!"

"And quoted the good Book," Mrs. Tyson said with a smile. "Just like a pastor's wife."

Elizabeth gave her a hug and sent Jo an encouraging smile before going to join Brandon in the parlor, where the Browns and Sheriff Fuller were waiting, sitting on the mismatched chairs.

"You know how fond Elizabeth and I have become of the boys," Brandon was saying, his polite smile once more on his face. "Would you mind telling us more about their mother?"

"More?" Mrs. Brown exchanged glances with her husband as if puzzled by the request.

"Yes," Elizabeth encouraged, taking a seat near

Brandon. "Was she fair-haired or dark like the boys? Do they have her eyes or mannerisms?"

"Oh." Mr. Brown chuckled. "I recall her hair was fair, like the missus'. And she had a real nice smile."

"Sweet girl," his wife agreed. "Always good to her kin. That's why we know she would want the babies raised by family."

Elizabeth clenched her fists to keep from commenting. Now that she knew the truth about the couple, she felt every lie. They never called each other by name, afraid they might use the wrong one, perhaps? And Mr. Brown had called his place a spread, a ranch, while his wife talked about a farm with horses. Elizabeth wanted to throw it all in their faces, but no doubt they'd find a way to explain everything. For once, she could only be glad for Brandon's composure.

"I'm sure she would approve of family," he said to the couple. "She was your aunt's child, did you say, Mrs. Brown?"

She nodded, handkerchief springing to her hand. "That's right, Pastor."

"So your aunt married a Smith?" Jeb drawled, eyes narrowing.

Mr. Brown frowned at him. So did Mrs. Brown. "No," she said. "Harriet married a Smith. Her pa was a Wentworth."

"And when exactly did she wed Mr. Smith?" Jeb asked.

"About a year before the boys were born," she supplied.

Had they rehearsed that the lies fell so easily from their lips? Elizabeth wanted to stand, shake out her skirts and leave the room in protest, but she knew she had to see this through.

Brandon leaned forward. "And they lived near you, in Fredonia?"

"Yes, of course," Mrs. Brown said. "We told you all this already."

Her husband shook his head. "I must say I'm disappointed in you, Pastor. Don't think I can't see what you and the sheriff are doing."

Brandon raised his brows, though Elizabeth knew he was sure of his purpose. "What are we doing?"

Mr. Brown pushed out of his chair, face reddening. "You and your missus just want the Lone Star Cowboy League's money to raise those boys. Can't be easy making do on a minister's mite in these parts. Well, I say for shame. Now, turn over our kin, or I'll swear out a complaint against you right here."

Brandon nearly gritted his teeth. Just when he'd thought he had the Browns ready to admit to their lies, the man had turned the tables on him. But he had no doubt the fellow had just confessed his own motives for wanting the boys. He was after the Lone Star Cowboy League's support. And Brandon chilled to think what might have happened to the triplets once the Browns had been given the money.

Before he could speak, however, Elizabeth swept to her feet. "The shame, Mr. Brown," she said, voice ringing, "is on you. We know that the babies' mother wasn't named Harriet Smith."

Mrs. Brown pressed her fingers to her lips. "Oh, dear. Poor Harriet must have been so distraught at the end. What did she claim to go by? Beth Wallin? Samantha Everard? Anne Fairchild?"

Was she trying to guess? Brandon didn't wait for her to stumble upon the right answer. "We also know her hometown. Sheriff Fuller sent a telegram there this morning, and the answer confirmed that a local rancher's wife was delivered of three babies almost a year ago."

"Doesn't mean those are your boys," Mr. Brown insisted. "Seems to me you're looking for any reason not to let those babies go to their family."

"On the contrary," Brandon told him. "My wife and I were willing to give up the boys to family, but it turns out you aren't related."

Mrs. Brown sniffed. "Oh, Pastor, how could you say such things when we have been open and aboveboard?"

She had to be one of the most convincing liars he'd ever met, but the tearful reply only reminded him of Elizabeth's so-called friend Florence, and he was now certain that lady's tears had been just as false.

"The question is, ma'am," Sheriff Fuller put in, "how could *you*? You tried to take advantage of our good nature. We may be openhearted in Little Horn, but we aren't fools." He rose. "I'll have to ask you both to come with me. I'm waiting for an answer from a few other towns. Instead of asking about the Browns this time, I asked whether anyone had news of a couple of your description swindling folks out of their money. I have a feeling the answers will be enlightening."

Mr. Brown squared his shoulders, head coming up to meet Jeb's gaze. "Now, see here, Sheriff. I don't much like you maligning my good name."

Jeb shrugged. "Far as I can see, it's not even your

name. But I have a jail cell just waiting to welcome you, whoever you are."

Mr. Brown blanched. His gaze shot to his wife, who let her face cloud further.

"I'm sure this is all a mistake," she said, twisting her handkerchief in her fingers. "How were we to know our Harriet wasn't the mother of your boys?" She laid a hand against her brow. "Oh, this is terrible! Dear Harriet must still be out there, alone and friendless!"

"That's right," her husband said, taking her arm to help her to her feet. "Our search isn't over, darling. We need to catch the next train out. Sorry, Sheriff, but I must insist. A woman's life may depend on it."

Jeb crossed his arms over his chest. "The life of Harriet Smith, runaway mother of triplets?"

"*Sick* runaway mother of triplets," Mrs. Brown reminded him. "It's such a tragedy. Oh, I don't know how I can bear it." She buried her face in her hands and sobbed.

Brandon wasn't sure whether to applaud her acting or turn away in disgust.

"There, now," her husband soothed, edging them toward the door. "We'll go home, check with the neighbors. Maybe she wrote while we were gone."

Jeb blocked their way. "You'll be free to leave Little Horn once I've verified you aren't wanted for any other crimes."

Mrs. Brown raised her head and clutched her heart with one hand. "Wanted! Why, Sheriff, what have we done besides tried to help three little babies?"

"Impersonation," Brandon supplied. "Accepting money under false pretenses."

"Attempted kidnapping," Elizabeth added.

"Kidnapping!" Mrs. Brown's gaze went from one determined face to the other. "But it was just a mistake!"

They were still protesting as Sheriff Fuller led them from the room. As soon as the door shut behind them, Brandon grabbed Elizabeth around the waist and swung her around. "We did it!"

"We did it," she agreed, grinning at him.

Brandon lowered her to her feet. "But there's more."

"More?" She looked at him quizzically.

Last night had been a start, but he wanted to make sure she shared his dreams for their future. "We have our boys back. We can be a family. A real family."

She stilled in his arms. "You mean a mother, father and children?"

"A husband, wife and children," he clarified. He went down on one knee, gazing up into her dear face, hands holding hers as he longed to hold her close. "Elizabeth Stillwater, I love you with all my might. I've always loved you, and I always will. Will you be my wife? Will you let me be your husband?"

Elizabeth clasped his hands and gave them a tug to raise him to his feet. This moment, this feeling, was everything she wanted. She thought her answer must be shining from her eyes.

"Yes, Brandon," she said. "Nothing would make me happier than to be your wife and the mother to your sons." She dropped her gaze. "And perhaps our daughters."

In answer, Brandon pulled her close. His kiss pledged his devotion, promised a wonderful future. This time, nothing and no one would keep them apart.

At length, he drew back. Elizabeth gave him a smile

she hoped mirrored the joy she felt. "I do have a request of you, husband."

His smile blossomed. "Anything, wife."

"You were prepared to adopt the boys. What do you think about adopting Jo and Gil as well?"

He laughed. "I think Casper Magnuson will demand to know why I was so determined to open a children's home if I intended to give the orphans a home in the parsonage."

Elizabeth chuckled. "You can convince Casper Magnuson. You have before."

He sobered. "But I don't have to this time. Fannie and Frederick have already asked me if they could adopt Jo and Gil."

She knew Fannie would be a marvelous mother for the two. "Do you think Jo and Gil will mind living in the children's home when they are no longer orphans?"

"I think they'll thrive there," he said. "It seems they've already proven they have a heart for the lost."

Elizabeth had told him her suspicions that Jo and Gil were the Good Samaritans who had been looking out for the triplets. He had agreed that the way they slipped about town would have made it easy for them to go unnoticed for so long. Gil's woodworking skills had allowed him to craft the blocks from wood leftover at the children's home. The fact that the siblings were the Good Samaritans also explained why the gifts had appeared at the church when Elizabeth had been staying at the boardinghouse with the triplets. Jo and Gil would have had a hard time delivering gifts or doing good deeds without being seen there.

A gurgling noise from the doorway told them they

had company. Theo was up in Fannie's arms, and Jasper and Eli clung to her skirts on either side.

"I take it the Lone Star triplets will be staying in Little Horn," she said with a fond smile.

"In Little Horn and in our family," Brandon assured her. He strode forward and picked up Jasper. Elizabeth went to lift Eli. To think, she'd get to see them grow tall and strong, in the eyes of the community and God. And she'd get to share that joy with Brandon. Tears blurred her vision as she gazed at her husband.

"Easy there, Mrs. Stillwater," he said, though it seemed to her his eyes were moist as well. "What will our sons think if they see their mother crying?"

"They'll know that sometimes joy comes out wet," she said, taking a step toward him. Brandon met her halfway in a kiss.

"Mama," Eli said, patting Elizabeth on the shoulder.

"Papa," Jasper said, patting Brandon.

"Fam-lee," Theo said, reaching for them all.

"Family," Brandon agreed. "Forever."

Chapter Twenty-Two

A week later, the Little Horn community gathered once more for a wedding. In fact, necks craned and folks stood on tiptoe to catch a glimpse of the bride. Dorothy Hill stood tall and proud, and Tug Coleman nearly burst with joy, as the two pledged their love.

From the front pew, Annie sobbed on Jamie's shoulder and later told everyone at the reception that her wedding, scheduled for a month's time with their parents' blessing, couldn't be more beautiful. And more than one member of the community paused in the receiving line to admire the diamond ring on Annie's finger, a gift that had united the family twice over.

"You saved us quite a bit of money, Pastor," Casper Magnuson said, clapping Brandon on the shoulder where he stood with Elizabeth and the boys overseeing the festivities. "The Hills and Colemans can help each other now with no incentive from us, and those swindlers won't be bothering Little Horn again."

Jeb Fuller had discovered more than one warrant out for the Browns' arrest, and the couple had been remanded into the care of a deputy from Mason County.

It turned out they had even stolen their names from an elderly couple near Fredonia. The so-called Mrs. Brown had once been an actress, specializing in tragedies, and her husband had made a living as a cardsharp. Apparently the stories in the newspapers, which had included the boys' names, had lured the couple into thinking they could pose as the triplets' relatives to earn the reward money and more.

But Jeb's outreach to the other communities had also brought a sadder response. Betty Lane, the triplets' mother, had returned to West Falls, Texas. The doctor there reported she had passed away a month ago, leaving no other family. Elizabeth had cried to think of the lady missing so much of her sons' lives. But she would always be grateful for Betty's sacrifice, because it had given Elizabeth her boys.

Now she was determined to find homes for the other abandoned children in the area. Two more orphans had joined Jo and Gil in the children's home, and the girl could be heard chattering away with them now as she showed them around the reception, explained the workings of the town and introduced them to everyone.

"That's Pastor and Mrs. Elizabeth," she said, her voice sounding more sure each day. "They're nice. And those are Jasper, Theo and Eli."

"They've had four mothers," Gil told them.

"And they were in the papers for miles around," Jo added. "They're famous."

The other two orphans, both boys, one a little older and one a little younger than Gil, looked impressed.

Four mothers. Betty Lane. Louisa Stillwater. Caroline McKay. And now Elizabeth. She was so thankful she and Brandon could keep them, their adoption approved by the league. But Jo was right, Jasper, Theo and Eli had captured the hearts of the whole town.

She glanced around, meeting smiles from Louisa and Bo, Caroline, David and Maggie. Even Mrs. Arundel and Mrs. Hickey were beaming at her.

"What has you smiling, Mrs. Stillwater?" Brandon asked, leaning closer.

"Our people, Mr. Stillwater," she answered. "Our friends and our family. Like the boys, I am home."

* * * * *

Dear Reader,

Thank you for joining me on Elizabeth and Brandon's journey. Having written two stories set in Little Horn, the people and place are near and dear to my heart. In 2016, the first series included *Stand-In Rancher Daddy* by Renee Ryan, *A Family for the Rancher* by Louise M. Gouge and my own *A Rancher of Convenience*. If you haven't read the first two books in the 2017 series, try *The Rancher's Surprise Triplets* by Linda Ford and *The Nanny's Temporary Triplets* by Noelle Marchand.

When I was pregnant with my first son, the doctor thought I might be carrying twins. My first thought was, how wonderful! My second was, how am I going to take care of two babies? It was probably a good thing it turned out to be one special little boy. My hat's off to Elizabeth, Louisa and Caroline for so capably loving Jasper, Theo and Eli.

I love to hear from readers. Visit me at reginascott. com, where you can also sign up for an alert to be notified when the next book is out.

Blessings!
Regina Scott

MONTANA COWBOY'S BABY
Big Sky Country • by Linda Ford

Cowboy Conner Marshall doesn't know the first thing about fatherhood, but he's determined to do right by the abandoned baby left on his doorstep. As the doctor's daughter, Kate Baker, helps him care for the sick baby, they forge a bond that has him wondering if Kate and baby Ellie belong on his ranch forever!

THE ENGAGEMENT CHARADE
Smoky Mountain Matches • by Karen Kirst

In order to protect his pregnant, widowed employee, Ellie Jameson, from her controlling in-laws, Alexander Copeland pretends to be her fiancé. But can this temporary engagement help them heal old wounds...and fall in love?

THE RENEGADE'S REDEMPTION
by Stacy Henrie

With nowhere else to go, injured Tex Beckett turns to his ex, Ravena Reid, who allows him to stay on her farm under one condition: he must help her with the orphans she's taking care of. But what will she do if she finds out he's an outlaw?

LONE STAR BRIDE
by Jolene Navarro

When Sofia De Zavala's father discovers she dressed as a boy to go on a cattle drive and prove she can run the ranch, he forces her to marry trail boss Jackson McCreed to save her reputation. Now she must convince Jackson their union can become a loving partnership.

LIHCNM0617

Get 2 Free Books,

Love Inspired® HISTORICAL

Plus 2 Free Gifts—

just for trying the Reader Service!

Cowboy Conner Marshall doesn't know the first thing about fatherhood, but he's determined to do right by the abandoned baby left on his doorstep. As the doctor's daughter, Kate Baker, helps him care for the sick baby, they forge a bond that has him wondering if Kate and baby Ellie belong on his ranch forever!

Read on for a sneak preview of
MONTANA COWBOY'S BABY by **Linda Ford,**
available July 2017 from Love Inspired Historical!

"Did anything you tried last night get Ellie's attention?" Kate asked Conner.

"She seemed to like to hear me sing." Heat swept over his chest at how foolish he felt admitting it.

"Well, then, I suggest you sing to her."

"You're bossy. Did you know that?" It was his turn to chuckle as pink blossomed in her cheeks.

She gave a little toss of her head. "I'm simply speaking with authority. You did ask me to stay and help. I assumed you wanted my medical assistance."

No mistaking the challenge in her voice.

"Your medical assistance, yes, of course." He humbled his voice and did his best to look contrite.

"You sing to her and I'll try to get more sugar water into her."

He cleared his throat. "'Sleep, my love, and peace attend thee. All through the night; Guardian angels God will lend thee, All through the night.'"

Ellie blinked and brought her gaze to him.

"Excellent," Kate whispered and leaned over Conner's arm to ease the syringe between Ellie's lips. The baby swallowed three times and then her eyes closed.

"Sleep is good, too," Kate murmured, leaning back. "I think she likes your voice."

He stopped himself from meeting Kate's eyes. Warmth filled them and he allowed himself a little glow of victory. "Thelma hated my singing." He hadn't meant to say that. Certainly not aloud.

Kate's eyes cooled considerably. "You're referring to Ellie's mother?"

"That's right." No need to say more.

"Do you mind me asking where she is?"

"'Fraid I can't answer that."

She waited.

"I don't know. I haven't seen her in over a year."

"I see."

Only it was obvious she didn't. But he wasn't going to explain. Not until he figured out what Thelma was up to.

Kate pushed to her feet.

"How long before we wake her to feed her again?" he asked.

"Fifteen minutes. You hold her and rest. I don't suppose you got much sleep last night."

There she went being bossy and authoritative again. Not that he truly minded. It was nice to know someone cared how tired he was and also knew how to deal with Ellie.

Don't miss
MONTANA COWBOY'S BABY by Linda Ford,
available July 2017 wherever
Love Inspired® Historical books and ebooks are sold.

www.LoveInspired.com

SPECIAL EXCERPT FROM

Love Inspired®

*Nell Stoltzfus falls for the new local veterinarian in town,
James Pierce. But their love is forbidden since he's
English and she's Amish. If Nell follows her heart,
will love conquer all?*

Read on for a sneak preview of
A SECRET AMISH LOVE by **Rebecca Kertz**,
available July 2017 from Love Inspired!

"You said your *bruder* was called out on an emergency,"
Nell said. "What does he do?"

"He's a veterinarian. He's recently opened a clinic here
in Happiness."

The strange sensation settled over Nell. Despite the
difference in their last names, could James be Maggie's
brother? "What's his name?" she asked.

"James Pierce." Maggie smiled. "He owns Pierce
Veterinary Clinic. Have you heard of him?"

"*Ja*. In fact, 'twas your *bruder* who treated my dog,
Jonas."

"Then you've met him!" Maggie looked delighted. "Is he
a *gut* veterinarian?"

Startled by this new knowledge, Nell could only nod
at first. "He was wonderful with Jonas. He's a kind and
compassionate man." She studied Maggie and recognized
the family resemblance. "How is he a Pierce and you a
Troyer?"

"I am a Pierce." Maggie grinned. "Abigail is, too. But
we don't go by the Pierce name. Adam is our stepfather,

and he is our *dat* now." Maggie's eyes filled with sadness. "I was too young to care, but James had a hard time with it. He loved Dad, and he'd wanted to be a veterinarian like him since he was ten. He became more determined to follow in Dad's footsteps."

Nell felt her heart break for James, who must have suffered after his father's death. "You chose the Amish life, but James chose a different path."

"And he's doing well," Maggie said. "My family is thrilled that he set up his practice in Happiness."

Later that afternoon, James arrived to spend time with his family.

She recognized his car immediately as he drove into the barnyard. James stood a moment, searching for family members. Nell couldn't move as he crossed the yard to where tables and bench seats had been set up. Soon, James headed to the gathering of young people, including his sisters Maggie and Abigail.

Nell found it heartwarming to see that his siblings regarded him with the same depth of love and affection. James spoke briefly to Maggie, clearly delighted that he'd handled his emergency then decided to come. She heard the siblings teasing and the ensuing laughter. Maggie said something to James as she gestured in Nell's direction.

James saw her, and Nell froze. Her heart started to beat hard when he broke away from the group to approach her.

Turn your love of reading into rewards you'll love with
Harlequin My Rewards

Join for FREE today at www.HarlequinMyRewards.com

Earn **FREE BOOKS** of your choice.

Experience **EXCLUSIVE OFFERS** and contests.

Enjoy **BOOK RECOMMENDATIONS** selected just for you.

PLUS! Sign up now and get **500** points right away!

Earn **FREE REWARDS**
Join Today!
HarlequinMyRewards.com

MYR16R